Suzy Vivian

The Blue Orb

The Blue Orb

Copyright © 2021 by Suzy Vivian. All rights reserved.

Additional Copies:

www.amazon.com
www.barnesandnoble.com

Published in the United States of America

ISBN softcover: 9781956895087
Library of Congress: 2021915089

To my wonderful sons, Matt and Scott.
You have been such a delight to me.

Contents

Prologue

Hundreds of years ago, in the land of Uranallee, there was a very powerful wizard. He was the most powerful wizard the world had seen in many lifetimes. His name was Xyrene. He was tall and very thin. He was stooped over with age and from his lifetime of study and work in the magic arts. He had tufts of wispy white hair around his ears. He kept it short most of the time, but it had grown longer of late. He had neither the time nor the inclination to tend to his hair because he was concerned about something of greater importance. He wore a long robe of black velvet that was tied to his slender body with a gold cord. At the neck was a tall collar. Both the collar and the front of his robe were embroidered with special runes in gold thread, marking his position as the most powerful wizard of the realm. He also wore soft slippers of black velvet lined with lamb's wool. They kept his feet warm in the cold castle where he lived. His black velvet hat was padded and rolled. It, too, was embroidered with gold thread.

He was nearing the end of his life and wanted to leave something of power as a legacy to the world. He thought about his legacy for many months. He finally decided that an orb with special powers would be the perfect bequest. He set out to find all the information he could regarding the powers found in a special blue stone—azurian—seen only in the Jade Mountains, where there are many dwarf mines to this day.

Xyrene had studied many of the ancient writings about magic. In an alcove at the far side of the library, he had found an ancient scroll among the many books and scrolls kept there in the castle. This particular scroll was kept at the back, where it was unlikely to be found. He had searched there many times before, but he had overlooked it because it was small and written on plain parchment instead of the usual material used for important documents. He grew more and more excited as he read it. The scroll told of ways to empower stones of special composition with magic that was otherwise unheard of. This was exactly what Xyrene had been looking for. He memorized the spells. Then he sent one of his acolytes to the Jade Mountains to purchase one of the pure blue azurian stones mined there. He knew it would be costly, but it would be worth every ounce of gold he would have to spend. He was very specific about the size and weight of the stone to be purchased. He would have preferred to go himself to be sure of what he was getting, but his acolyte, Murzhog, was very reliable and meticulous about following his requests.

Murzhog returned with the perfect stone after many months of traveling and searching the mining communities in the Jade Mountains. Xyrene was so pleased with the stone Murzhog found that he promised him that he would have the stone when he died. Murzhog had hoped for this very thing as he traveled and searched for the precious stone. He smiled in gratitude, knowing he would have the power soon. The old man couldn't live much longer, after all. Such power as Xyrene envisioned was exactly what Murzhog was after, and it was why he had joined the wizards in the first place. He always acted the obedient acolyte when around any of the powerful wizards in the castle. He could not risk the possibility of detection. He would be thrown out or have his tongue cut out.

Xyrene was anxious to begin work on his precious orb. He took the stone to his workroom and spent many hours sculpting the stone and smoothing its edges until it was a perfect round orb. He did the work himself to be sure it was perfect. He would take no chances with this precious stone and his legacy. Xyrene debated what powers he would instill into his orb. He decided that it should be capable of amplifying directed thought with just a few words of power. This would mean that if the person holding the orb wanted to make the land more fertile or the cattle more productive, it would be so, given the proper words of power. Unfortunately, the orb would also respond to powerful emotion as well. Xyrene had not intended the latter to be the case, but he was not as careful as he thought he was when imbuing the orb with his power. When the orb was used, a blue fire would be emitted that would cause the results sought by its user. He was a very optimistic wizard and somewhat naive for one of his age. He had lived sheltered among other wizards like himself all his life. He never thought that there might be someone who would use his orb for evil purposes.

As Xyrene began to pour his magic into the orb, he noticed that it began to change. There were swirls of color inside it that looked like clouds, but they were more than that. If he looked closer, he could see the shapes of the runes embroidered on his robe. This was alarming since the runes had power in themselves. He had not realized when he began the spell that it could do such a thing. He was worried and almost decided to destroy the orb. There would be too much power in it if he continued.

Murzhog said, "Master, if the orb has such power, think what a legacy it will be of your own power! Who could doubt that you are the most powerful wizard the world has ever seen?" So with such flattery, Murzhog convinced Xyrene to complete the orb as he had planned.

Xyrene finished working on the orb and decided to try it out on his own cattle to see whether it would really help them be more productive in giving milk and producing young. He held the orb and thought about healthier, more productive cattle. He said the proper words. Blue fire shot from the orb and spread out for what appeared to be several miles around Xyrene's castle. Xyrene could not imagine what that could mean. Had the orb become so powerful that it would affect everything for many miles around? He pondered this for a week and began to see the results of what the orb had done. Most of the cows had become pregnant and were giving much more milk than normal, but it also affected the chickens, rabbits, and sheep. As the next few months progressed, it became obvious that it would be the most prolific year in the land near Xyrene's castle.

A side benefit was that more of the women in the community became pregnant. Xyrene was delighted, but he was also a bit wary. He had only intended for the cattle to show some improvement. Another thing he had not expected was that he was exhausted from making the orb and using it. The orb seemed to have used the wizard's strength to do his bidding. It appeared that using the orb would come with a price.

Murzhog noticed Xyrene's decline and decided he would not have to wait much longer after all. Xyrene was fading fast. Murzhog thought it might be from forming the blue orb, but he did not realize it was also from using it.

Within six months, Xyrene could no longer get out of bed. He called Murzhog to his bedside one evening when it was evident that he would not be able to talk much longer.

Murzhog knelt by his master's bedside in order to hear him better.

Xyrene whispered, "Murzhog, you must hide the blue orb. It is too powerful for any man to use. It could kill them and possibly anyone else within miles of its location. I am afraid that I have made a terrible mistake in creating it. In my desire to leave a legacy of my power, I have created something with the potential to create much evil." Xyrene was fading fast. Talking was extremely trying. "I … have always trusted you to do my bidding … please don't fail me now … Promise me that you will … hide the orb where it can never be found."

Murzhog smiled at his old master and said, "But, Xyrene, it is your legacy. I would keep it and use it only for good. You saw what it has done for the people of this land. They are ready to worship you for what has been accomplished. I cannot destroy or hide this thing of beauty and promise that you have created."

Xyrene was alarmed at this, but he was too weak to protest too much. He reached for Murzhog's hand and tried to pull him closer. Grasping Murzhog's robe, Xyrene said, "You will destroy yourself … and all who are near you if you … use the orb … It will kill you … even as it has killed me … I'm afraid … that is my legacy."

Murzhog was young and could not imagine anything happening to him that would not be good. He wanted the power and was anxious to get it. To calm his master, he said, "I will do as you ask, Master. I see that it would be wrong to use the orb. I will hide it as you say."

Xyrene must have seen the lie on Murzhog's lips because he said, "Murzhog, you will die." Xyrene fell back on his pillow and breathed no more.

Murzhog closed Xyrene's eyes and said, "Thank you for the warning, but I think I can handle the orb. I have far more strength than you ever did. And the power of the orb is worth the risk." Of course, Murzhog was deluding himself. No one was as powerful as Xyrene—even in his old age.

Murzhog called for the servants and told them that Xyrene had died. They hurried out and called for the physician to confirm his death. Murzhog made the arrangements for Xyrene's state funeral. The people of the land were saddened by Xyrene's death. He had been a powerful wizard and had helped them. However, they were not surprised. It was well known that Xyrene's health had been failing for months. Xyrene had not had time for a wife or children, so no family came to mourn him. All his old friends had died years earlier.

After the state funeral, all went back to normal … or so it seemed.

Murzhog had the blue orb to himself. He pondered what he would do with it first. He must be very discreet. He had watched Xyrene use the orb and knew what to do. He was keeping the orb in a black velvet bag that he lined with lamb's wool to keep it safe. He locked it in a chest in his room. Murzhog felt confident that he could protect and keep the orb a secret from prying eyes.

What he did not know was that one of the servants had been hiding in the anteroom to Xyrene's bedchamber and had heard all that had passed between Murzhog and Xyrene. He had discreetly followed Murzhog to his room and watched through the partially open door as Murzhog hid the orb in the small chest. The servant, Dagmarnic, smiled to himself. He knew he would be able to get the orb sooner or later.

Months later, Murzhog came home from a party very late. Dagmarnic was helping him undress and get into bed. Murzhog was very drunk. Dagmarnic had been waiting for a time when Murzhog would be incapacitated. Now was Dagmarnic's chance to get the orb. When Murzhog was fast asleep and snoring loudly, Dagmarnic took the key from around Murzhog's neck.

All was going well for Dagmarnic. He opened the chest and brought out the bag that contained the orb. Unfortunately for Dagmarnic, he was unaware that Murzhog had planned for just such an eventuality. He had cast a spell on the chest. Anyone who opened it without saying the proper spell would be incinerated on the spot. As soon as Dagmarnic picked up the bag, he was set ablaze. Within moments, all that was left of him was a pile of greasy ashes.

Murzhog was aroused when he heard Dagmarnic's screaming. He was alarmed when he saw the flames, but when he realized what had happened, he smiled. His little trap had worked marvelously. He regretted the loss of Dagmarnic. He had been a good enough servant, but he could not be sad that the man died trying to steal his precious orb. The smell of burnt flesh was overpowering. Murzhog called for his servants to clean up the mess. He let it be known that Dagmarnic had died while trying to steal from him. He warned them that the same thing would happen to anyone else who tried it. It proved to be a very effective deterrent. No one dared go near the chest or steal anything from Murzhog from that day on.

Murzhog decided one day in early spring that he would like to try out the blue orb for himself. He had delayed using the orb partly out of fear—though he did not recognize it as such—and partly to hide the fact that he had the orb. The other wizards would have punished him for possession of a relic with so much power. The wizards were very protective of the power they held. Murzhog knew that Xyrene had left all his notes in his private library and office. He had found them soon after Xyrene's death and kept them in his chest with the orb. He drew both out of the chest after speaking the words of power and set both the orb and the scrolls on the table in his room. He found the words to make himself richer and more powerful. He was excited to think he could use the orb for this purpose. He had been reading the powerful words Xyrene had written and found just the right combination to get what he wanted.

He focused on the orb and began to say the words. As soon as he started, he felt the strength draining from him. He could not imagine what was happening. He was focused on himself and his selfish desire for money and power. For those in the area, that was fortunate. It was not so fortunate for Murzhog. He could feel a change coming over him. He began to feel light-headed, and his strength failed. The blue orb was pulsing with a mysterious blue light.

Just as he was beginning to think he would die, the feelings stopped. The blue orb grew still, the blue light faded, and all became quiet. Murzhog was thinking it was not so bad—that maybe he could handle it. Suddenly he was filled with excruciating pain. He opened his mouth to scream, and blue fire shot out of his mouth and his eyes. He could not stop screaming. He was in such pain. He fell to the ground and never rose again.

He did get his wish. Within a very short while, there was an increase in the money coming into the realm. Carters and merchants were bringing bags of gold and putting them on the steps of the castle where Murzhog had lived. They didn't seem to know why, but they felt compelled to do it.

After that, no one dared touch the orb. It was walled into Murzhog's tomb, and none could enter. None dared enter. The other wizards knew better than to try to use the orb or approach the tomb. However, every once in a while a strange blue light would shine from under the door to the tomb. The orb seemed to have a life of its own.

After hundreds of years, the castle crumbled and turned to dust. It was said that the area around the castle was haunted. No one dared enter the valley where it once was. No one knew what had happened to the blue orb. No one could be certain, but it had not been seen for hundreds of years.

Then a very strange thing was reported. A man by the name of Kaylub found what appeared to be a blue stone with strange swirls inside. It had been crusted with dirt and debris from so many years in the ground. The man polished the stone and wondered at its beauty. He took it to a nearby wizard, Zenitten, and showed it to him. This wizard had heard legends of the blue orb and wondered whether this could be it.

Zenitten was a rather fat man with greasy, shoulder-length hair. He lived alone and kept to himself. He used his magic when called upon, but he preferred when people stayed away. As he pondered the possibility that he could have the blue orb of legend, he began to sweat. He knew he must be very careful in using it. If legends could be believed, he needed to be very careful—or die trying. He knew many words of power, and as he held the orb, he felt its pull. He wanted to use it. In fact, he needed to use it, but what would he do with it?

He decided to try something very simple. He would say the words of power that he had used to try to bring rain to the area. There had been a drought for two years, and the crops were dying. He had used the words before, but the results were not impressive. He had been able to summon a few stray clouds but nothing substantial. He decided to try the words while holding the orb. He said the words he knew and waited to see what would happen. He noticed a slight weakening as he said the words of power. He felt even more as the clouds rolled in. It began to rain for many miles around the wizard. He had forgotten the words that would break the spell and was weakening by the minute. He became very afraid as he frantically looked for the words he needed. He finally found them in his *Book of Power*. He said the words rapidly and carefully. The rain was building to a gale, but he finally stopped the spell.

The rain gradually abated, and a watery sun began to leak through the clouds. The power of the orb amazed and terrified the wizard. He was not a young man, and it took him weeks to regain his strength. His servants were very concerned about his health. The people were very impressed that Zenitten had accomplished such a great task. The crops were growing, and the people would not starve during the winter. Word had been passed along that Zenitten had brought the rain.

Zenitten, though drawn to the power of the orb, was fearful of its use. It had a strange power over him. As his strength returned, he forgot how terrified he had been when he had first used it. By chance, there was a king in the land. King Mordent was very powerful and cruel. He heard about the orb Zenitten had used to bring the rain. Mordent coveted the power it represented. He sent one of his messengers to Zenitten to be brought before him.

Zenitten feared King Mordent. He suspected that the king would want to take the orb from him or at least control Zenitten's use of it for his own cruel ends. King Mordent was known to torture any who tried to thwart his plans for power. He used the foulest means to get information from those he considered to be a threat to his power. He preferred to get the information personally. He enjoyed the screaming and the smell of blood and sweat as he performed his evil acts on his unfortunate victims.

Zenitten happened to be holding the orb as he thought of a way to prevent the king from getting the orb or controlling his use of it. He spoke aloud one of the particularly painful death spells he knew and directed his thoughts to the king. He had not consciously meant to do so. Once the words were out of his mouth, he knew he had made a terrible mistake. Power left his body as the spell wove its way to the king.

Zenitten fell to the ground, and his servants ran to help him. He said, "Go to the king … go to the king," as he was carried to his bed. The orb fell from his limp hand as he was placed on his bed. One of the servants ran to the king's palace. He didn't know what he would find there, and he was terrified.

Zenitten asked for his *Book of Power* to be brought to him as the pillows propped up his head. He found the words to counteract the spell and hoped he was not too late. He fumbled for the orb and not finding it, had his servant look for it. It had rolled under the bed. His servant handed him the orb and bowed out of the room.

As Zenitten's servant ran through the town's narrow streets, he became more and more anxious. There were crowds typical of a morning with hawkers and booths for merchants selling everything from food to cloth. He had to push his way through. Finally, the gate to the palace came into view. He forced his way through the milling groups of villagers and arrived at the palace just as the screaming started. He rushed to the door to the king's dining hall and found the servants in an uproar. They were saying that the king had been eating his dinner and doubled over in pain. Blood poured out of his mouth and ears. He started screaming and fell into his plate of half-eaten calves' liver. He was dead instantly. When the screaming started, the palace guards came running. The servants feared that they would be held responsible for the king's death. If so, they would be put to death in a most unpleasant manner. The guards questioned all who were present when the king died. The palace magistrate was called in, and the investigation began.

As soon as the guards were heard coming down the hall, Zenitten's servant ran back to the wizard to tell him all he had heard and seen. Fortunately, Zenitten recovered as soon as the king was dead. He felt so good that he got out of bed and told his servants to bring him food. It appeared that when a spell was broken, the power of the orb was cut off. Zenitten knew instinctively that he had found something very important for using the blue orb. He must remember that, before he used the orb for any purpose, he must account for the breaking of the spell before it was too late. Zenitten became very rich and powerful.

There was still a price to be paid for using the orb. Zenitten became a greedy and jealous old man. He wanted more and more power and wealth. All the people of the realm feared him. Zenitten was slowly going mad. The orb gained more and more control of him as time went by. Zenitten began to shrivel and become more and more embittered. Finally, when one of his servants came to help him dress, he accidentally knocked the orb off its pedestal. Zenitten thought the man was trying to take the orb. Zenitten reached for the orb, but he missed it and fell to the floor. The fall caused his hip to shatter. Zenitten screamed and cursed the servant. The servant picked up the orb and placed it back on the table.

Zenitten's curse was so vile that it woke something within the orb. The orb glowed blue fire, flashed across the land, and killed everyone within several miles. Everything was leveled, and no tree, animal, or bird survived. The land was covered in ash, and blue smoke was seen for many miles. So ends our story of the blue orb— or does it?

Jasmine In Trouble

The night was dark. The rain lashed the earth and created quagmires where the road had been. A young woman by the name of Jasmine rode on a black horse, running desperately through the night, racing against the sound of the wolves. They were closing rapidly. In a few more yards, there would be shelter in the castle. She urged the horse faster as hope bloomed for the first time in three days. The horse was tiring, but he seemed to sense that safety was close at hand. He pushed harder to beat the wolves to the castle and the promise of safety.

Zarcon, a great wizard, felt a strange stirring in the realm to which he claimed power. He was aware that the witches had come into possession of an artifact with great magical powers. He feared it might be the legendary blue orb. He had hoped the orb was lost forever, but now he was not so sure.

Zarcon suddenly sensed that there was someone in desperate need and the person was coming toward his castle at a frantic pace. He felt the need to climb the stairs to the top of the castle walls to see if anything would appear so he could understand what was happening.

He rose from the chair in his office near the castle gates and left the room to climb to the top of the wall. He was aging, and the climb was somewhat difficult for him. He did not often venture up the stairs. When he made it to the top and looked out over the meadow, he could hear wolves howling and a horse coming fast out of the trees just beyond the meadow to the south.

Zarcon called to the guards below to open the gates quickly. The wolves were running close behind the rider. He feared they might be the wolves controlled by the witches. If so, the rider had cause to fear. The witches were relentless when they felt they had been wronged. This could explain the reason for the wolves and the desperate rider. He would save a life if he could.

The large, white, granite castle seemed to rise out of the ground as she approached. Jasmine could see a man watching from the parapet to signal the men below to open the gates to the castle. She raced for the gates, and they opened just as the need was greatest. Just then, the wolves broke out of the forest. A slim shaft of light broke through the gates, and Jasmine and her horse slipped inside. The gate was quickly shut and barred. Seconds later, the lead wolf slammed into the gate with a howl.

Zarcon came down the stairs near the gate and asked, "And who has the wind and rain blown into my castle this night?"

Jasmine started to fall off the horse and was caught by one of the guards.

Zarcon was shocked when he realized it was Jasmine. When she was able to stand, Zarcon said, "What if the wolves had caught you? Fortunately, I sensed something coming, and I thought it might be someone in desperate need when I heard the wolves howling. I climbed to the parapet to see for myself. I was concerned that someone was in trouble. I'm glad I did. You may have been wolf bait by now. Come with me to a place that is warm and dry. We will talk." He looked to the guard that had helped Jasmine off her horse and said, "Micah, please help this young lady, will you? I fear she has had a rough time of it and needs some assistance just now."

Micah put his arm around her waist to help her walk.

Jasmine whispered, "First, will you please take care of the horse? He has been more than valiant in getting me here safely."

The other guards took the horse to the stable and assured her that he would be well cared for.

Zarcon led her to the room just off to the side of the gate where he had his small office. It was warm and had a nice fire in the hearth. Micah helped her into the room and left.

Jasmine looked at Zarcon and sighed deeply. The young woman from the Jade Mountains was exhausted from the days and nights spent running in terror since the wolves had started chasing her. She carried a black leather pack on her back and set it beside the small bench near the fire. She removed her rain-soaked cloak and set it on the bench. She wore black knee-high boots, black leather pants, and a rough-spun white tunic belted at the waist with a black leather cord. She had short black hair and a pretty face. She looked much younger than her years.

Zarcon looked at Jasmine and said, "Ah, Jasmine! It is good to see you and in one piece. How did you get here without the wolves getting you first? How far have you come? What brings you to me? What if the wolves had caught you?"

Jasmine sighed and said, "If they had caught me, you wouldn't have the blue orb now, would you?" She reached into her pack, opened a black velvet bag, and produced an orb the size of a man's fist. It seemed to glow once it was out in the room. Swirls of color inside appeared to be like mist.

Zarcon gave a sharp intake of breath. He came forward into the light of the small lantern on the table in the center of the room. He was tall and thin and had a hawk nose and large blue eyes. His white brows met in an angry crease above his nose. He had a long white beard and a robe of deepest blue. Jasmine knew he was the wizard Zarcon.

"Long we have feared this orb was back in the world. How did you get it? I thought you were gone from this land. No one has heard from you for months." Zarcon was so relieved to see her, and he was very happy she had come to him with the orb.

Jasmine was small—even for someone from the Jade Mountains. Many would pass her by, thinking she was a child. This made her even more dangerous. Zarcon knew how independent and dangerous she could be. He had been concerned about her whereabouts for several months.

Jasmine knew that Zarcon was worried about her and wanted to hear all that had happened. The orb was too important to take anyone into her confidence while she was hunting it. Now that she had it and the witches were after her, she knew she needed to trust him and ask for his help. She managed a small smile and said, "If you want to know what I've been through, you'll have to wait until I catch my breath and have something to eat. I'm starved and exhausted. In case you've forgotten already, I was being chased by wolves a few moments ago!"

"Yes! How thoughtless of me not to take your safety and health into consideration as soon as you came through the gate. I will call for food and a room for you immediately. We'll talk in the morning." Zarcon eyed the orb as Jasmine put it back in her pack. He was drawn to it, but he knew it was too dangerous to hold. It was very unsettling to know the orb was a reality—and was in his castle. He had hoped it was just the stuff of legend. Now that he had seen it with his own eyes, he was very worried.

As if reading his mind, Jasmine said, "Zarcon, I know you had hoped the orb was a thing of legend, but you must face the reality of it. I'm sorry to burden you with it, but I had nowhere else to turn. You are my only hope for keeping it out of the hands of the witches." Jasmine caught his look of concern as the orb disappeared into her pack. Jasmine knew it was unfair to burden Zarcon with such a weight, but he was the only wizard strong enough to be of any real help. She knew she must trust Zarcon and rely on his judgment in the days and weeks ahead. She struggled a bit with the knowledge. She had learned the hard way not to trust until trust was earned. She would take no chances with the orb—even though she needed his help.

Zarcon sighed and rang a bell near the door. Almost immediately, a tall, dark woman in a simple white robe and a belt of leather appeared. "This is my friend Jasmine. She has had a rather rough night. Greta, would you please bring her something to eat and prepare one of the rooms for her? She will be spending some time with us here at the castle."

Greta hurried out to do Zarcon's bidding.

Zarcon looked at Jasmine with concern. "We will take care of you, Jasmine … and that accursed orb." He feared it would be the beginning of something more than he was prepared to deal with. He was aging and felt it in his bones. This challenge, he knew, would be all he could endure and possibly more. The witches were a powerful, evil bunch. He knew he was more powerful, but the magic drained him at an alarming rate lately. He hoped he was up to it.

Greta reappeared with a bowl of thick beef stew, a round of cheese, some crusty bread, and a flagon of sweet wine. She set them on the table.

Jasmine smiled her gratitude, and Greta went to prepare sleeping quarters for her. Jasmine ate heartily and was soon drooping over her plate. She was so exhausted that having her hunger assuaged meant that her body could finally relax. She felt safe in the castle, and the warmth from the fire was lulling her to sleep.

Zarcon rang the bell again, and Greta helped Jasmine out of the room. He frowned slightly at the thought that the orb was now a reality. He was grateful that Jasmine had it in her possession. If this truly was the blue orb, the power of it was beyond price. It must be guarded from any who wished to use it. Jasmine would be a worthy companion for the trials that faced them now. In the past few months, his suspicions had been raised regarding the surfacing of it. And now he had actually seen it—if only briefly. It was said to be in the possession of the witches, and that was intolerable. They were much too evil to possess something with so much power. So far, nothing alarming had occurred. In time, it would surely be made known what the witches would do with it.

Jasmine half-leaned on Greta as she helped her from the room. "It's not far to the room I have prepared for you." Greta led her down one short hall and turned right at the end. There were rooms on both sides of the hallway. She led Jasmine to the first one on the right and opened the door.

The room was cozy, and a large bed was centered on the wall to the left. A fire on the hearth warmed the room nicely.

Greta helped Jasmine undress, and she slipped into a warm flannel nightgown that was held out for her.

Jasmine said, "Greta, I have known Zarcon for years, off and on, and I have never seen you here before. How is it you know Zarcon?"

"Oh, that is a long story and better left for another day. You need your rest, but if you require anything at all, I will be glad to get it for you."

"I appreciate all you have done for me. Thank you for your kindness."

As Greta left the room and closed the door, Jasmine used the warm water and soap Greta had left to wash her face and hands and get ready for bed. It felt good to get some of the grime off. She would bathe in the morning. She took the orb out of her bag and held it in her hand. It was truly beautiful. She felt some of its power. It could draw her in if she let it. Fortunately, her power was not great enough for the orb to use. She was fascinated by it, but she knew she could not hold it for long. She hesitated for a moment before putting the orb back in the bag. She hid the bag in the back of the sideboard by the bed. She climbed into bed and was asleep as soon as her head hit the pillow.

Jasmine slept fitfully that night. She kept hearing the cry of the wolves in her dreams. She knew what would have happened to her if the wolves had caught her. They would not have hesitated to rip her to shreds. She also knew they were after the orb. She was sure these particular wolves were sent after her from the witches' coven.

The witches were enraged at the loss of the orb. They would stop at nothing to get it back. The leader of the pack was a big gray male. He was known to be particularly vicious. Thinking of him made her curl into a ball and tremble. Strong as she was, in her weakened state, she could hardly bear to think of what that wolf would have done to her.

Morning came, and the rain still fell. The clouds were so dark that it was hardly evident that daylight had come. The only good thing that could be said about the weather was that it would slow anyone on the roads. The roads were mucky and hardly passable, even for a horse and rider, much less a wagon or carriage. It was unlikely that the witches would leave their castle in this weather— orb or no—especially since they had the wolves to keep track of the orb.

Zarcon knocked on Jasmine's door to check on her condition. She let him in and smiled at his look of concern. She told him she was doing well considering.

He was glad to hear the energy coming back into her voice. She had been so exhausted the night before that he feared for her health. It was lucky that she was young. He could tell that running from the wolves had taken a toll on her. She had lost some weight since the last time he saw her. Her eyes had dark circles under them, but he knew Greta would take excellent care of her.

Zarcon reluctantly said, "Now that you have the orb, we must begin to plan our course of action. Are you up to spending some time doing so? I would like to know how you came into possession of such a powerful artifact. Is it true that the witches had it in their possession?"

Jasmine knew what he meant and knew that they must decide what to do with the orb and how to protect it. She said, "I will tell you everything as soon as I am ready. I will have Greta get you when I am ready to join you. I need a bath and a change of clothes. I have been on the trail for a long time."

Zarcon said, "Certainly. I will send Greta to you immediately if you're ready."

Jasmine smiled and thanked him. She knew the rain wouldn't last much longer. The witches would be on the hunt again soon enough, especially since they knew where to find Jasmine. The wolves would lead the witches to Zarcon's castle; that was a certainty. There seemed to be a special connection between them and the witches that she did not understand.

It was with a great deal of delight that Jasmine bathed in the tub Greta and some of the servants had brought in and filled with hot water. She could let the stress and worry of the past several weeks slip away for a few moments. The water helped relax her aching muscles. Her headache was also getting better now that she felt safe. She soaked until the water began to cool.

With regret, she called for Greta. Greta brought in a large, warm towel to help her dry off and dress. She stepped out for a moment and came back with breakfast for Jasmine. Jasmine was still weak and was grateful for Greta's help. She was normally very independent, but she realized that she really appreciated Greta and all she was doing for her. The time spent running had almost cost her life. She could not have gone another day. Her state of weakness was unsettling. She hoped her body would recover quickly for what was to come. She would need all her strength to deal with the orb and the witches.

Greta had cleaned Jasmine's clothes that morning and set them out for her. Once Jasmine had bathed and dressed and eaten the breakfast Greta had provided for her, she asked for Zarcon. When he arrived, she followed him to his study.

Zarcon led her down one of the many hallways that drew closer to the central area of the castle. They passed through an archway and into a large open area with large windows and a circular space used for gatherings. They went through this area and into another hallway at the other side; to the left was a large door that admitted them into Zarcon's study. There were shelves lined with books on three of the walls. The ceiling was very high. The fourth wall was filled with large leaded-glass windows that opened onto what appeared to be a garden in warmer times. It was a beautiful room with dark oak shelves and furniture. A massive, ornately carved desk was set just in front of the windows. In the center of the room was a table that served as a place for Zarcon to eat when he was working or as a place for planning or study. There were eight chairs set around the table with padded leather seats and high backs that were also ornately carved.

Jasmine sat across from Zarcon. He unrolled a map in front of them. Zarcon asked Jasmine to tell him how she had obtained the orb. He was fairly certain that Jasmine got the orb from the witches since they had recently come into great wealth and had moved into a castle of their own. They had no obvious means of support, and Zarcon could not help but think that the orb had something to do with all of that. It was reputed to have that kind of power, and much more besides, if old rumors could be trusted.

Jasmine told him that she had heard that the witches were in a castle in the Rimeron Valley. She finally found the castle there in the forest just outside the village of Castlebrook. She told him that the castle was an ugly thing with demons mounted on the walls and two forbidding-looking towers at either end. It was built with black granite and had a brooding air about it. Jasmine had watched the witches coming and going for many days. She dressed as a child, sat on the rocks near the castle, and talked with the villagers about what the witches had been doing recently. She stayed in an old inn where she could see if the witches left and how long they were gone. No one had noticed her as she watched. She dressed in ragged clothing and kept mainly to herself. Jasmine noticed that one of them seldom left the castle. Every day at about midday, she slept in a chair by a window overlooking the garden. This occurred without fail. She noticed that there were only two guards by the gate during the day. The other men seemed to be gone from the castle. She could also see the stable where the guards kept their horses just inside the gates. Soon she had a plan to get the orb.

A few days later, Jasmine got lucky. She had just left the inn with her backpack when she saw the other witches leaving the castle in a coach. They left the sleepy witch behind. The witches' armed guards had not yet returned, and the drawbridge had been left down. She could not have gotten into the castle if it were up. The moat contained some really frightening fish, and suspicious-looking bones were visible deep within the murky green water.

Jasmine crept across the wooden bridge and into the castle. The guards were talking softly to one another just inside the gate. Jasmine crept up behind them with a knife hidden in her hand. She said, "Would one of you come and help me with my horse. He seems to have caught a stone in his hoof."

One of the guards smirked and said, "Now, why don't you just go over to the smithy and have him help you?"

Jasmine smiled at him and said, "I just thought that a big man such as you could help a young girl in distress. My horse is in pain, and I don't want to make him walk any farther than I have to before he is helped. Could you please come for just a moment?"

The guard could not resist her plea. "Well, far be it from me to refuse the request of one so young and pretty. I'm sure I can help you." Under the ragged clothing, she was very pretty, and he was more than happy to go around the corner with her.

The glint in his eye told Jasmine he was planning on entertaining himself with her for a time. He seemed sure she would be easy prey. Unfortunately for him, Jasmine had other plans. As soon as they were out of earshot, she tripped the man and slit his throat before he could sound an alarm. He made no sound at all as he hit the cobblestones. Jasmine wiped the blood off on the guard's pants.

She climbed the wall of the building by using the bricks for foot and handholds, and she crouched on the roof for a few moments. She was counting on the other guard getting curious. It didn't take long, thankfully. Just as he rounded the corner and called the other guard's name, Jasmine jumped on his back and stabbed her short knife into the back of his neck, severing his spinal cord. The man dropped like a sack, dead as he hit the ground. Jasmine jumped off his back as he fell. She left the castle wall and went to the stables. She found a big black horse that looked strong and healthy. He must have been one of the witches' favorites. She hurriedly put a saddle and bridles on him and left him there while she tried to find the orb. She kept to the walls and quickly made her way to the main entrance to the witches' quarters.

Jasmine went up to the door and tried the handle. It was not locked, which was another stroke of luck. However, it must mean that the other witches would not be gone long. Jasmine quietly opened the door and walked in. The witch was sound asleep and did not stir when Jasmine quietly shut the door. Jasmine had seen blue lights in the upstairs bedroom and realized the witches must have the blue orb. She hurried up the stairs.

At the top of the stairs, Jasmine turned left and followed the hall to the door at the end. That door was locked, but Jasmine had special tools to enable her to pick any lock. After inserting the tool into the lock, she was able to open the door in seconds. Jasmine knew the witches would have the orb in a safe or strongbox hidden in that room. She searched quickly and found a box under the bed. This lock was a bit tricky, and Jasmine was getting nervous that the other witches would return before she could get out.

When she heard the click that meant the lock was conquered, she was surprised that the witches had not put a spell on it. She had feared that something nasty would happen to her when she opened the lock. She assumed that they were probably feeling very secure in their castle. Jasmine reached into the box, drew out the black velvet bag, and opened it to find the blue orb inside. She almost laughed aloud at the sight. She had been seeking this orb ever since she suspected there was something more to the witches' sudden wealth than their talent with magic would account for.

She stuffed the black velvet bag inside in her pack, slung it over her back, and crept out of the room. She quietly closed the door and hurried along the hall to the staircase leading to the front door. As she reached the bottom of the steps, the witch stirred in her sleep and opened her eyes. The witch started screaming and rushed to catch Jasmine before she could escape. Jasmine darted out the door before the witch could get near her.

Jasmine ran to the stables and jumped on the back of the big black stallion she had saddled earlier. Together they ran from the castle. She could hear the witch screaming and crying, but she did not leave the castle or pursue Jasmine. That was a relief for Jasmine. She put as much distance between herself and the castle as she could. She knew the other witches would not be long in coming back from their errand or whatever they were doing. She knew the witches would send their wolves after her as soon as they found out what she had done. Fortunately, she had planned for a long ride and had packed jerky, hardtack, and a skin of water in her pack to allow her to keep going.

Jasmine rode steadily for three days, following streams and small creeks as she could and resting when the wolves were far enough behind her. They always picked up the scent and came on howling and barking in fury. It was a desperate race. She had been at the end of her endurance when the rain started and made the road a slippery mess. Until then, she had made good progress in keeping ahead of the pack of wolves. As she tired, the horse did too. The wolves started gaining on her as she pushed her horse to go faster. Zarcon's castle could not have come at a better time. She knew she was failing, but the horse was amazing. He seemed to find strength deep inside that pushed him to the castle gates just as the wolves were snapping at his heels. He had literally saved her life.

"And you know the rest of the story, Zarcon. I ran for my life with the wolves close behind. I was afraid I wouldn't make it. When I saw your castle appear in the night, it gave me hope. As you know, I got here just in time to avoid being torn to shreds by those wolves."

Zarcon looked at Jasmine with new respect for all she had accomplished in getting the orb from the witches. Her strength and endurance were incredible in one so slender and young. "You amaze me, Jasmine. I am so grateful you were able to acquire the orb before the witches could do any real harm with it. They must be so furious right now. I wouldn't want to be that sleepy witch. She must be in a great deal of trouble. Have you felt the pull of the orb at all? There are tales of its attraction for anyone who possesses it." "Yes, but just a bit. I think it's because I have such a small amount of magic. I know a few things, but I have no real power. I think the orb affects those it can manipulate in more powerful ways. I also keep it in the velvet bag it came in. I will not touch it if I can help it."

Zarcon was relieved that there was a way to contain the orb. He had been concerned about Jasmine and the risk she was taking in traveling with it. He had heard the rumors and was afraid not to believe them. He could feel the pull of the orb every minute of the day and night since she brought it into his castle. It was a very dangerous object. He would not succumb to its power. He could not afford to. If he did, all would be lost—and he knew it.

Zarcon looked at Jasmine with pride and asked, "Do you know the history of the orb?"

Jasmine thought a minute and said, "You know, I only know a little about it and its power. Would you mind telling me its history? I know you have studied it for a number of years."

"I would be glad to tell you all I know … Many hundreds of years ago, in the land of Uranallee, there was a very powerful wizard. I'm sure you've heard of Xyrene. It is said that he was nearing the end of his life and wanted to leave something of power for a legacy to the world when he was gone. He had decided that an orb with special powers would be the perfect bequest. He set out to find all the information he could regarding the powers found in a special blue stone, azurian, seen only in the Jade Mountains where there are still many dwarf mines to this day. I'm sure you are familiar with the area, Jasmine. Have you seen the azurian stones? They are quite rare, thankfully."

Jasmine was thoughtful and finally said, "You know, I have heard of them, but I did not know that power could be added to them. I have not seen one myself."

Zarcon said, "I have not seen the stones either. I am hoping there are none of these stones left in the world. They are much too dangerous. It is said that Xyrene had studied many of the ancient writings about magic. He had found an ancient scroll that told of ways to empower stones of special composition with magic that was otherwise unheard of. This was exactly what Xyrene had been looking for. He memorized the spells and sent one of his acolytes to the Jade Mountains to purchase one of the pure blue azurian stones. Xyrene was willing to pay whatever it cost to get one. His acolyte finally returned with the perfect stone. Xyrene, in gratitude, made the mistake of promising to give the stone to his acolyte when he was gone.

"Unfortunately, that is what the evil acolyte was hoping for. It was the power he wanted.

"Xyrene perfected the stone himself. When he finished the work, Xyrene decided that his stone would be able to amplify directed thought with his power words. As Xyrene empowered the orb, it began to change.

"Jasmine, did you notice the swirls of color inside that looked like mist but are more than that?"

"I did. It is so fascinating to see. I was drawn to it as I watched the colors swirl. I can see how a person with power would have a difficult time staying away from it."

"That is indeed part of why it is so dangerous. I imagine the witch, Zora, is addicted to it by now and will struggle to maintain any level of sanity without it. It is suspected that Xyrene was not as careful as he thought he was. He was worried that there would be too much power in it if he continued, but his evil acolyte was able to convince Xyrene to complete the orb as he had planned.

"Xyrene finished the work of the orb and tried it out on his cattle by saying the proper words. His cattle were affected—and so were all the farm animals for several miles. In the next few months, it was obvious that it would be the most prolific year they had seen in a very long time.

"Xyrene was delighted, but he discovered that he was exhausted from making of the orb and using it. The orb used the wizard's strength to do his bidding, and using it would come with a price.

"The apprentice noticed Xyrene was fading fast. He thought it might be from the forming of the blue orb, but he did not realize it was also from using it. Xyrene knew he was dying, he tried to get his acolyte to promise to destroy the powerful orb. When it became apparent that his assistant was planning to keep the orb for his own use, Xyrene told him he would die if he used the orb.

"Well, as the great wizard took his last breath, his acolyte kept the orb and hid it, thinking he was strong enough to handle the orb. He was wrong, of course. After Xyrene's death, life in the village seemed to return to normal.

"Xyrene's assistant finally tried to use the orb. He said the words of power, began to feel lightheaded, and his strength failed. The blue orb was pulsing with a mysterious blue light. Just as he was beginning to think he would die, the feelings stopped. The blue orb grew still, the blue light faded, and all became quiet. Then suddenly, he was filled with excruciating pain. He opened his mouth to scream, and blue fire shot out of his mouth and eyes. He could not stop screaming. He fell to the ground and never rose again.

"After that, no one dared touch the orb. It was walled into the acolyte's tomb where none could enter and none dared. It is said that a strange blue light would shine from under the door to the tomb and that perhaps the orb had a life of its own.

"Hundreds of years later, after the castle had crumbled and turned to dust, the area was said to be haunted. The legend of the blue orb was lost for a time. Then a farmer was searching for one of his sheep in the area where the orb was last thought to be. He tripped over a stone that was buried in the dirt and found a blue stone crusted with dirt and debris. He took the stone to his farm and polished it. He took it to the wizard, Zenitten, who figured out that it was the ancient blue orb. He felt its pull and the need to use it.

"History tells us that Zenitten, in an effort to end a drought in the area, discovered that he must account for the breaking of the spell before it was too late. Otherwise, the orb would continue to take the power or strength of the user. In this way, Zenitten became very rich and powerful.

"But Zenitten became a greedy and jealous old man. He was slowly going mad. The orb gained more and more control of him as time went by. Then Zenitten fell, blamed his servant, and spoke a nasty curse that woke something within the orb. There was such a blast of power that everything was leveled. The land was covered in ash, and blue smoke was seen from as far away as Landpur. That is the last anyone had heard of the orb until now. That is why we must keep the orb out of the witches' hands. The power in it is just too great. Do you understand what we are up against with possession of this orb?"

Jasmine sighed, "I knew it was very dangerous, but I had not known the full history of it. I am even more terrified of the witches and what they could do if they ever get the orb back. What are we going to do now?"

They talked for a while longer about the witches and what they might be planning now that Jasmine had the orb. They were both very concerned. The witches were very powerful and had learned many spells that would do much harm if they were to get close enough. Jasmine and Zarcon decided they needed more help in that department. Zarcon was very strong, but he was aging, which was enough to convince them that they could not continue in the fight alone.

As Jasmine and Zarcon finished their conversation, Greta came into the room and asked if they would rest and eat something.

Jasmine and Zarcon realized they had been talking for hours. It was time for a break to rest their minds and bodies from their concerns.

Greta brought bowls of thick stew with crusty bread and tea made from the water from the spring under Zarcon's castle. It was delicious and strengthening to them both. Greta joined them as they chatted and were able to forget for a time the danger they were in.

As night drew in, the three of them settled around the fireplace and talked of other things. Soon, they went off to their rooms for the night. It was to be an early morning. Plans needed to be made for how to proceed—and where to go to get the help they were going to need. Zarcon had an idea, but he needed some time to think it through.

Witches In A Rage

Zora looked at her sister with disgust. She could barely contain her rage and nearly screamed, "How could you have slept so soundly that you didn't hear Jasmine in this very room? We all heard the rumor that Jasmine was in the area. We knew she wanted the orb. Why could you not have forgone your nap for once? We were only gone a few short hours. Now we have lost the orb because of you."

Zora was the high priestess of the witch coven. She was short and rotund with long graying hair that stuck out in every direction. Her face was round, and her cheeks had spots of bright red, which was a small indication of the rage she was trying very hard to control. She wore a shapeless black gown made of silk. Her hands trembled with rage. She wanted desperately to choke her sister, Magg, but she knew that would only aggravate the situation. *How could Magg have been so stupid?* Jasmine had slipped into their castle while the other witches had been away. Magg had been left to guard the orb, but she had fallen asleep by the window where the sun was warm and comforting. She had always taken a nap in the afternoon. She couldn't help herself, but this was a disaster! Jasmine had even killed two of the guards. It was difficult to believe that such a small woman could do so much damage in such a short time.

Magg was taller than Zora—but not by much. She was also plump and had the same unruly hair. Hers was ash blonde. She was also somewhat lazy, but she had certain gifts that the other witches needed at times. They couldn't just send her away—or worse—and now they had to deal with the loss of the orb. Zora and the rest of the witches were willing to kill to get it back. The others might have killed Magg if Zora were not her sister.

It had happened, of course, while Magg slept. When Magg took her nap, she slept so soundly that it was almost impossible to wake her. It was obvious now that Jasmine had bided her time and noted the habits of the witches. She had waited until the other witches were gone and sneaked in during Magg's nap. The orb had been kept in the special box in Zora's bedroom, but that would not have been difficult for Jasmine to figure out. Jasmine had probably noticed the strange blue light coming from Zora's bedroom certain nights and wanted to look at the orb. The more she used it and held it, the stronger the pull became. She could hardly bear to leave it alone anymore. She began to tremble just thinking about it being gone and no longer in her control. Without the orb, the witches would have to worry about their income. That alone was frightening to them. It had been so easy with the orb. Zora could just use it to call money to them. They didn't have to worry about where it came from. It was just there when they needed it. Zora had noticed a slight weakening of her strength, but she chalked it up to "too much to do." Before the witches found the orb, Zora had read everything she could find about it and how it was controlled. She was obsessed with getting it. She knew it had to be someplace. Something that powerful did not just disappear.

Zora had gathered the four witches of her coven to seek the orb in the area where it had last been seen. The name of the blast zone was

Desolation for very good reason. Nothing grew there, and no animal would live near it—even though it had been several hundred years since it was ruined. The five witches had camped at the edge of Desolation and spent many weeks searching the ruins for any sign of the orb. Finally, when they were searching near the center of the ruins, they felt something calling to them. Zora was affected the strongest and could pinpoint the source of the attraction. She and the other witches took turns digging. They finally broke through what appeared to be a small room. They all screamed in delight when they saw a bright blue light shining through the small opening. They dug frantically, pulling away the stones, until the hole was big enough for one of them to get inside and retrieve the orb.

Of all five witches, Anesthia was the most slender. So, it fell to her to crawl into the hole. She was just able to slip through and crawl down to the floor of the small room. She could see where she was because of the light from the orb. She stood up in the small space and admired the orb for a moment. Zora lost patience and screamed, "What's taking you so long? Hurry. I want to see it for myself!"

Anesthia smiled her most evil smile and said, "Don't worry. You shall have it soon enough. I was just admiring it for a moment."

Zora said, "Well, stop it and bring it out *now!*"

When Anesthia picked up the orb, it sent a thrill of power through her body she had never felt before. The thought came to her that she could destroy the other witches and have it all to herself. She contemplated the idea for a moment and then realized she could not do it. There was too much at stake to try to wield the power herself. At least for the moment, she needed her sister witches. She climbed up to the hole, handed the orb to Zora, and finished climbing out of the hole.

Zora took the orb and held it lovingly. The other witches crowded around to gaze at the prize they had finally won. The beauty of the orb was almost hypnotic. With a great deal of reluctance, Zora placed it in a black velvet bag.

The witches knew they could finally have all they desired. They could rule the world and fulfill their most evil passions now that they possessed the orb of legend. They could hardly believe it, but it was true … now it was gone! And they knew Jasmine had taken it. She would pay dearly for that. She would not live to tell the tale if they could help it.

It was known that Jasmine had no problem getting into any lock that was made. She had the skills and tools to get into anything, and she was dedicated enough to tackle them all. Well, she had definitely been dedicated in getting the orb from them. She was in and out of the castle before Magg could do anything but scream. Fortunately, the other witches came home not long after Jasmine left. As they had approached the castle, Magg screamed that Jasmine had taken the orb. Jasmine had only been gone for an hour.

They had sent the wolves after Jasmine as soon as they realized what she had done, but since the wolves had been far from the castle, it took extra time to answer Zora's call. The wolves had failed to catch Jasmine or get the orb. They would pay for that failure. The wolves would try very hard to get back into the witches' good graces. After all, they knew where Jasmine was. Magg would also pay for the loss of the orb. It would take time, but she would pay dearly.

Magg was young for a witch. She was only twenty-three in human years. She was also very naive. That's why Jasmine could get to her. It had probably been foolish to leave her at the castle to guard the orb in the first place, but that was neither here nor there now that the orb was gone.

Along with Zora and Magg, the five witches in the coven included Heleren. She had high cheekbones and full red lips. Her eyes were sea green, and her hair was deep red. She was fuller figured than the other three witches. She loved the color red and wore it at all times since they found the orb. Her gowns were all the same shade of deep red, much like the color of blood. Velvet and silk were her favorites. She wore a black velvet cloak when the weather was cool.

Heleren had lured many an unwary man to an unhappy fate with her charms. To say she was beautiful was not quite accurate. She had a way with men that went beyond her physical attributes. Of course, part of it was the magic. The men she chose seemed to fall for her the minute they laid eyes on her. The purpose was to use these men for her pleasure. Heleren's pleasure was not limited to the physical. She also took delight in the mental control she could exert over others.

There are many stories of her using men. She had sent one to his death by asking him to throw himself off the Tanganee Bridge, just for her amusement. The man did it. He left a wife and three children behind. Of course, that never bothered Heleren. It was all part of the game she played. Magic definitely had its uses. Heleren used her magic to manipulate and humiliate. She especially enjoyed humiliating men. It was said in quiet circles that there was once a man who had lured her into his arms only to laugh and leave her when she told him she loved him. She was so humiliated that she swore it would never happen again. She had never let anyone get close again. Heleren became very bitter as time passed. It was becoming more and more difficult for her to find pleasure in anything except causing pain. She was in the coven to find satisfaction. She hoped their plan for ruling the world might help give her some interest in life and living.

Anesthia had short, spiky white hair and cold blue eyes. She was very beautiful, but her heart was like stone. No one could guess her age. She was still slender and graceful with a few lines around her eyes, but nothing else hinted at her true age. Since they found the orb, she preferred to wear blue silk that matched her eyes. She knew the effect it had on those around her. She also wore a long dark blue velvet cloak. Anesthia stayed in the coven for the sole purpose of gaining power over those she considered lesser inhabitants of the land. She felt that her life would be so much more interesting if she had power over others. She delighted in killing animals and sometimes humans for the same reason. It was such an exhilarating experience when she could watch their lives flow out of their bodies. Many thought she used her magic to bring their life essence to her. It was suspected that this was the manner in which she seemed never to age. In any case, it was wise to give her a wide berth.

Myshella was the fifth witch and probably the worst of the lot. She was cruel to all. She had long, curly black hair, cold, black eyes, thin lips, and a long, straight nose. She was tall and thin and had dark skin. She may have been beautiful at one time, but life had changed her looks to become cold and hard. Now she enjoyed nothing quite so much as bringing pain to anyone who crossed her in any way. Any perceived slight was worthy of the most severe punishment. She wore black at all times. She preferred her gowns to be made of silk, but lightweight wool was good in cooler weather. She wore black leather pants under her nearly black wool cloak. She could almost disappear at night when she wanted to. With her magic, the eyes of those who looked would pass over her without seeing her. The person would only feel a cold wind and shiver.

The coven had survived for many years. The witches were absolutely driven to conquer all. As the coven sought the return of the orb, there was nothing they considered too harsh or cruel.

Zora gathered the other witches to her to plot the recovery of the orb. "We must plan our attack as soon as we know what we're up against. The wolves will lead us to her place of refuge. We will wage war on any who try to protect her."

Anesthia smiled. She loved the sound of that. War meant using the tools she possessed. If power over others could be had, she would have it.

Myshella thought for a moment and smiled. It was the kind of smile that would freeze the blood of a scorpion. Myshella would linger over her victims and prolong their deaths for as long as possible. Hearing their screams pleased her.

Zora said, "We must follow the wolves with our scrying pool. They have only been gone a short time. Once we know who is protecting Jasmine, we will act."

The other witches nodded for their own reasons. The coven was strong, but they were not loyal. The witches worked together for a common goal and nothing more. Besides, it was convenient to let Zora lead. After all, she did possess the stronger gifts. One of those gifts was the very inconvenient ability to detect a traitor. She would know almost immediately if one of them decided to go out on her own. They needed each other, at least for the time being.

Zora led the others to the scrying room in the lower chambers of the castle. They went through an iron-bound door and walked down the cold, narrow staircase in single file. Zora lit a torch as they moved through the next doorway. It was very dark with no windows or slits in the stone walls. They came to a wide landing that opened into the bowels of the castle. The large room had a stone bowl on a pedestal. In the back of the room was a spring from which Zora filled the bowl. The water was dark and smelled of sulfur. No one knew for sure where it came from, but it had been there for centuries.

Zora looked into the magical water, mumbled an incantation, and waved her hands over it. The water cleared, and the witches saw the wolves running through the forest.

"This could take hours," Magg said.

Zora slapped her. "If you hadn't lost the orb, we wouldn't be here at all. I would advise you to be very, very quiet and pay very close attention to what is happening here. The wolves could find Jasmine at any time. We must be alert and vigilant. You will take the first watch. If you know what is good for you, you will not fail me again!"

Magg held her cheek in shock. Her sister had never struck her before. She knew how much trouble she was in for losing the orb. She would not fail Zora—no matter what. "I will do as you ask." She did her best not to let her tears show. The other witches would see it as weakness, and there would be no end to their teasing.

The other witches watched the exchange and smiled. It truly was a moment to remember. They decided to relax for a bit and hope the wolves were close to Jasmine. It was getting more and more interesting.

The hours passed. The witches had food brought down at intervals. Each witch took her turn watching the scrying pool. Finally, on the evening of the third day, the wolves were almost on Jasmine. They were shocked to see that she was riding one of their horses, the big black stallion. They realized how she had gotten so far so quickly. They cheered as the wolves closed in on her. They were howling in anticipation. Jasmine disappeared into a large castle, and the witches watched in horror as the lead male wolf slammed into the gate. The wolves continued to prowl around, looking for an opening, but finding none, they lingered, hoping to see Jasmine again. The large castle was in a valley near the edge of a forest. It was white granite with very high walls, which was not what the witches had expected. They were hoping for a small cottage with no one around. It was going to be much more difficult than they had hoped for.

"Now what do we do?" Magg asked. "That's Zarcon's castle. How will we ever wage war on one as strong as he? He probably has the orb now! This is terrible!"

The others were worried, but they were able to hide their concern. They had to get the orb back. It would just take longer and require better planning, but they would eventually win. They had no doubt.

Zora shook her head. This was grave news. She wanted to slap Magg again, but it would be futile. Magg was so upset that she probably wouldn't feel it. Zora looked the other witches in the eye one by one and calmly said, "We must have courage. We are all strong, and together we are surely a match for Zarcon. He is old. We have to plan very carefully and take our time about this. War is what we declare here, and war is what we will prepare for." Zora smiled her most wicked smile with a terrible gleam in her eye.

Three of the witches looked at each other with varying degrees of smiles. Their eyes were alight with the prospect of taking on Zarcon and Jasmine. The future was exciting and intimidating.

Magg cowered in the corner. She did not feel good about any of this. She remembered all that she had heard of Zarcon and his impressive power. Perhaps she was the wisest one of them all. Only time would tell.

Plans Made

Zarcon had known the moment that Jasmine showed him the orb that he would need reinforcements. There was no doubt that the witches would be plotting to get it back. He pondered through the night who he should call upon to help. There were many who would be willing to help, but there were not many who would want to go up against the witches. The list was short. Zarcon had his own army within the castle, but waging war against witches would require a special kind of talent. He knew the man he must call, but he hesitated to bring him into the problem. The man was Donavan. He was a man with many talents. Unfortunately, he had retired from the world and was living alone. Donavan had sworn that he would not be disturbed and didn't want visitors the last time Zarcon had tried to communicate with him. He had his reasons and wouldn't discuss them with anyone. However, it was general knowledge that it had something to do with the murder of his family while he was away fighting in the Wolf Wars five years before. He had sworn that he would not become involved in the world's problems again. He had served his time, and it was time to rest. He often said, "Let others do the dirty work now. I have had enough of it."

Zarcon needed Donavan because he was strong and smart. He also had some magical powers that would be of value at this perilous time. Donavan could deflect the witches' spells for short periods. It was very draining on Donavan to use his magic, but he could do it if called upon. Zarcon also hoped Donavan could be taught to use other forms of magic. The ability to block spells was very rare and probably indicated other hidden powers. Zarcon would have to pay Donavan a visit soon. He needed him desperately. The wolves had already come sniffing around. He knew Jasmine would be coming with him. She was a valuable ally. Besides, Jasmine held the orb. The problem was convincing her of the necessity of going to Donavan. He knew that Jasmine was not overly fond of him. She had not trusted him since their last meeting. It would take some time for her to learn to trust him at all, and trust was something they needed on their mission.

Zarcon began to make plans for the journey. It would be long and arduous, but it was necessary if they were to have any chance of succeeding against the witches. Things had to be taken into hand right away for them to have any hope at all.

Zarcon called Greta to his library early that morning. She was always close at hand. She seemed to know when he was upset and when he might need her. Greta was much more than a servant to Zarcon. She was his confidante and close adviser, and he valued her intelligence and wit. Besides, under those frumpy clothes, she was a very attractive woman. He had decided Greta would be coming with them. He needed her insight as well. She could sense things that he sometimes missed.

Zarcon would also bring his great hound. Voltar would be able to warn them if the wolves came within two miles of their group. He had a gift for that. They would need Voltar on the journey. Zarcon also had the strongest horses in the country. He bred them for endurance and strength. No horse could outrun or outdistance his beauties. All of them were a deep russet. Anyone in the land would know one of them on sight. They were magnificent.

Jasmine was almost sad that the rain had stopped that morning. She woke to sunshine coming in her bedroom window. The roads would dry out, and it would be much easier for the witches to travel. The witches would know where she was soon enough. She was hoping Zarcon had a plan for them to get out of here. Jasmine had slept late that morning. She took off the nightgown Greta had brought her the night she arrived and bathed again in the big tub Greta and the servants had brought in that morning with hot water and thick towels. All of Zarcon's servants were kind and helpful. She relaxed in the tub until the water began to cool. She dressed in the clothes she had brought in her pack. She wore her black boots, a slim skirt of gray silk, and a shirt that was also gray silk. Greta had made sure they were cleaned and ready to wear.

When she was ready, Jasmine went down the hall to meet with Zarcon. She was hungry, and Greta had told her that breakfast was waiting as soon as she was ready to eat. Her mouth watered as she came closer to the dining room. She could smell ham and potatoes. As she entered the dining room, she could see that there was also hot bread and cheese. Greta had placed a large pitcher of cool berry juice on the table.

Zarcon looked on as Jasmine ate. He had finished his breakfast and had been waiting for her to come down to eat. He said, "How did you sleep? Have you rested well? I'm glad to see that you are up and ready to talk this morning. We must assume that the witches were watching the wolves come here. Would you be willing to leave soon?"

Jasmine was relieved that Zarcon was already thinking as she was. She knew they had to get away. "I slept well. Thank you. I want to leave as soon as possible, but where will we go? Do you have a plan?"

Zarcon smiled. "I have a plan, and I hope you will be willing to go along with me."

Jasmine thought, *Where could he be thinking of going that I would not want to follow?* She said, "Where would that be, Zarcon? You know I can't stay here any longer. The witches will be coming soon."

"I want you to think about this before you give me your answer. Are you willing to do so?"

"Yes. Please just tell me." Jasmine was becoming impatient. *Is he stalling? Why can't he just say it?*

Finally, Zarcon said, "I have been thinking, and I have decided that we must seek the aid of Donavan. He has the strength and intelligence, among other valuable assets, to help us in our fight against the witches. I know you have had issues with him in the past, but these are going to be difficult times, to say the least, and we need all the help we can muster."

Jasmine thought about his proposal. She did indeed have issues with Donavan. During the Wolf Wars, he had offered to take her to Synkana. The city was not far from where they were. He had left one night when the wolves were howling and never returned. There was some talk that a witch was in the area, but he had never come back to explain what had happened to make him leave her alone. How could she trust him now? Zarcon seemed to think Donavan was important to the problems they would be facing. If she said no, Zarcon would honor her feelings, but how could she allow her pride to rob them of the help he thought they needed? She said, "I would consider the journey if you can explain why Donavan is so important to us."

"Donavan has some magic that we will need desperately. He can actually block the witches' spells for short periods of time. It tires him greatly, and that concerns me, but if he can help us, even for a short period of time, I would prefer to have him there. There is one catch.

Donavan has not left his small cabin in years. He says he wants to be left alone. You have heard about his family during the Wolf Wars?"

"I heard that they were killed, but I never heard the details."

Zarcon didn't know how much he could tell Jasmine. It was a terrible story. "Donavan had been out with his patrol one dark night. He left his wife and two children at home. They should have been safe. There was no reason for the wolves to track them to his home, but they did find his family. They circled the house, howling. Donavan's wife, Zerina, took the children to the cellar and pulled the heavy wooden door over the entrance. Again, they should have been safe. However, there was a witch with the wolves that night. She was said to be short and round with graying hair that stuck out from her head in every direction. She was laughing as the wolves were howling. It was a terrible sound. Farmers from a mile away said they could hear the racket from their farms. Suddenly, a fire could be seen in the distance. The witch had thrown a torch onto the roof of the wooden farmhouse. It caught fire immediately. The wolves blocked all the exits as Donavan's family tried desperately to get out, but there was no escape that evil night. Donavan arrived just as the roof collapsed on his home. The witch and her wolves were gone by then. He was never the same. I think he went a little mad after that. I'm counting on him having enough rage left for the witches to help us now."

Jasmine was shocked and saddened by the news. She said, "I had no idea the death of Donavan's family had been so horrific. It explains a lot. The night he left me might have been the very night his family was killed. I heard the horrible howling of the wolves. I am ashamed of the anger I have harbored all this time. I know I must forgive him. If I had only known, I might have helped in some way."

Zarcon replied, "You could not have known. It really was a terrible time in the history of this land. Donavan was trying to do his duty, and it cost him his family. Let's hope he has had enough time to recover."

Zarcon and Jasmine spent the rest of the day planning what they would need for their journey. Greta joined them as soon as the household was settled for the day. She wore a red silk gown with white embroidery on the hem and bottom of the long, belled sleeves. It was slender with a high neck. She looked beautiful. Her clothes managed to hide her charms. Zarcon smiled to see her in such a fine dress. Jasmine was pleased to see Greta. She was beginning to think of her as a friend. They talked of the upcoming journey. They planned on leaving in two days, hoping that Jasmine would have her strength back by then. They knew they had to leave soon. Time was not on their side.

As the sun was setting, Greta looked out the window at the valley below. She happened to catch a glimpse of several wolves milling around the meadow at the base of the castle walls. "Zarcon, Jasmine, what do you make of that?"

"Zarcon! Those are the wolves that were chasing me! I'd know that big gray male anywhere."

The wolves circled the open field and howled in frustration. The leader barked a command, and the other wolves followed him back toward the witches. They left in a hurry and howled as they ran. They could be heard for miles. It made the hair on the back of everyone's necks stand up, especially Jasmine. She knew how relentless they were.

Zarcon said, "The witches must have called them back. They know where you are. The witches have ways of watching that I am not entirely sure of. They must be following the wolves with whatever power they possess. They know where Jasmine is for now—but not for long."

"You saw the wolves. We must leave tomorrow. The witches will need some time to decide their next course of action. If we leave right away, we may have a head start."

Jasmine said, "I'm all for any advantage we can get. Let's go as soon as we may."

Greta had no more desire to remain at the castle if the witches were coming. It was time to move on.

"I'm bringing Voltar. He can smell a wolf from two miles away and a witch from a mile away." Zarcon smiled. "Any advantage we can find is one I want to have with us."

Jasmine smiled too. It would be one of the few adventures she did not have to face alone. She was glad for the company and protection it provided—even if it meant that she was not as free as she was used to being. There were too many risks involved not to use anything she could to save the orb from the witches. The power of it was too great. With the orb, it wouldn't be long before they would be able to rule the world. That must not happen. If it cost her life, Jasmine would not allow that to happen. She was fairly certain that Zarcon and Greta felt the same way. If they could convince Donavan to join them, they might have a chance of keeping the orb away from the witches. Zarcon's powers were formidable, yet if he felt the need to have Donavan with them, it must be important.

Greta, Jasmine, and the servants spent most of the day packing what they would need. Zarcon worked out the details of their journey in his library. Jaron, the stable master, was informed that the expedition would begin in the morning so he could have the horses ready. He was a strong, good-natured, man with dark curly hair and soft blue eyes that seemed to smile and put others at ease. He was also the smith and had learned something of the health and welfare of horses. He wore a leather apron most of the time. He would be needed on the mission to keep the horses healthy and sound. Zarcon asked if he would go with them to whatever waited for them with the witches. Jaron was more than willing to go fight the witches. They had caused his family some problems over the years. He would mention things every once in a while that would make others suspect he hated the witches with good reason.

Terrence, the master-at-arms, was asked to choose ten of his best men to take with them on the mission. Terrence was tall and powerfully built with a large mustache that drooped to his chin. His dark skin and eyes missed nothing. He was handsome by most measures, and his features seemed chiseled from granite. He was very competent and thorough. He considered himself to be Zarcon's bodyguard and had saved the wizard's life many times. He would not have allowed Zarcon to leave him behind on such a dangerous mission.

Zarcon called the head servants and workers to his gathering room and said, "I have gathered you here to tell you some grave news. You all know that Jasmine has come to the castle while being chased by wolves sent by the witches. You also know that there is a group of us leaving the castle for an undetermined amount of time. What you don't know is that the witches have sent those wolves to find us and to allow them to know where Jasmine is. Some of you may have seen the wolves circling the meadow this morning."

Many of the servants gasped, and some nodded. They knew what it could mean for their safety, especially if Zarcon were gone.

Zarcon continued, "I am going to ask you to do something that will be hard on all of you. I am going to ask you to leave the castle as soon as we leave in the morning. Gather any belongings that will help you survive in the forest and leave. If the witches come here and find us gone, they will seek some form of revenge on all who are left. You've heard the stories, and you know they are ruthless. Please make sure that everyone leaves within two days. I wish I could protect you, but our mission is of utmost importance. We will do all we can to destroy the witches, but you all must leave. Do you understand what I am asking of you?"

They all answered, "Yes."

One of the servants asked, "Where should we go? There are no towns or inns near here."

Zarcon said, "I am aware of that, and that is why I suggested that you gather anything that will help you survive in the forest for a few weeks. I can't know how long we will be gone, but the witches will come. Take any weapons you can carry from the armory. The wolves might come with them. I don't need to tell you what that means. I won't be taking all of the soldiers, so you won't be without some protection, but you must hurry and put as much distance from here as you may. I know there are some caves a few miles up the ravine to the north. Perhaps they might provide some shelter as well as protection from the wolves."

The servants grew fearful at that and left with the resolve to be gone as soon as they could gather up their belongings and food from the castle. Zarcon was relieved to hear them talking thus. It was a relief to know they would leave and find safety in the forest. He only hoped that the witches would leave the wolves at home. He didn't want to think about what would happen if the wolves found his people in the forest. His soldiers would help protect them, and the weapons in the armory would serve them well. Beyond that, he could only hope for the best for them.

Zarcon found Greta after the meeting and held her close while he tried to calm himself. It was a fearful thing they were going to undertake.

Greta held him for a time. She had rarely seen him so upset. Maybe he knew something she did not. Her level of apprehension rose considerably. She looked up into his face and softly asked, "What concerns you, Zarcon?"

"I'm at a loss as to how to save everyone from what is coming. It suddenly struck me that we are leaving all within the castle to a possibly horrible fate. I hope they all leave as I have advised them."

Greta replied, "You can only do what you can do. The rest is up to them." Zarcon's group agreed to go to bed early that night. They had to leave at first light. It would be a very long day. Jasmine realized she would have to ride one of the big horses that Zarcon prided himself on. She hoped he had one that was a bit smaller. Her ride on the big black horse when she was running from the wolves convinced her that big horses were not exactly comfortable for her size. That horse had saved her life, but she wasn't sure she could handle it again. Her legs were still sore.

Zarcon was thinking of her and had a small horse that would do nicely. He was going to sell it because it was born so much smaller than the other horses he preferred, but he decided to keep the mare because she was so pretty and full of fire. Zarcon took Jasmine out to meet the horse just before dinner so she could get to know her before they would have to leave the next day. Jasmine loved the horse as soon as she saw her. The mare's name was Ruby because her coat was a beautiful light russet color unlike the other horses, which were roan. Ruby seemed to be a throwback to some other line. Zarcon could never figure out why she was so different from his other stock. And now he was doubly glad he had kept her. As Jasmine approached Ruby, she spoke to her in quiet tones, words that were not really words, just soft sounds to soothe her. Ruby responded and came to Jasmine to nuzzle her hand, which held an apple for Ruby. Jasmine had gotten the apple from the kitchen as she passed through on her way to the stable. Jasmine stroked Ruby's neck and head and helped Jaron saddle her.

As Jasmine climbed into the saddle, Ruby whinnied but stood still. Jasmine knew then that the two of them would make a great pair. She was excited to be off on the journey. Jasmine rode Ruby around the stable yard for a few minutes to get to know her temperament, and Ruby was content to do so. Jasmine was almost reluctant to dismount, but it was time to have their evening meal and get ready for bed.

Greta and Zarcon were both tall, so the other horses in the stable were fine for them. Zarcon rode his favorite stallion. Phantom was large—even for the horses Zarcon raised. He was strong and spirited but easy for Zarcon to handle.

Greta's horse was a mare named Scarlet. Her horse was gentle and strong. Greta knew her horse well and looked forward to what lay ahead. Greta was not without gifts of her own as they faced the witches. She, too, would be a great asset to their endeavor. She was still working out what her powers were and what advantage they would be against the witches, but she could almost read minds and emotions with her observations of people. Perhaps she would be able to warn the others of what the witches planned before it was too late.

Zarcon knew he needed the ten soldiers, including Jaron and Terrence, because he was not foolish enough to imagine they could travel through this rough land without protection. He did not want to bring so many that they would be noticed. They also had several pack animals to take care of the need for food and shelter on the trail. Hunting would supplement their diet, but other necessities would need to be brought with them.

They ate dinner with Jaron and Terrence that night. Zarcon needed to know if all was ready and whether any problems or concerns needed to be addressed before the morning. Greta brought in roast venison from Zarcon's forest and vegetables from the castle garden and roasted potatoes. They ate with gusto, not knowing when they would have another meal like it. They went to their respective rooms early and tried to settle in for the night. Most slept fitfully, but at least they were resting. Jasmine was more tired than she expected after the activity of the day. This worried her a little since they would be riding all the next day, and swiftly, but she knew she would do whatever she must.

The next morning was cold with a mist on the ground. Winter was coming. After a hurried breakfast, they gathered in the stable yard to mount up, each with their own thoughts. There was some trepidation since none of them knew what to expect, and all feared what could happen. They would be facing the witches at the end of this mission, an unsettling thought at best.

When all were mounted up and the packhorses were loaded, they headed for the gates of the castle. Voltar was barking with excitement, happy to be leaving the confines of the castle. The rest of the group was somewhat solemn. Yet, as the sun broke through the mist and the dawn was bright and sunny, their hopes rose. The situation didn't look quite so gloomy. There were a few clouds left over from the storm that had passed the day before. The road was finally drying out enough for travel. It seemed a good omen for the first day of the expedition. Jasmine felt hope rise as they finally set out. The threat of the witches' wrath seemed far away, if only for a while. There would be plenty of time to worry about that in the days to come. Jasmine smiled at Greta, and they rode side by side for a time. Voltar stayed close to Zarcon as he rode. The big dog was known by the horses and did not cause them any alarm as they traveled.

Terrence rode in the lead with the two scouts who would ride ahead and look for places to rest and camp for the night as the day wore on. He knew enough about the witches to be wary. He also knew that if the wolves had been here, it would not be out of the question that they could be watching even now. He was hopeful that they had gone back to the witches to report, but one could never be sure about the witches and their wolves. Terrence had been with Zarcon for many years and never in all that time had he felt such a dread for what might lie ahead. To deal with witches such as these after all these years, when he was no longer at his peak, filled him with apprehension.

The day remained clear as they rode west through the forest. There was a single track to follow. Trees grew close to the trail and shaded their passage. The sun dappled the forest floor as it shone through the trees. The weather was pleasant and not as cool as it had been. This part of the land was mainly unpopulated by even the meanest of farms.

Zarcon preferred the solitary life in the forest to that of towns or cities. It would be a while before they came near any sort of village. That was why Zarcon was very careful to plan for the pack animals. They would need a backup if the game was not plentiful enough for their group. This could be an even greater problem given that the wolves had been in the forest only the day before. It was likely that the wolves had taken a large share of the game animals as they returned to the witches' castle.

They rode for three hours and finally stopped by a small stream to eat, rest, and check the horses. Jaron was very good with the horses and could provide care if anything went wrong. He was also very good-natured and enjoyed the company as much as caring for the horses. Zarcon was glad he had asked him to come. Jaron had been eager to participate in such an important mission. He longed for adventure but never had the opportunity to travel very far from Zarcon's castle. There had never been reason. He was young and very strong. He was confident that he would be able to help if things got rough as they journeyed. He looked forward to the challenge, but little could he know what was ahead for them all. For now, he was happy to be able to care for Zarcon's beautiful horses. He checked each one of them carefully, making sure none had rocks in their hooves that would cause damage to the horses. All was well for the first part of the journey. Jaron had expected nothing less.

When he finished checking the horses, Jaron walked over to Zarcon and said, "The horses are doing well. They are so strong. I'm always impressed with their stamina. You have done well in breeding them, Zarcon." Jaron loved the horses and was very proud to be chosen to oversee their care.

"And you have done well caring for them. I am so grateful you chose to come with us. Thank you again."

The other men in the party spoke to one another quietly as they ate and prepared to ride once more. They knew that life was never boring when Zarcon was on a mission, so the anxiety was evident. They only hoped they would be ready when the time came to fight. In this area, there could be anything from wolves to bandits. It was very important to be wary. Terrence was especially anxious, given what little he knew about the mission they were on. He counseled with Zarcon whenever he could get him alone. "Zarcon, please let me know if you need anything at all to make your travel more comfortable. If there is anything I can do to help, you know you can count on me."

Zarcon was thoughtful for a moment and then said, "Terrence, you know that is the reason you are here. I know that you are aware of my needs and are watchful if I tire. I will count on your discretion as well. Thank you for your concern. I am feeling quite well just now."

Terrence bowed his head in acknowledgement and headed back to the others to give instructions regarding the placement and order of watches through the coming night. They would be stopping for the night in another few hours.

Jasmine and Greta ate in silence, each with her own concerns. They each knew that the forest was full of surprises, and they wanted very much to be on their way again. It seemed that everything was quiet this day. The thought crossed Jasmine's mind that the wolves may have had an impact on the forest population. Even the birds were relatively quiet. She felt the hairs on the back of her neck rise at the thought that they could be anywhere, possibly watching them even now.

Finally Zarcon ordered them all to mount up. They were ready to travel once again. The soldiers all carried longbows, arrows, short swords, shields, and knives. Their shields bore Zarcon's emblem: a star with a flame below it. The men also had the emblem on the left breast of their uniforms, which were gray tunics over black pants. They also had silver braids on the shoulders and along the bottoms of the tunics. Their uniforms also included dark gray cloaks with a silver clasp in the shape of a flame.

Zarcon wore a dark red cloak with silver flame clasp, a silver gray tunic, and black wool pants. Greta also wore black wool pants and white cotton tunic with her dark hair tied back with a leather thong. Her cloak was black velvet, heavy and warm. Jasmine wore her black riding cloak, black leather pants, and white muslin tunic. She wore a pack with her few belongings and, of course, the orb. Zarcon was the only one of the party who was aware of that fact. She also carried weapons. She had a longbow and short sword as well. She was very good with weapons. She had lost her own weapons when she fled from the witches' castle and the rest during the chase through the forest when the wolves were after her. It felt good to have some once more. Zarcon had allowed her to choose whatever she needed from his considerable supply in the armory. The group also carried more subdued clothing in their packs. They knew they would need them later on when they must disguise their passage as farmers or merchants when they came to the more populated areas of the country, but they wanted to start the mission in their uniforms to remind them of the seriousness of the journey they were about to take and in respect for Zarcon.

They continued west as the day wore on. Terrence led the way through the more familiar areas this close to the castle. They stopped again close to a clearing. There was a small creek that would allow the horses to drink and grass for them to eat. The party would eat here and set up camp. It was also hoped that there would be game to supplement their diet. The meadow was promising. If all else failed, they could fish the creek in the morning. As a group, they unrolled their bedding. One of the men cooked some beans over the fire. They drank water from the creek and talked quietly. They were feeling the effects of the long ride.

Voltar ran among the group, looking for attention and handouts. He finally settled down near Zarcon after they had all eaten. The sun was close to setting, and they wanted to be settled for the night before it was dark. Jasmine had been tired at the beginning of the ride, but Ruby was a great horse and matched Jasmine's spirit and strength. She was able to enjoy the ride after all. She was becoming hopeful that the journey would be successful, even if it was too early to feel that way.

Witches Making Plans

The witches left the scrying room to plan their battle with Zarcon and Jasmine. They climbed the stairs through the castle until they reached the main level. Their war room was located in the south side of the castle where the sun shone through the longest part of the day to give them more daylight. They stood around their war room table and looked at the map there. Zora pointed at the place in the forest to the south that was the area of Zarcon's castle. The wolves had shown the way. It was fairly remote, which made their plans easier to implement since there would be few people around to worry them or raise any alarm.

Zora had been thinking of what to do and finally said, "I would like to take one or two of you with me to Zarcon's castle to survey the area and see if we can find a weak point in which to enter the castle without Zarcon's being aware. We know that the castle is heavily guarded and probably has wards placed on its entry points to sound alarm if anyone tries to enter without leave to do so. If we find that we cannot enter, then we may take it down if necessary." The other witches smiled at that. "We will also take the wolves with us to set the mood, if you know what I mean." Zora laughed an ugly little laugh that made Magg want to cry. She did not have a good feeling about any of this. If only she had not lost the orb to Jasmine, but in Magg's heart of hearts, she knew Zora was better off without it. That orb was taking over her life. It was an addiction that would undoubtedly end with Zora's death. The orb seemed to hold that kind of power over her sister. Magg had seen the look in Zora's eye when she held the thing. It made Magg's flesh crawl to think of it. Now that the orb was gone, it seemed that some of the witches' powers went with it. She wasn't sure if the others noticed that bit of bad news, but she had, and it made her very nervous to think what Zora would do if she realized what it meant in the coming battle with Zarcon.

The witches had planned on Jasmine staying at Zarcon's castle for some time to recover from the time she spent running from the wolves. Surely Zarcon would want her to rest up. They knew Jasmine to be a very small and slender woman. Most of the women the witches knew who were built like that had no stamina at all. They were blinded by these thoughts and their own pride, even though they knew that Jasmine had been able to ride for three days before she finally made it to Zarcon's castle. How she had eluded the wolves during that time was a mystery as well. They could not fathom anyone with that kind of intelligence and stamina.

They decided that, instead of waiting for the wolves to come back, they would go to the castle themselves and see what was going on. Surely they could get to the castle before anyone there could make plans. Who knew what Zarcon would do under the circumstances? Hopefully they would be able to catch them unawares and get the orb back very soon.

In their rage at losing the orb, they were also reluctant to take on Zarcon without some kind of plan. Zora decided to take Anesthia and Myshella with her. She knew that those two would be able to help take care of any resistance they might find there. She also knew that both of them would enjoy the process of interrogating anyone. She also thought it best to have the others in reserve in case they did come up against serious resistance from Zarcon or his people. The other two were told to be ready to leave if the big gray leader came back for them.

The three witches ordered their coach and four loaded with food and supplies. They rode in the coach and slept in their tent as they traveled. The men who drove the coach also put up the tent each night and prepared food for the witches. The three of them were in a hurry, so they drove the men and horses mercilessly. Nevertheless, it took four days of travel before Zarcon's castle finally came into view. They had taken a small track that was very seldom used by people living near the castle. It was rough—but a shorter route than the road most traveled. The fact that they stopped to eat and sleep slowed them down. By going the way less traveled, they hoped to arrive without any notice. Zora called the wolves to her as they traveled. It didn't take long for the wolves to find them on the road. She had the wolves follow quietly behind just in case they would be needed for protection.

Fortunately, most of those left behind in the castle had followed Zarcon's warning and had hidden in the forest. Everyone knew the power the witches could bring to bear against castle walls, especially if they were angry. They had taken all the weapons and food from the castle they could carry in wagons. They also had what was left of Zarcon's horses to help carry some of the load. They finally found a series of large caves up in the mountains several miles from the castle to hide in as Zarcon had suggested. They were able to barricade the entry to the caves with brush and large stones they were able to roll in front of the entrances in case the wolves found them. It would be easier to defend if the wolves could only enter one at a time.

Unfortunately, there was one group of people that did not believe the witches could possibly get into the castle or harm them. They loved their homes and didn't want to risk hiding in the forest for who knew how long. It was just ridiculous that the others thought the witches were that powerful. The thought of them getting into the castle was unsettling, but they were convinced that it just could not happen—power or no power. So they stayed and put a large and strong length of wood to bar the gate. They also hid deep within the castle, thinking they could not be found. They would just wait it out for a few weeks if necessary. They had plenty of food and other supplies to get them through.

The witches arrived at the castle just as the sun was going down. Zora had the coach pull up to the west wall of the castle furthest from the gate. Zora and Anesthia descended from the coach to inspect the wall for any hidden doors or secret entrances. They were not happy at finding nothing. As they got back into the couch, Zora ordered the men to take them to the north side. On inspecting this side of the castle wall, they could still find no secret entrance. So, they got back into the coach and ordered the men to go to the east side. As they searched this side, they could at first find no entrance. The witches were becoming extremely frustrated.

Zora finally said, "Well, it looks like Zarcon has hidden secret entrances to his castle even better than we thought. I guess we will have to take the direct approach."

So it was that they went around to the entrance gate of the castle that they had watched Jasmine go through. They got out and walked up to the gate. Zora tested the gate and found it to be made of solid oak and very securely barred. Zora tried one of her spells on the crossbar. It very nearly took her head off when it sent a wheel of fire at her. Zarcon had prepared the little surprise for her. Fortunately she was short enough that it whistled just above her head. Anesthia swore loudly in fright. Myshella was standing far enough back that she observed the reactions of them both and grinned wickedly.

There was no response from inside after the noise subsided. Zora was very irritable by now. She marched up to the castle gate and yelled up at the castle wall, "Hello, the castle." They got no response from anyone inside, so Zora called out again, "Hello, the castle. We wish to speak with you, Zarcon."

There was, of course, no answer from within. Zora called again, "Hello, the castle. This is Zora the high priestess of the witch coven. Answer me now or face the consequences."

Nothing happened. The group hidden in the depths of the castle could not hear her yelling.

Zora was becoming very angry. Once more, she shouted at the castle, "Hello, the castle. I am warning you. You had better open the gate, or I shall open it for you."

There was still no response from the castle. Zora decided to stand a few yards back from the gate and fire a warning volley at the gate, just to let them know she meant business. She waved her hands around in her special incantation. Red fire began to form between her hands. She launched it at the castle gate. It hit with a thundering crash, and the heavy oaken gate and the heavy wooden bar burst into flames. Gradually, as the fire died down, it could be seen that there was a large hole through the center of the gate. Still, there was no response from within. She had been certain that Zarcon would come to the turret above, say something to her, or respond in some other way to her use of magic. It infuriated her that there was no response at all. How could he be so stupid? Couldn't he see that she meant business?

Gradually, it began to dawn on her that perhaps there was no one to respond. This was terrifying. That would mean that they had all escaped. That could not happen! She decided to go in and find out for herself. She ordered the other two to come with her. Together, they walked up to the gate and looked in. Nothing moved inside. No sound could be heard. They pushed the gate open. The fire had burned through the bar across it. They walked in and looked around the immediate area. Still, nothing moved. The wolves followed them through the gateway and started sniffing around.

They walked through the portcullis and into the central area of the castle grounds. There were small homes and shops for taking care of the needs of those living inside. The castle itself was to the right of the gate. They moved to the castle entrance and tried the main doors. They were, of course, locked. In frustration, Zora pounded on the doors. Having no answer, she drew back once again and formed the ball of red fire, not as large this time, and sent it to the locks on the doors. They burst into red flames, and the doors swung open. Zora and the other two witches burst into laughter. This would have been fun if the others had only been here, but they were becoming more aware that Zarcon and Jasmine had very likely escaped.

As they moved through the castle, the witches became more and more enraged. It appeared that they had been outmaneuvered, but then they noticed a movement to the right of where they were standing. It was a small dog running down the hall. They followed the dog and noticed a door that was slightly hidden by tapestries inside one of the larger rooms. The door was slightly ajar, and the dog had disappeared at this very point. The door was not locked, so Zora pulled it open. The witches could hear quiet murmuring from far below. They just looked at each other and smiled evilly. Now it was getting good; Anesthia and Myshella would have someone to torture after all. They would even have a dog to kick. They decided to teach Zarcon a lesson. When he came back from wherever he was, there would be a big surprise waiting.

They decided to approach quietly, just in case there were guards with weapons held by those below. It was surprising that there were no guards at the door. Did they really think they would be safe here? It was amazing. As the witches approached the stairs leading lower into the castle, the sounds became clearer. The people there seemed to be having an evening meal and were completely unguarded. Perfect!

Doven, one of the few soldiers who had stayed, felt the hairs on the back of his neck rise suddenly. He felt he was being watched— as did the rest of the group. He pushed his plate to the side and reached for his weapon, a short sword that was close at hand. Clarit, his friend, was startled by the move and said, "What is wrong?" Just then, a fireball hit Clarit in the chest. It blew all the way through him and hit the wall behind him. The others started screaming. The witches came slowly down the stairs after having announced their presence so dramatically. It would now be a slow dance of pain for those left alive. All three were smiling in anticipation of the fun to come.

Doven hid his sword behind his back as the witches descended the stairs, looking for an opening to attack them. He knew that at least two of the other men had long knives in their boots. He only hoped they would use them. With sudden clarity, they all knew they would most likely die this day. It was just a matter of time. Zora knew that her fireball had caught them by surprise, and it gave them the advantage if they could use it quickly. She spoke in a menacing voice, "Well, well, well. What have we here? It looks like we are going to have some fun after all. I was so afraid you had all gone away. I'm so relieved that you foolish people decided to stay. You are going to tell us where the others have gone, especially Zarcon and whoever went with him."

Just then, the little dog barked and lunged at Myshella. He managed to take a sizeable chunk of flesh out of her leg before he was killed with a spell that separated his head from his body. Blood was everywhere as he fell to the floor. Mayhem broke out at that. Doven moved quickly and was able to slash Anesthia's arm and face before he was killed when Zora stopped his heart. The others continued to scream and yell at the witches in defiance. There were three men and four women with two children left in the room. None of them had fighting experience. They were like lambs to the slaughter.

"The rest of you won't get off so easily." Zora smirked. She was sure of herself and her sister witches. "You will provide the evening's entertainment for us. We are so pleased you are here."

Anesthia was bleeding profusely from her arm and face, and Myshella was limping from the dog's bite, but both were so enraged at the attack that they didn't notice the pain.

Myshella grabbed one of the women and used her long fingernails to dig out her eyes while she screamed in pain, blood pouring down her face. She left her for the moment to put a spell on one of the men who tried to help the woman. The spell made his throat close over so he couldn't breathe. He shuddered and fell to the floor, scraping at his neck frantically until he turned blue, convulsed once more, and died. One of the men with a knife frantically ran for Zora with his blade drawn, but he was too far away and tripped over one of the bodies and landed just short of Zora's feet. Zora took great pleasure in squeezing the life out of his heart slowly and painfully. He finally gasped, clutched his chest, and died.

Anesthia saw one of the children hiding under the table. She caught him by the arm and pulled him out. He was trembling with fear. He said, "You will kill me, but I tell you now that you are one of the ugliest women I have ever seen." Anesthia was going to take her time with the little brat, but with that remark, she lost control of her power and turned him to ash on the spot. He screamed for only a moment and was gone. Anesthia fed on his soul and grew younger as the group watched in horror.

The women who remained tried to hide the last child from the witches. Myshella saw what they were doing and grabbed another woman and held her head back by the hair while she blew her poisonous breath into her lungs. The woman struggled not to inhale, but in the end, she had to draw a breath. The poison entered her body and began to dissolve her organs slowly. The woman started screaming and crying from the pain. It was too terrible to bear. Myshella smiled, knowing what would come. She died an hour after the witches left. She could only moan on the floor in terrible pain.

Zora smiled at the last man as he stood in front of one of the women to protect her. He said, "No, please don't hurt Mandy. Please don't. Take me instead."

Zora answered, "I think it would be more fun for you to watch what I do to her, don't you?" The man started crying and lunged at Zora's throat. Zora ducked and kicked him in the rear as he sprawled out on the floor. Zora caught the woman's arm as she tried to get away. Zora made sure the man was watching while she made the woman stand before her. Zora took the man's knife and made him tie her up with a rope over one of the beams in the ceiling just high enough that her feet did not touch the floor. He was sobbing as he did so. "There will be time enough for you later," Zora said with a growl. "Now watch."

Zora told Mandy to open her mouth. She refused, so Zora used her magic to make her open her mouth so that she could use her magic again. Zora sent a spell out from the castle and called stinging flies to her. Suddenly, the room was filled with flies that could not only sting but also devour flesh. Zora directed the flies to go down Mandy's throat. She started to scream as Zora looked on with a smile. Zora was able to kill with a thought; she could also keep a person alive and conscious far longer than they would normally have under such conditions. Mandy screamed her pain as Zora kept her mouth open to the flies. The pain was so great that she shook violently, but her body would not lose consciousness. The flies that could not get down Mandy's throat began to devour her flesh. When Zora finally had had enough, she stepped back to admire what she had done. The woman was still alive, but barely. She had lost a lot of blood. Her flesh was still being eaten by the stinging flies, and she could not scream anymore. The flies had filled her mouth and nose and were crawling into her organs.

The man, however, was screaming and crying for Zora to kill Mandy and himself quickly. Zora just smiled and left the woman for the time being. The woman's eyes were pleading for death, but it was not to be until Zora had had her pleasure from the woman's pain.

Zora decided it was the man's turn. She decided to prolong his pain for as long as the woman stayed alive so he would witness all of her suffering. She started by chanting in a low voice to call the green death spell. It appeared at the top of the stairs and curled its way down the steps. It was a tendril of green mist that crept along the stone to Zora's outstretched hand. Once she had control of the mist, she sent it into the man's chest. He started to scream as the green death opened his chest and began to melt his organs. His eyes were like saucers as he watched the mist do its work. He was trembling from terror and pain.

The woman was still barely conscious and silent. Zora decided she could end it for the man as soon as she died. It wasn't long. He was glassy-eyed from shock and pain but still conscious and looking at the woman with such grief to know that he had kept them here to die like this. If only he had been wiser. Too late, he knew. He felt his life force leaving his body as he watched hers do the same. Anesthia came closer and inhaled their soul power as they finally died. She looked even younger now. Zora was angry with her for doing so when it was her entertainment that she was stealing from, but she let it go, knowing that it would keep Anesthia happy for a time at least.

There were two women, one blinded, and one child left huddled in the corner of the room where it was darkest. They were hoping the witches would forget about them. The witches smiled at each other and knew that they each got one more to play with. Myshella took the hand of the woman she had blinded and jerked her from the corner where she was hiding. She tried to twist away, but Myshella was too strong. The witch knew that the woman would not see what was coming, so she took her time, her sister witches watching with anticipation. Myshella whispered, "Be calm, my little one. I have a painful surprise for you."

The woman moaned. "Please don't hurt me anymore."

Myshella chuckled softly at that. "It will only hurt as long as I want it to."

The woman screamed, "No! Please!"

Myshella loved it when they begged for mercy. It gave her such a thrill. She grabbed the woman by the hair and began a spell such that she slowly took the woman to death in the most painful way imaginable. When she was done, Myshella felt a great sense of accomplishment; this is what she lived for.

Now it was Anesthia's turn. She decided she would like best to take care of the remaining child. When she grabbed the little girl from the woman next to her, she had a fight on her hands. The woman must have been her mother because she fought like a tiger to get the child back. Zora had to intervene with a spell to make the woman lose her strength so Anesthia could get the child away. The little girl was terrified and angry at what she had seen the witches do to the others. She had secreted a knife in her dress and brought it out just as Anesthia grabbed her. The girl managed to plunge the knife into the witch's side before she was killed. Anesthia lost control once more and killed the girl with a shock from her fingertips. The girl died with a smile on her face. Anesthia was so angered by the attack that she then incinerated the body. The knife was still in her side.

Zora knew a little bit about healing—not her favorite thing to do—and it came in handy in times like these. She used her power to heat the knife as she pulled it out so that the wound would be cauterized. She then checked Anesthia's body for the extent of the injury. Fortunately, the knife had missed anything vital and had only severed a few minor blood vessels. So the cauterization was all that was needed. Anesthia breathed a sigh of relief when Zora told her.

Zora looked over the last woman and smiled her most wicked smile.

The woman shrank into the corner, quietly saying, "No. Please leave me alone. Haven't you done enough?"

Zora laughed at that. "Not quite. You are still alive, are you not?" The woman moaned in horror of what was to be her death. She had gone into shock watching what the witches had done to her family and friends. Now it was her turn, and she was almost numb from it all.

Zora contemplated what to do. This was just too much fun. She thought, *So many victims and so much time to play with them.* Zora was tiring. It had been a long day, and it was getting late. Zora decided to end this one quickly after all. She looked at the woman, not with pity, but with the knowledge that she was tiring. She concentrated on the woman's heart and slowed it down. The woman felt faint and fell to the floor. The pain started soon after. Zora squeezed the heart tighter and tighter. The woman cried out as her heart finally stopped beating, and she died. The other two witches were somewhat disappointed, but they were tiring as well. It was time to quit for the night. They did enjoy the moaning of the one woman still dying as they left the room.

The room where they had done their dirty work was splattered with blood and other gruesome evidence of their passing. They walked up the stairs slowly but with a sense of satisfaction for the thing they had accomplished. The wolves were waiting just outside the door of the castle as they emerged. They had heard the screaming and had been howling to be part of what the witches were doing. The wolves nearly went mad from the smell of blood on the witches' clothing. Zora had to reprimand the big gray male for trying to tear off Anesthia's gown.

He had managed to bite Anesthia on the leg as he did so. At Zora's reprimand, the big wolf whimpered and skulked away.

The men had set the tent up just in case the witches needed it. They had also prepared food for the evening meal. It was stew that they had in a pot over the fire. The witches came through the gate, and the men were terrified by the look on their faces and the sight of all that blood on their clothing and in their hair. Anesthia was still bleeding from the cuts on her arm and face. Zora had promised to fix them after they had something to eat. They were actually starving from their exertions of the night.

Zora ordered Cardeegan to fetch water for the three witches to wash up with. He sent two of his men to bring buckets of water from a well that was found in the courtyard of the castle. Zora and the others went into their tent and washed the grime off their bodies as best they could. They changed into some clothing they had brought with them and had the men burn the dirty dresses they had removed. It felt good to get the filth off them. Zora had a self-satisfied smirk on her face all evening. The other two witches were in a particularly happy mood as well. Anesthia acted like a young girl after Zora healed her wounds. She felt so young. The reason was more than likely that she had used the life essence of her victims to prolong her life.

The witches decided to sleep in the castle after they ate. It would be good to sleep in a bed after the rough journey they had taken to get to Zarcon's castle. Zora was delighted with their night's work and said, "Aren't you both glad you came along on this little excursion? We have had some fun even though we did not get the orb back yet."

Myshella said, "Yes, I am glad I came. I imagined that everyone I killed was Jasmine or Zarcon. I only wish it had been. I'm counting on you, Zora, to heal that cursed dog's bite on my leg. It is hurting badly now."

Anesthia said, "I enjoyed using the people for entertainment. It's just that I'm the one who was hurt the most. It makes me very angry. I also count on you, Zora, to finish healing my wounds."

Zora said softly, "Of course, my darlings. I will heal you both now. It is time we were sleeping and resting up for tomorrow's entertainment." She quickly and efficiently healed both their wounds, though it made her very tired to do so. She would never admit it to either of them. She knew that if they suspected her weakness, they would take advantage of it.

The others asked, "What entertainment are you talking about? There are no more people here in the castle. We've checked everywhere."

Zora smiled and said, "You just wait and see. It will take all three of us to accomplish what I wish to do. I'm so glad you both are here to help me with it." And with that remark, Zora would say no more about the matter.

They found rooms in the castle to sleep in for the night, using their magic to find their way around in the dark. It was just a matter of using a little power to make a small light to follow. They knew the layout of the castle pretty well from their explorations earlier.

They slept well that night. It had been too long since they had had so much to entertain them in one night. It was exhausting but worth it. Anesthia and Myshella spent part of the night wondering what Zora had in mind for the morrow. It would be interesting, if they knew Zora at all.

When morning came, the witches rose late. They felt refreshed and ready to head back to their castle. The men had prepared breakfast for them. It was fried bacon, potatoes, and some cheese mixed together on the griddle they took with them. After eating, the witches gathered around Zora to find out what she had planned.

Zora said, "Even though we had some entertainment last night that was very satisfying, I want to do more for Zarcon's surprise if and when he returns here. I am still angry that we did not get the orb back. They have outsmarted us this time, but they will pay for it. I wish to use the Black Wind to utterly destroy his castle. He won't have a home to come home to. What do you think?"

Anesthia and Myshella were both stunned by the proposal. They had heard about what the Black Wind could do but had never thought to use it themselves. This was an interesting idea. They looked at each other and nodded.

Anesthia said, "We would like to leave such a surprise for Zarcon. We would be happy to help you with it."

So it was agreed. When everything was packed up to leave, Zora ordered the men to take them a few hundred yards away from the castle and wait. The witches got out of the carriage and walked a few paces from it. They stood conferring for a few moments and then started an elaborate incantation. They were so angry at the loss of the orb that all they could think of was revenge. Choosing to use the Black Wind was very unwise. As they spoke the spell, black smoke began to form in the air around them. It grew thicker and thicker as they continued to speak the words of magic. Lightning flashed, the smoke began to swirl, and the wind grew stronger around the witches. The smoke and wind gradually increased in intensity until it was raging. The thunder and lightning were almost deafening. It grew larger and larger until it dwarfed the castle. As the wind grew more intense, the witches began to smile with glee. They extended their arms as if to push the mass of smoke and wind at the castle walls. It hit with the sound of an avalanche, and the castle started to break apart from within.

The wind and lightning tore at the castle until it was crumbling piece by piece. Suddenly, there was a tremendous roar, and the castle collapsed in on itself with a sound like gigantic rocks grinding together. As the lightning and thunder and smoke and wind died down, it could be seen that the castle was no more than a pile of rubble. Fires still burned within the mass, but it was gone. The witches laughed until they had tears in their eyes. It was the most fun they had had in a very long time. Zarcon would learn to foil the witches. It just wasn't right.

Cardeegan and the other men stayed close to the coach and struggled to keep the horses in line throughout the commotion. They were strong men, but this was almost too much for even them. The witches' laughter was also frightening. There was an element of insanity in it. They were fast becoming something even these men feared.

Zora was not quite done with Zarcon and his people. She had a feeling that the other people from his castle were not too far from there. So she sent the wolf pack after them. She knew the lead male would be able to find them. She sent him a message to kill any they could find.

The villagers hiding in the caves had heard the great roar of the castle being destroyed. They knew then that the witches had to be in the area. They realized what it meant for those who had chosen to remain in the castle and mourned their loss. They only hoped that their deaths had been quick and that the witches had not found them. They could not know what the witches had done. They were fearful of the wolves, so they kept no fire for fear the witches would send the wolves looking for them. They also made sure their weapons were ready and at hand. They were prepared if the wolves showed up.

The wolves ran from the castle, and the big gray male howled in triumph when he got the scent of those who had left the castle. The wolves would have some fun of their own this day. They followed the trail left by the villagers. It was easy enough to find. Their trail led to the caves a few short miles from the castle. When they found the caves and started barking and howling at the entrance, the people inside were ready to defend themselves.

The first wolf to break through the brush of the first cave was cut down by one of the soldiers who carried a long sword. The next wolf charged through the hole left by his brother. He was able to get past the soldier and attack one of the men inside. They wrestled on the floor, the wolf's teeth inches from the man's face, snapping and growling as they fought. The man finally managed the strength to toss the wolf aside long enough for the first soldier to stab him in the heart. He died with a yelp. More wolves gathered at the entrance and struggled to get through the brush but could only get through one at a time. They howled in frustration. When the lead gray found that the other wolves from his pack were cut down, he was angered and charged the entrance himself. He was met by swords and was struck by an arrow in his left flank. His anger cooled with the pain. He howled and leaped back through the brush to leave the cave. He knew then that the effort was futile and called the rest of his pack to him. They howled in anger as they left the scene.

The villagers still inside the cave cheered as they heard the wolves leaving. Fortunately, no one was hurt badly in the attack. The man who fought the wolf was scraped up a bit but had no serious injuries, just a few teeth marks on his arms. After the wolves left, they remained quiet and tried to relax until they were sure the witches and their wolves were gone for at least a time. They sent a runner to the villagers in the other caves, telling them what had happened with the wolves and that it was hoped they would not return. The others were glad to hear that two of the wolves had been killed. Those wolves had always been a threat in the land. The people remained in the caves a few more days just to be sure the wolves would not return.

Zarcon's plan had saved their lives. Zora and her sisters left the scene of destruction they had caused and climbed back into their coach. Zora told the men to get moving. The wolves would follow them when they were ready. The witches were exhausted from the exertions of the spell and the labors of the night. Their coach rolled out, and the witches laughed again. This was a day they would not soon forget. The destruction of the entire castle was worth the effort. As they headed for home, they plotted what their next move would be to find Zarcon and that nasty thief, Jasmine. Revenge, they were sure, would be sweet.

They stopped after three hours of travel to rest the horses and eat a quick meal before continuing on. They wondered why the wolves had not returned to them yet, but assumed that they were keeping the villagers busy. They discussed the possibility with glee. After finishing their meal and loading their coach, they made ready to leave. They took the main road on the way back to their own castle. It was a better road and would provide some comfort for the witches. There was no longer any reason to remain out of sight of the local people. The noise of the castle coming down would warn them that the witches were abroad in any case. There was a small village some fifteen miles ahead that they hoped to come to that evening where they could perhaps spend the night at an inn.

Cardeegan and the other men were also glad to be closer to some civilization. It was rough for them as well. They enjoyed being away from the witches' castle but would have preferred to be without the witches even more. This journey had been especially interesting with what happened at the castle. They had felt the surge of power as the Black Wind had come forth and were shocked that the witches would call it. They knew about the Black Wind—as did all the people familiar with witchcraft. They just hoped they would not be around when the Black Wind came back for retribution, as they knew it would. The legends regarding using the Black Wind were widely known. The men held their thoughts private as they contemplated the proper time to leave the employ of the witches. It would not be good to tell them of their desires; they would each have to leave secretly and alone. Cardeegan would not allow that to happen, and they knew it. They would mostly fantasize what it would be like to be somewhere else, anywhere else for that matter. They were getting close to the small village of Skirville. The witches were looking forward to a nice hot meal and a bed to sleep in. They were tired of sleeping on the ground, even if it had only been for a few nights. They anticipated sleeping under a roof this night.

As day turned into night, the witches entered the village and decided to stay at the small inn near the main road. It was called the Black Stone Inn. The inn was made of wood that had weathered to a gray color. Any paint that might have been on it was peeling in patches or long gone. The door was barely hanging on two of its hinges. The windows were filthy, and it was impossible to see into the common room.

It was very quiet as they entered the inn, and there were no people around except for the innkeeper who was dozing by the fire in a large chair. The inn proper was quite small with a bar and four or five tables scattered around the room. The fireplace was set in the center of the wall opposite the bar. A young woman came around the bar and asked them if they would like a meal and a room. She was short and fat with greasy brown hair.

Zora answered with a growl, "Of course we do. It's getting late, and we haven't eaten, you dolt! We will also need someone to take care of our coach and horses for the night. Our men will also need a meal and some straw to sleep on."

The innkeeper roused himself at the sound of voices. He jumped to his feet when he realized it was the witches who were speaking. He grew increasingly uneasy as Zora became angry. No one could trust these witches to leave you as they found you, especially if you were foolish enough to anger them. He put on his best smile and said, "Good evenin', ladies. How about some wine while you wait for yer meal? I'll also get our very best rooms ready for you all, heh. We … we … are honored by your …presence." Catrin looked at him as though he had suddenly lost his mind.

He continued, ignoring the girl, "Me name is Willikins, and this here young woman is my daughter, Catrin. We are at your service." He bowed awkwardly as he said the last.

Zora looked him up and down and decided that the two of them together did not promise a great deal of intellectual capacity. She said, "Thank you. My sisters and I will sample your wine. We have traveled far this day and would like to relax for a bit before we retire for the evening. We shall sit here by the fire and await our meal and the wine, but do hurry; we are not long on patience."

Willikins had heard tales of the witches' supreme lack of patience. He began to tremble as he brought out the wineglasses and some of the best wine he had to offer them. He dearly hoped it would be good enough. He walked to their table and placed the glasses in front of each of them. He also set the bottle in the middle of the table. He waited while they tasted the wine.

Anesthia spoke first, her patience completely gone. She yelled, "Is this truly the best you can do? I've tasted better in the portside taverns of Celestinia. Surely you can do better than that!" Anesthia knew this was very likely the best he had. She wanted him to make a mistake so she could have a turn torturing the fool. She enjoyed having the opportunity to torture those idiots at Zarcon's castle, but you just couldn't have too much of that kind of fun. Destroying the castle had been exciting, but she was still hoping for additional activities as well. She was hoping this ignorant innkeeper would provide her the opportunity.

Willikins replied, "Milady, I regret that the wine is not to your likin'." He was sweating by this time. "We just got this here delivery today. I have not tasted it muhself. I'll bring up a bottle from the cellar, one we've had for a while. I am hopin' you will find it more to your likin'. I would not wish to displease milady." He gave her a gap-toothed grin, hoping it would calm her a bit. It only made her lose her appetite.

Anesthia smiled a tight smile and bowed her head to dismiss him to his errand. She looked at Zora and frowned. It didn't look like the innkeeper was going to rise to her bait. What a disappointment. Of course, she could always turn him into a toad just on principle, but it was too soon to tell if that was all she was going to get to do to him. Maybe later on she would think of something unpleasant for his fate.

The innkeeper returned and poured the new bottle of wine into new glasses for the witches. The witches took a sip. They decided to let the innkeeper off the hook.

Zora said, "This is adequate. Is the meal ready yet? We are starving."

Catrin had been working on their meal from the kitchen in the back. They had some pork that had been slow roasting all day and some potatoes to go with it. She had baked some bread earlier. They also had some fresh-churned butter for the bread. Catrin put the plates of pork, potatoes, and bread and butter on a tray and scurried out from the kitchen to put on the table for them. She said, "Here's yer meal. Please let me know if I can get you anythin' else that we have to offer. I'll just go and prepare your rooms now." At that, she dipped a quick curtsy and left hurriedly, nearly running up the stairs.

Willikins followed his daughter upstairs to get the rooms ready. They still needed to make the beds with clean sheets. It was rare that they changed the sheets, but this was an emergency. They knew that if they did not please the witches, they would regret it. They opened the windows to air out the rooms. They did smell a little musty. Hardly anyone came this way anymore. Willikins could only hope the witches might be inclined to pay them a little. If not, hopefully they would at least be able to go on living.

Catrin was thinking much the same thing as they prepared the room. She had also heard tales of the cruelty they visited on those who displeased them.

The witches were discussing what to do while the two were away.

Zora said, "We must be careful here. If we do anything to harm these people, where will we stay the next time we come through here? Many of the shopkeepers and farmers have already left because of the tales that are told about us. We will find other opportunities to enjoy ourselves in the very near future, I'm quite sure."

Anesthia frowned again. She was not happy and told Zora so. "I would really like to show this man what comes of displeasing us. It would be something to remember the place by. I'm getting nervous and unhappy. I would just hurt them a little. It would make me feel better. Now you tell me I can't. What am I supposed to do?" She frowned and pouted at that.

Zora hated it when Anesthia pouted and whined. Zora actually pitied her. Anesthia's desire to harm others was becoming an obsession. How could she be useful in the war that was coming if she couldn't control herself? Zora would have to consider what to do about it later. Right now, she was just too tired. It truly had been a long day, and she was feeling it now. The food had turned out to be adequate and filling. That was about all anyone could ask in this remote area. At least they would be sleeping in a bed tonight, be it ever so humble. The beds had better be clean.

Willikins and Catrin came down the stairs just as the witches were finishing up their meal. They both hurried to the table and removed their dirty dishes.

Willikins asked, "How was yer meal this evening?"

Zora said, "It was adequate. We would like to retire now if our rooms are ready."

"They sure are. We've made 'em ready for ya."

The witches rose from their chairs and followed him upstairs. The rooms were at the end of the hall. They were next door to each other. The rooms were fairly small with a decent-sized bed and small wardrobe across from the bed. There was a candle on a small table beside the bed. Willikins lit the candle in each of the rooms just before he left. The women went to their rooms and prepared for the night. Catrin had set a basin of water on the dresser in each of the rooms. There was a towel and bar of soap there as well. The women washed up before going to bed. It felt good to wash off some of the grime from their travels.

The witches slept soundly that night. When the sun came up, they dressed and went downstairs for their breakfast. Willikins and Catrin had prepared sausage and eggs with biscuits and gravy for the women to eat. There was also fresh milk and berries picked from the bushes out back of the inn. The witches ate heartily. They pushed themselves away from the table, and Zora said, "That was a better meal than we have expected. We are going to be leaving now. Will you see that our men are fed and ready to leave?"

Willikins said, "We've seen to that, milady. In fact, the men are outside with yer coach and horses ready to go right now."

Zora was surprised. Maybe this man was smarter than he looked. He might bear watching. A man with initiative could be dangerous. Nevertheless, Zora thanked the man and walked out of the inn to their coach, where indeed the men were waiting to leave.

The innkeeper and his daughter were never so grateful to see the backs of any travelers as they were to see the backs of the witches that morning. Both gave a heavy sigh of relief and almost staggered from the release of tension of the past hours.

Suddenly Willikins grabbed his head and screamed. He felt as though his head was about to explode. Catrin helped him back into the inn and eased him into a chair by the fire. Gradually the pain subsided, but it left him with a droop to the left side of his face that never healed. He could barely talk intelligibly for the rest of his life. He knew the white-haired witch did this to him, and he hated her passionately. He had seen her looking at him and moving her lips as she stepped into their coach.

In any case, the witches were at last on the road home as the sun rose higher in the sky. Anesthia was strangely quiet and had a smirk on her face that was unsettling the first few hours on the road. The others could not guess why, although they had heard the scream as they left the town. They would be home tomorrow evening if all went well. The trip was tedious as they traveled back to their castle. They stopped for their midday meal and rested the horses for an hour before setting out again. The day was cool, but inside the coach, it was stuffy. They could hardly wait to be home. One more night on the road would be all they had to face.

As the sun began to set, Zora called a halt for the night. The men set up camp and prepared the meal. The witches were grateful that this was the last one before they were home again. The ground was hard and lumpy, and they had a difficult time sleeping.

By then, Anesthia was in a particularly bad mood. Her lust for blood was causing her to be very short-tempered and angry. Her little spell on Willikins hardly sufficed to satisfy her in any meaningful way. Zora had to keep telling her to settle down and keep quiet. Anesthia, in turn, was sharp with her sister witches and would not calm herself and sleep.

By morning, the witches were all cross and out of sorts. Zora knew she had better regain control of Anesthia or she would have problems she could not handle later on. She said, "Anesthia, you will both calm yourself and maintain some semblance of cordiality with us—or you will ride one of the horses the rest of the way home."

Anesthia gave her an evil look, thought better of her desired response, and finally said, "Zora, I beg your pardon. I have been under a lot of strain on this adventure and do not appreciate the restraints you have put on me to leave the innkeeper and his daughter alone." At that, she kind of smiled inwardly. "I really need to vent some of my frustration, but I will do as you ask and try to calm myself for the remainder of the journey." She struggled to control her rage at the very idea that she could be made to ride a horse all the way home from here. It was unthinkable. The men would lose respect for her as well, and she could not countenance that in any way. So she took a deep breath and forced herself to bury her emotions for a time. There would surely be time for bloodletting soon. Maybe she would have to practice on some woodland creatures if things did not improve soon enough.

Zora was able to relax a little watching Anesthia force herself to be calm. It also gave her some satisfaction to know that she still could control the witch. She smiled to herself, knowing she was still the leader of the coven. Even Anesthia did not dare challenge her when it came down to it.

Myshella watched the exchange with some trepidation. It would not do for the two witches to get into a war just now with the worry over getting the orb back. They really did need to be united in the effort. She was also able to relax a bit when Anesthia finally backed down. Myshella was becoming increasingly concerned for the sanity of both of them. They were not handling the stress of the situation very well. If they could just hold it together until they could get the orb back.

The journey was somewhat quieter and easier on the nerves, and they continued without Anesthia's constant complaining and fidgeting. Myshella was able to relax and even doze a bit, knowing that Zora would be able to handle any problem Anesthia might create.

The three witches looked forward to being back in their castle and telling Heleren and Magg of their adventures. They would all have a laugh about Zarcon's castle. That at least was a happy thought. The fact that the nasty thief, Jasmine, had escaped again with the blue orb was very troubling indeed. Something must be done, and quickly, to get it back, but what could they do? They had not come up with anything on the return trip. They had tried to think but were just too tired and distracted. It had been difficult to sleep in tents for so many nights. They were not used to hard living and longed for the comforts of home.

It would also be good to talk as a coven. Zora was sure that between them something would come to mind. Finally, the castle could be seen in the distance. Zora was particularly proud of how the castle appeared ominous as they approached. It was huge and black with two large towers and plenty of demons on the walls. She was especially fond of the moat. It held man-eating fish that could turn a man's body into a skeleton in just moments. How delightful! There were a few skeletons in the moat, which made it very effective as a deterrent for anyone foolhardy enough to try crossing the moat. The people of the town never went near it. It was just the occasional traveler who would hear tales of great wealth and try their hand at thievery.

The coach and men approached the drawbridge, and it was lowered as they approached. The sun was lowering in the sky as they crossed the bridge and headed through the portcullis. What a delight it was to be home! Now they could get down to business and plan their attack on Zarcon and Jasmine—if they could just find them. Ah, but they would in due time. It was just a matter of who had the most patience. Of course, Zora forgot that she didn't have any.

As they entered the courtyard just inside the gate, they could see through the coach window that their sister witches were waiting for them on the steps leading up to the castle door. Heleren looked beautiful as always, but Magg looked haggard. Zora looked at her sister and wondered what could possibly be going on. Magg wasn't pretty by any stretch of the imagination, but she looked really worn out and a tiny bit scared. Well, Zora would get to the bottom of it soon enough. Right now, she must present herself as the true high priestess that she was. She stepped out of the coach as soon as her servant opened the door for her and held her hand as she did so.

Zora walked up the steps to the castle with her head held high. She said, "How goes the castle? Has all been well while we have been gone?"

Heleren responded, "All has been well. We missed our dear sister witches. Have you regained the blue orb? Is Jasmine dead? What about Zarcon?" Heleren was putting voice to the fears they had been living with since the three had left the castle. They had been worried that something might have happened to prevent Zora, Myshella, and Anesthia from getting the blue orb back.

Zora was annoyed that they would start with the questions so soon after they had arrived. She started to say something out of impatience but caught herself. Now was the time to work together. She must put off the questions, however, until she could refresh herself with a bath and some food.

She said, "Sisters, we have just arrived from a long, tiring journey with much to tell you. Please let us change, refresh ourselves, and have something to eat before we get down to business."

The others were embarrassed, but Heleren said, "Just tell us if you have the blue orb."

Zora did not want to tell them that she and the others had failed, but it looked like she would have to give them something. She said, "We will discuss it soon enough. Now let us through so we can recover from our journey."

Heleren was not happy, but she let them pass. Sometimes there was no getting information from Zora if she didn't want to give it. She only hoped Zora hadn't noticed Magg's state of mind. Heleren had lost patience with the woman and had given her nightmares for her hand in the loss of the blue orb. Magg had woken screaming several nights in a row. Heleren loved the sound, but if Zora found out she was causing the nightmares, she would be in big trouble. Two nights ago she had stopped, hoping Magg would be able to recover, but Magg had another nightmare last night that was not of Heleren's doing. Sometimes the nightmares developed a life of their own. How was Heleren to know that Magg would just keep having them? This was just too inconvenient right now.

Additionally, how was Heleren to know that the three would be coming back so soon? They had thought they would be gone at least another week. Oh, well. It couldn't be helped now. Hopefully Magg would not realize what had happened to her and would just think it was something she had eaten.

The three witches marched into the castle and up to their rooms. They told the servants to bring them warm water for baths and clean clothing to change into. They also ordered the cooks to prepare a meal for them when they came back downstairs. The other two witches followed them in and sat in the library to talk.

Magg asked softly, "What do you make of that, Heleren? Do you think they recovered the orb?"

Heleren replied, "I am very much afraid they did not. Don't you think Zora would have made a big show of having the orb if she did? I think we are in for a war if they haven't recovered it. You know how desperately we need that orb to accomplish all we wish to do."

Magg sat in the corner chair, curled up in a ball. She was still afraid. The nightmares had been terrifying. She had dreamed over and over again that the wolves were chasing her. She had the blue orb and was running through the forest. She could hear the wolves getting closer and closer. She ran to Zarcon's castle, but when she got there, no one would open the door to let her in. When the wolves caught her, they began to bite her and tear at her flesh. She started screaming and couldn't stop. She had been unable to go back to sleep the rest of the night. Now she feared sleep. The dreams wouldn't stop. Maybe Zora could help her. She had asked Heleren, but she had refused. It was as if she didn't want to help. What could that mean? She would have to ask Zora about that too. Zora was finished with her bath and had dressed in her favorite gown. She wanted to look her best when she faced the others. Her maid tried to do something with Zora's unruly hair but only managed to tame a few of the strands. The rest seemed to have a life of their own and flew about Zora's head. Zora was thinking of what to say as she prepared herself to go downstairs. It was unthinkable that they had failed to get the orb back. She would have to be very careful how she presented the problem. Heleren could be very difficult in times like these. She felt the prickle of sweat down her back as she braced herself to go downstairs.

Anesthia and Myshella had finished their baths as well. They were both starving and could hardly wait to get downstairs to the food. They were not concerned about what Zora would say to the others. They knew it really was her problem as to how to present their failure to Heleren. They were just grateful it wasn't up to them. As for the trip itself, there had at least been some entertainment, but they didn't have the orb—and that was something that could not be ignored. They were ready to go downstairs, and Anesthia knocked on Zora's bedroom door to see if she were ready to come down as well.

Zora answered her knock, and they went down together. Zora whispered to the other two, "We will talk with the others as soon as we have eaten. Don't say anything until then. I have to collect my thoughts as to how to tell them what has happened."

Anesthia said, "I agree with you. I won't say anything." Myshella just nodded.

The three witches walked down the stairs and went into the dining room. The others had been waiting for them. All were hungry and ready for the evening meal. They had been so concerned for the outcome of their sister witches' journey that they hadn't been able to eat much the few days they had been gone. Their future was so tied up with the recovery of the orb that they couldn't bear to be without it.

The servants had prepared Zora's favorite meal of roast duckling, boiled game hen, roasted vegetables, crusty bread, butter and preserves, and blood pudding for dessert. Zora's mouth watered at the sight. She had missed the meals at the castle. They were always so delicious. Zora had hired the best chef in the land to cook for them. Yes, she was so glad to be home. They all ate heartily. Magg and Heleren were anxious about what had happened. Magg was finding it difficult to concentrate on her meal when she could see the wicked gleam in her sister's eyes. She knew something unwholesome had happened. She hoped that no one had been hurt this time.

When the meal was cleared away, Zora asked them all to follow her into the library to discuss what had happened on their journey and what they would do in the near future.

The witches followed her into the library and sat in their favorite chairs by the fire. All eyes were on her as Zora began, "Dear sisters, Anesthia, Myshella, and I have had a hard few days. We journeyed to Zarcon's castle as we had planned. When we got there, all was quiet. We called to Zarcon to come and meet with us. He did not respond. We called two more times and still no response. I cast my red fire at the castle gate. It blew a very satisfactory hole in the middle of it." The other witches cheered at that. "So we went inside. Nothing moved. We looked in every home and every part of the castle for any who might be hiding inside. We finally found an unfortunate group of people who were hiding in the rooms below the castle. We had some sport with them, which was very satisfactory."

Magg began to tremble. She knew what Zora meant by that remark, and it made her sick to her stomach. *Those poor people*, she thought. *How horrible it must have been for them.* Magg didn't ask any questions. She knew she would not want to hear the answers.

Zora continued, "We had planned on finding Zarcon and that nasty thief, Jasmine, and exacting our revenge, but alas, it was not to be." She made a point of looking sad at this statement. "But all was not lost. At least we had some fun. Isn't that right, girls?"

Myshella and Anesthia both cackled delightedly. Magg cringed at the sound. She didn't like the coldness in their eyes. Heleren frowned at that last remark. How could they have missed getting the orb? Nothing would make up for that loss. It was an outrage! She could feel her magic weakening the longer the orb was gone. She was pretty sure the others were having the same problem. That none of them spoke of it was unnerving. She said, "So what you are telling us is that you failed to retrieve the orb!"

Zora had feared Heleren's rage, and now she had to face it. In an effort to soothe her, she said, "As you so accurately have stated, we did indeed fail to retrieve the orb from those thieves. However, with some careful planning and your help, we shall succeed! But we need to work together on this. Make no mistake: it will be a challenge like we have not faced before. I am sure, between us, we will find the way to get back what is rightfully ours. What do you say, Heleren? Are you in?"

Heleren knew Zora had her. She could never back out now. It was imperative that the orb be recovered for their use. She said, "You know I am loyal to the coven and will do all I can to retrieve the orb. I am just so disappointed that you failed in your first attempt. Yes, we can get it back if we work together. Thank you for reminding me." That last statement galled Heleren, but she knew she must get along and go with whatever Zora planned. Hopefully she would have the opportunity to contribute to that plan. She didn't like feeling left out.

Magg watched this exchange between Heleren and Zora. As she watched them, she became very agitated. She could see it in Zora's eyes that there was more to the story than she had revealed so far. She hesitated but finally asked, "What else did you do?"

Zora just smiled. "We did something very gratifying. Can you guess what it might have been, dear sisters?"

Magg looked from Zora to Anesthia to Myshella and was frightened by the looks on their faces. This couldn't be good. With a dread she could not hide, she said, "Have you done something to Zarcon's castle?"

Zora gave a wicked laugh and said, "Very good, Magg. We have indeed done something to Zarcon's castle. We have leveled it! It was very pleasing to watch its destruction. We couldn't have done it ourselves, so we used the Black Wind to do so." Even though Zora was smiling as she said that last, Magg and Heleren gasped in shock. Myshella and Anesthia both smiled knowingly. They must have forgotten that no one used the Black Wind with impunity. It was the most dangerous spell known to the coven. Magg was terrified by the news. It appeared that Zora was finally going too far with her use of the magic. She feared what this might mean for them all. Surely Zarcon would be able to feel the use such powerful magic. It might tip him off that they were seeking his total destruction if he hadn't figured that out already. Zarcon was much smarter than her sister witches were giving him credit for, and they didn't even realize it yet.

Zora could see the dismay on Magg's face. "Magg, why does this news upset you so? Aren't you pleased that we have destroyed our enemy's castle? Surely it pleases you to know that he has no home now—not that he'll ever need it." The rest of the witches burst into loud laughter at that, all except Magg. Between the news that the Black Wind had been used and the nightmares she had been having lately, nothing could cheer her up.

Magg said, "I am glad that you have caused Zarcon grief, but I hope it won't bring ill on us all because of what you have done." The other witches scoffed and laughed even louder at her fear.

Zora kept laughing, but in the back of her mind, she was a little concerned about Magg and her lack of response to the news of Zarcon's castle. Zora would find out what was bothering Magg, but it would have to be later. Right now, she just wanted to bask in the happy feelings generated by the destruction she and her sisters had caused for Zarcon. They may not yet have the blue orb, but at least they had caused Zarcon some grief, along with anyone who had lived in the castle—not to mention the special pleasure they had with the families that were still there. That was cause for satisfaction, at least for a time.

Finally, as their laughter quieted, Heleren said, "Magg is right about one thing: the Black Wind will exact a price for its use. How do we prevent that from happening? We don't have that kind of power without the orb!" Heleren was just beginning to see the foolishness of using the Black Wind and feared for her own safety—if not for the others.

Zora quit smiling. She had put that little bit of information away. *What would they do indeed? Well, that couldn't be helped now.* Zora tried to appear calm and said, "Don't worry. We'll get the orb back before anything can happen. Rejoice with me while we think of Zarcon's reaction to his beloved castle being gone when he returns, if he returns." The other witches smirked at that. Magg just hung her head and tried not to cry.

While it was true that the witches had destroyed the castle using the Black Wind, it was also true that there was a price to pay for its use. Zora had no idea what she had unleashed on the world by doing so. Only time would tell whether the witches would be able to stand against it or fall victim to the consequences of it.

Magg was still very agitated. "How do we get the orb back, sister? I have been so worried. I have had nightmares since you left to recover it. I have been hoping that you could help me. I haven't slept in days. In fact, I'm afraid to go to sleep."

Heleren flinched; there was no hiding the truth now. How would Zora react? Would she suspect that the nightmares were Heleren's doing? She began to sweat as she watched Zora. It could go very badly for her if Zora found out what she had done.

Zora sat for a moment, stunned by what Magg had said. She did suspect that Heleren was at the bottom of this. She also had a good idea why she had done it. Magg had earned some form of punishment for letting the orb out of their hands, but were nightmares really appropriate? Zora knew of the power of Heleren's dreams. With some concern, she said, "Tell me about your nightmares, Magg."

Magg recounted the wolves chasing her and tearing her apart and how she woke up screaming every night since they began. Zora could see the toll the dreams had taken on her. In just a few nights, Magg was a wreck. She wouldn't be much good to any of them at this rate. Zora looked at Heleren and asked in her sweetest voice, "Heleren, do you know anything about this?"

Heleren swallowed when Zora used that tone. She knew she was in trouble, "Well … you see … it was Magg who lost the orb, really. I was angry with her and wanted her to pay for what she did. I stopped the nightmares two nights ago, but she seems to still be having them. Sometimes they do that. I'm sorry. Myshella might be able to do something for her." Heleren tried to smile at that, but she was too afraid of Zora's reaction.

Magg gasped. "You did this to me? I have spent these last nights tortured by these horrible nightmares—and you did it to me?"

Zora could see that Heleren's curse had caused a bit more damage to Magg than had been intended. It was possible that Magg's sense of guilt was causing the nightmares to continue. It was time for it to end before Magg was senseless from lack of sleep. "Myshella, can you do something for Magg? We need her to be functioning if she is to be of any help to us."

Myshella sighed. "Of course I will try. It's the least I can do for the sister of my high priestess." She looked at Heleren with a smug expression. It was just too good to be true that she would be asked to fix one of Heleren's curses.

Zora looked at Heleren and said, "I will not punish you this time. Magg deserved to be chastened for her hand in the loss of the orb, but this is where it ends. No more punishment need be delivered. Magg gets the message, don't you, Magg?"

Magg shivered. "Yes, sister." She was shocked that Heleren would do such a thing to her. She hoped that Myshella would be able to help her. She really was suffering from the nightmares and lack of sleep. Because of them, she could barely stand—much less walk and think straight.

Heleren inhaled deeply. She hadn't realized she was holding her breath through Zora's response. She was well aware that Zora could kill with a thought. It wasn't the death alone that was terrifying. Zora had sharpened her skills to include all manner of unpleasant journeys to that end. Zora did not enjoy torture as much as Anesthia did, but she was still very imaginative when it came to painful deaths.

Heleren was relieved when Myshella asked Magg to follow her out into the hall. It was bad enough that her spell had been found out. The humiliation of having Myshella fix the spell was almost more than she could bear.

When they got out into the hall, Myshella put her hands on Magg's head, said a few words of incantation, and pushed her away.

Magg staggered as she tried to regain her balance. She was just able to do so. She was not prepared for the rough treatment. She did, however, notice immediately a lessening of the fear and was able to think more clearly. She said, "Myshella, what was that for? You could have warned me that you were going to treat me so rough!"

Myshella just smiled and turned to go back into the parlor with the other witches.

Magg followed close behind with some trepidation. Things were getting worse for her. If only she had been able to stop Jasmine before she got away with the orb. Oh, well. That couldn't be changed no matter how much she wished it to. In her heart of hearts, she was actually glad it was gone, but she dared not admit it to her conscious mind for fear Zora would detect her insubordination.

Magg and Myshella resumed their seats and sat quietly. Zora was ready to continue the discussion of more important matters. Zora said, "Sisters in darkness, we must find Zarcon and that little thief, Jasmine. Do any of you have an idea where we should start? I fear they may have sought the help of Donavan. He is a very real threat. You know he can block spells, don't you? We can only hope that Zarcon does not go to him, but there it is. If they do so, do any of you know where he might be located? I have heard so many rumors. I don't know what to believe. Some say he has moved far away from this place—perhaps even as far away as Uranalee. Others say he has a cabin in the mountains, but no one seems to know which one is true. What have any of you heard? Where could we start?"

Anesthia said, "I have heard that he lives near the coast and makes a living fishing."

Zora responded with some impatience, "That was years ago. Have you heard anything new?"

Heleren thought for a few more minutes and said, "I heard he left his home and moved to the Backlash Mountains to be alone. You upset him, Zora, when you killed his family, you know. Even if Zarcon finds him, it is very unlikely that he will leave his quiet little cabin."

Heleren smiled wickedly as she finished. She visualized the depth of feelings that must have driven Donavan to the mountains to swear off all contact with humans. She admired Zora for what she had done to him. Though she had no such depth of feeling herself, she enjoyed watching what those feelings would do to others.

Zora became very interested in what Heleren had just said. "When did you hear that? I must know."

Heleren instantly became anxious. "I heard it just six months ago. I was—"

Zora cut her off, "Where were you and what were you doing? Who told you?"

"I was just saying that I was in the town of Merrido near the Backlash Mountains. There was a man I had enticed to stay with me for a while. He professed to be an old friend of Donavan, though I thought it more likely that he was an old enemy. He said he had heard about his old friend staying in a cabin in the Backlash Mountains all alone and wanted it to stay that way. So this man had become angry that Donavan did not desire his company, and he came into town to get drunk. When I met him, he was well on his way. I coaxed him to come with me, which he did, and then I made him tell me all he knew about Donavan's whereabouts. I thought the information might be useful at some point in time. I had no idea whether it would be important or not. It was just fun to get the information out of the man." She smiled coldly at this last. The others knew what she meant. "It wasn't something we were particularly interested in, so I didn't think much about it. Do you really think Zarcon would go to him for help?"

"That's the point. We don't know where they went or who they might go to for help now. Maybe they won't go to anyone. Maybe they think that, now that they have the orb, they can do whatever they need to do alone, but I would think finding Donavan would be a good place for us to start at least."

"So, who goes and who stays? Should we all go together?" Zora wanted to know how they felt about an expedition to find Donavan and the others, if possible. She felt good about going after Donavan. She had held a grudge against him for decades. So, even if Zarcon and his band of thieves weren't going there, she could have a little fun with him anyway. She couldn't help but smile at the thought.

Myshella wondered at the strange look on Zora's face. "I would like to come. I think I can be of better service to you than staying here." She didn't want to be left out again. She needed to get out of the castle for a time before she truly lost it.

Magg was worried about being left behind again. "I would also like to come and help in any way I can. You know I have skills that could help get the orb back. Please let me come, Zora." She knew she was begging, but at this point, she had no pride.

Zora smiled at her sister and said, "Magg, I would like to have you come, but in your present condition, I think it wise for you to stay here and mend. Myshella, you may come and be welcome."

Magg frowned. She really wanted to get out of the castle for a time, but if Zora made up her mind, there really was no arguing about it. She seemed to shrink back into herself for a time. Myshella was gratified by this turn of events. So, Magg would be left behind again? Was Zora easing her out of the coven intentionally? Only time would tell.

Heleren was thoughtful. "I think I would like to come. There are bound to be men who need to be disciplined on the way. I may even be able to help with Donavan. That is an interesting situation to contemplate, don't you think?" She was nearly salivating at the thought. No man would hurt her again, but she would go out of her way to hurt them if she could, and she knew she could.

Zora said, "You may have a point, Heleren. I think you could be of service, yes indeed. Anesthia, what is your choice? Will you come or stay behind with Magg?"

Anesthia smiled. "And miss the opportunity to play with Jasmine? Not on your life. I'm in for sure." Her cold blue eyes shone with anticipation of what she could do to Jasmine. Zora shivered. This one was frightening on so many levels. She was just grateful that Anesthia was with them and not against them.

Zora gathered her power and said with authority, "So, it is decided: Magg stays and the rest of us go. Magg, we are not punishing you. We just want you to heal and be well. We will need you later, I'm sure. Maybe we could send for you when we find the thieves. Would that please you?"

Magg tried to smile. It was at least something to look forward to. "I will be fine here. Thank you, Zora, for thinking of me. I will anxiously wait for word that you need me. I wouldn't want to miss out on helping you regain the orb." Magg had a bad feeling suddenly that maybe she was glad that she would be staying home after all.

So, the witches spent the rest of the evening planning what they would need for the expedition. The excitement grew as they came closer to finalizing their plans and getting ready to leave. They decided that they would need to be gone in no more than two days. That would give them time to get all their packing done. Yes, it wouldn't be long now, and they would have the orb back and make those who had stolen it pay dearly for their treachery.

On The Move

As soon as things quieted down, Zarcon gathered the party together to discuss the day. "We have had a quiet ride today. We can be grateful for that. Be alert. We may not be so lucky from here on out. Things could become very interesting at any time. We will set watches every night. I will take the first watch tonight. Terrence will take second watch."

Zarcon was concerned that it had been such a quiet ride. He knew that couldn't last. He wondered about the day's ride. Could they be followed? He hoped not. He decided that he had better be much more aware of magic as time went by. Zarcon could detect using magic. He had to assume the witches could do the same. He worried that the witches might try to find them with their magic. He would not use his own unless it was absolutely necessary. He didn't want to give up their position too soon.

Zarcon sat on the ground and rested against a large tree with Voltar next to him. Zarcon's watch was nearly at an end when the big dog started to growl. Zarcon knew that growl meant wolves were nearing the camp.

After several minutes passed, Voltar bolted past Zarcon with a loud bark and attacked something in the brush about fifty feet from where he sat. Voltar attacked the animal as it tried to creep into the camp. The big dog easily killed whatever had tried to attack Zarcon and the camp. It struggled a moment and then lay still. Voltar stood over a wounded wolf, growling.

Terrence heard the noise and was instantly on his feet. He rushed up to Zarcon just as Voltar finished killing the wolf. "What is going on? I heard Voltar fighting. Has he killed something here? Are you all right, Zarcon?"

Zarcon led Terrence over to where Voltar was growling. The wolf looked like a large animal had clawed its side. The wound looked to be a few hours old and very deep. The poor animal was weak from the loss of blood. Zarcon wondered why a wolf would be in such bad condition. "What could have caused such a wound?"

Terrence was just as concerned and was worried about Zarcon as well. Zarcon looked pale and old. Terrence was hoping Zarcon could keep going but feared he was nearing the end of his endurance. Both men were very grateful to Voltar for his quick response in killing the wolf before it could do harm to anyone. Zarcon patted the great dog on the head, "Good work, Voltar."

Zarcon could see the concern in Terrence's eyes and said, "I'm fine. As you can see, Voltar has killed this wolf. I am concerned about this wound on its side. I don't think this is one of the witches' wolves. It is small for one of them, but what could have gotten to this wolf and caused such an awful injury?"

Terrence replied, "I have seen many things in this land that others would not believe existed, but I have never seen wounds quite like these. Look at the depth of the wounds again. I would say they are at least two inches deep. It's a wonder the wolf was not completely gutted. Another question is how did it get away?" Neither of them had any answers. Terrence was concerned as he took the next watch.

Zarcon found his bedroll and tried to sleep with Voltar close beside him. He did not sleep well. He kept thinking about the wounded wolf. *What could it mean?*

As the sky lightened, the group began to waken. Before they ate, Zarcon told them about the wolf that Voltar had killed. Greta and Jasmine were both shocked. Men were concerned that they had not heard anything. Terrence told them that he had heard Voltar fighting in the brush close by and rushed to see what had happened. He found Voltar standing over the wolf and had gone with Zarcon to examine it.

Terrence assigned two of the men to bury the wolf. No one could explain how the wolf could have been wounded like that. Apparently there was a larger animal prowling the area—not a pleasant thought for any of them. They ate jerky and hard bread and drank some water from the stream. They filled their canteens before setting out for the day. They didn't have time to fish or hunt. The group felt the need to move on quickly. Whatever wounded the wolf could surely be close by.

They mounted up and headed west again. They kept to the trail and talked softly with one another as the day passed. The forest was deep and still. The horses' hooves were quiet on the trail covered with pine needles and dead leaves. The silence was almost oppressive. There were few birdcalls, and no small animals seemed to be moving in the brush near the trail. The sun shined through the trees and speckled the trail as they rode through the forest. It was a beautiful day—if only they could forget about the wolf and what could possibly have attacked it. Fear was in the air as they quietly rode along.

Suddenly Zarcon felt a terrible pain in his head and fell forward on his horse. It was the feeling he got when powerful magic was being used. This was worse than anything he had felt before.

Greta and Terrence rode up to him quickly in grave concern. Zarcon had never acted like this before. Greta asked, "What has happened? Are you all right?"

Terrence grabbed the horse's reins and stopped him as he steadied Zarcon in the saddle.

Zarcon could only moan for a few moments and hold his head. Finally he said, "I have just felt the most powerful burst of magic I have ever felt. It can only be something the witches have done. I suspect Zora is up to no good. I only hope the castle is unharmed. I pray everyone has left as I urged them to do. Indeed, I fear for us all." Zarcon got down from his horse and vomited in the grass off the trail. His head hurt so badly. He couldn't help feeling ill.

Terrence was by his side in seconds. He stood by and helped Zarcon stand. Zarcon was very pale and appeared to be very weak. Greta also jumped down off her horse to help Zarcon. She was greatly disturbed by his reaction and his news. "Is there anything we can do to help you? Is there any way you can find out what happened without going to the source?"

Zarcon wiped his mouth, shook his head weakly, and said, "No, we must press on. This feeling only makes the need for speed even greater." He was able to clean himself off with a cloth Terrence provided. Greta brought him a drink from his canteen, and with Terrence's help, he got back on his horse.

The other members of the party were just coming up to Zarcon, concerned about what had happened. Zarcon told them all briefly that there had been a terrible release of magic such as he had never felt before, but there was nothing they could do about it now. "So we must press on. Donavan is now more important than ever to our cause."

The group was more concerned than before. Too many things were happening in the short time they had been on the trail. The powerful use of magic—in all probability, done by the witches— confirmed their fears. They were anxious to get to Donavan's cabin. Surely, if he would just choose to help them, they had a chance of stopping the witches from causing any more damage.

They continued on their way, trying to relax as they went. The next few days on the trail were relatively quiet, which was a good thing, given the state of tension they had been under. There was a fairly large creek that flowed close by the trail, and they had plenty of fish to eat and water to drink, which allowed them to preserve their other supplies for leaner times. The weather also cooperated, and the trail was fairly dry as time passed.

Zarcon's headache was gone, and he was able to sleep at night. Greta was grateful that he was doing better. It had been frightening to see him so ill. She was thinking that maybe things would be all right if they could just get to Donovan in time.

Jasmine was also concerned about Zarcon, so she was relieved to note that he was relaxing and able to focus on the trail and the needs of the group. Greta was a calming influence on everyone. She seemed to have some magic in that regard. Jasmine was drawn to her in many ways. They were becoming fast friends.

The track began to widen as the day progressed. Voltar was happily following the group, sniffing and barking at the forest animals that crossed the track. They were getting closer to human habitation. There were a few farms off the track, hidden among the trees. They rounded a bend and saw a small village just ahead that they would stop at long enough to replenish some supplies as well as find out any news before they found a place to camp for the night.

The village was called Moroville. It consisted of a single lane through the middle of the village with shops on either side of the road. The businesses were small with wooden planking to allow villagers to enter away from the road. They all had pitched roofs with wood shingles. They were painted bright yellow, orange, blue, and red. It gave the village a cheerful feeling. The people they passed were friendly and helpful when asked for directions as they entered the village.

They were told that, on the far end of town, there was an inn that was painted a bright blue and was called the Parrot. The owner always had a parrot in the common room that squawked and made a terrible mess just under his perch, but he was entertaining to the customers with his colorful vocabulary and choice of times to use it. Whenever the town cleric stopped by, the parrot said, "More booze over here." The man didn't drink, so no one knew quite why the parrot behaved the way he did. He just seemed to know what would embarrass or irritate someone the most.

As they rode into the inn's yard, Jaron took charge of the horses. Two of the men helped him take them to the stable in back of the inn so that Jaron could look them over and they could brush the horses down before going in to eat. After checking the hooves and legs of each of the horses, Jaron was satisfied that they were sound. He also checked with the stable hands to be sure they would feed the horses.

While Jaron was busy with the horses, Zarcon's group entered the inn and sat at a table in one corner—the better to watch others in the room and protect their backs. Jaron and the others walked into the inn as Zarcon stepped up to the bar. They found where the others were seated and joined them.

Zarcon walked up to the innkeeper, put two gold coins on the bar, and said, "We would like to have some ale and bread and cheese and perhaps some stew at our table in the corner when it's convenient. Also have you any news, sir, from the east?"

The innkeeper was short and rotund with a balding head. He wore a dirty apron tied around his middle. He was also a suspicious man and looked Zarcon over very closely for a few seconds. "I will have your ale and bread and cheese, along with some of my stew in a moment. As for news from the east, I've heard some strange rumors the last few days. It is said that a castle was leveled. It was suspected that a few people were left inside and were killed as it came down, but it is not known for sure.

Apparently the rest of the people had fled and hid in the forest. Would you know anything about that?"

Zarcon was shaken by the man's words, but he tried not to show it. That had to be the magic he had felt. There was no doubt that it was his castle since he would have been the only one to have his people escape into the forest. He said, "I may know the man who lived in that castle. What do you suppose caused the destruction of it?"

The innkeeper said, "It is said that the witches came to talk to the lord of the castle, known to be a wizard by the name of Zarcon, but finding him gone, they took some sort of revenge on his castle. There is also some suspicion that the witches may have spent some time torturing the people who died. I pity the poor man. Those witches have left him nothing standing. If you see the man, will you let him know what the rumors say?"

Zarcon was upset, but he said, "I will certainly tell him of the rumors and warn him of the witches' interest in his whereabouts. Do you have any other news?" Zarcon was barely able to contain his rage at the thought that the witches may have tortured anyone—let alone any of his villagers.

The innkeeper was silent for a moment and then said, "I have heard also that the witches have turned their wolves loose and have sent them to find this wizard." He whispered, "I have also seen a man in black who is asking questions. His name is Black Hawk. There are many stories about his talent for killing. He has been gone for a week, but I think the two issues are linked. What about you? He is asking after that selfsame wizard, Zarcon."

Zarcon thought for a moment and said, "It may be so. I wonder what this Black Hawk would want with a wizard."

Zarcon was shocked to hear about this Black Hawk. Who could be looking for him besides the witches? What was going on here? He must confer with the others. "I thank you for your news."

The innkeeper just smiled and went back to his work. He wasn't paid to think anyway. It did seem rather strange that this was the third incident in one week that people were asking for news from the east. *Hmm, funny that.*

Zarcon's group were talking quietly and waiting for their meal when Zarcon sat back down at the table. He said quietly, "I have some strange news to tell you. There is a man by the name of Black Hawk who has been asking around about me. Would any of you have an idea who this man might be or what he may be after?" Zarcon decided to tell them the rest of the news as they traveled. It would not be good to talk about his castle where others might hear. Terrence said, "I have heard rumors about a man by that name. No one really knows where he comes from, only that he is a hired assassin by trade and temperament. That he is looking for you is cause for concern indeed. It would be helpful if we could find out who has hired him and why."

"Who do you suppose he is working for that would want anything to do with me?" asked Zarcon. His voice betrayed his concern.

Jasmine and Greta were leaning closer to hear what was being said. Both were concerned for Zarcon's safety as well as the safety of them all. All they needed now was another enemy to deal with. Jasmine had also heard rumors of Black Hawk. She was fearful that, if even a fraction of what was said about him were true, they were in a lot of trouble. This was a man to fear. She decided to keep it to herself in any case. It would do no good to scare the others; they had enough to worry about.

Just then the parrot squawked and said, "Death is coming … death is coming." The crowd laughed nervously and went back to their business.

"That parrot is a nuisance." The innkeeper tried to lighten the mood. "Don't mind him. He's always been one for doom and gloom. He's just a stupid bird after all."

One of the patrons said, "That may be, but he has a nasty way of ruining a perfectly good evening. No one needs to hear his squawking anyway. It's a good thing the food is so good."

All laughed at that, and the moment passed.

Those with Zarcon finished up their meals and left the inn together. Jaron and two of the soldiers went to get the horses. The stable hands had just fed them. They each saddled their horses. Everyone mounted up, and they continued west toward Donovan's home. Jasmine was spooked by the parrot and said, "You know, that parrot was so annoying, but his last words bothered me. I am fearful that the bird might have some power of foretelling. It really gave me the creeps. What do you think of it, Greta?"

Greta was thoughtful and finally said, "I agree with you. I just hope that bird was just spouting off and doesn't really have powers of any kind. What do you think, Zarcon?"

Zarcon was close at hand, and after some thought, he said, "You know, the longer I live, the more I realize that I don't know half of what goes on or is possible in this world of ours. I detected no magic in the room, however, so the bird is most likely harmless. Don't let what he said get under your skin. He is just a silly bird after all." Zarcon was trying very hard to comfort the women. He was not so sure about the bird. It gave him a chill when he heard the bird talk about death. It was always in the back of his mind that they might not all survive this quest.

Greta and Jasmine and a few of the men breathed sighs of relief. Zarcon's words gave them some comfort. The atmosphere was a bit gloomy in the inn, and they were glad to be away from it. The day was sunny and warm for this time of year. It gave them a feeling of hope as they rode along the trail. They rode on for the rest of the afternoon and stopped for something to eat and to rest the horses as the sun began to descend. They were still following the creek. There was a grassy meadow to the left side of the trail where the horses could eat as well.

As the group rested, Zarcon told them that he had decided not to tell them something important while they were at the inn, but he needed to tell them now. He began, "The innkeeper told me that there is a rumor that a castle has been destroyed by the witches when they did not find the wizard Zarcon at home. I was also told that a few people stayed in the castle and were killed by the witches just before they destroyed the castle. The innkeeper said that the rest of the people left and were said to be hiding in the forest. I am so angry to think that they did not all leave. Then to think what the witches must have done to them is more than I can deal with." Zarcon had to pause to regain control of his emotions. Everyone else was in shock at his words and didn't know what to say. It was too horrible to contemplate.

After a few moments, he continued, "I am grateful that most of them listened to me before we left. I just hope they can survive until we return. I don't know if the wolves went with the witches, but the innkeeper did say that the witches were said to have released their wolves to find Zarcon. That, of course, is us. We must be very watchful for any sign of those wolves. Fortunately, Voltar is with us and will give us ample warning of their approach. Won't you, boy?" Zarcon patted Voltar on the head as he spoke. The dog nuzzled his hand and barked. "Furthermore, I believe that the witches used some really terrible magic to be able to actually level my castle and those within it. I'm fairly certain that was the cause of my headache a while back. I am really afraid they may have used the Black Wind to do it. If so, there is more unleashed on the world than we can know."

This was another shock for the group. Jasmine spoke for the rest of them when she said, "Zarcon, this is horrific news! What happens when the Black Wind is released? I've heard only rumors, but those are terrifying in themselves."

Zarcon decided he had better tell them the truth and all of it. They needed to be prepared for what might come. "When enough power is used to call up the Black Wind, it does the bidding of those who brought it to life. It will disappear for a time, but it will come back at some point to cause the caller much grief. Fortunately, it was the witches who did so. The Black Wind will call them when it decides it needs to use them for its own purpose. Those who have called the Black Wind have been known to have dreadful things happen to them later on. Sometimes the Black Wind waits for months, or even years, to do its work on those who dare to call it forth. I have seen wizards and witches who have spontaneously combusted, lost their magic forever, or suddenly start bleeding from their noses, ears, and mouths. Sometimes they develop sores all over their bodies and die in horrible pain. It just doesn't make sense that the witches would want to risk such a fate just to get revenge on us. I am seriously worried about their sanity. Zora, in particular, is very vindictive. I can't help but think she was behind the calling of the Black Wind."

Jasmine knew Zora had been using the blue orb. Her sanity was indeed in question at this point. She would have to talk with Zarcon about that when they were alone. She still did not want the others to be aware of the blue orb in her possession. The time would come when it would be necessary—but not yet.

They all had much to think about at this point, and since the day was getting late, they decided to move on and try to find shelter for the night. They would need a place that was defensible from the wolves. There was no knowing when they might show up. They mounted up and headed west once again, keeping the creek in sight. They filled their canteens and watered their horses before they left.

As the day wore on, they gradually noticed that there was no game to be seen. How could this be? It was very unsettling. They all hoped the answer would be a simple one. It didn't seem likely. As they traveled, they became more and more agitated. Nerves were on edge. Tempers began to flare. The horses became restive, pawing the ground when the group stopped for a meal or a rest. There was definitely something wrong. Zarcon could detect a small amount of magic, but he passed it off as something minor. He was hoping it was something in the natural world. They continued to travel, but their nerves were even more on edge as time passed.

A mist began to curl around the horses' hooves and crept through the trees. It was thick enough to obscure the ground around them as they rode on. Mason, the last man in the line, was watching the mist warily when he noticed red eyes in the midst of it. He started to scream when he saw long, scaly limbs with razor- sharp claws reaching for him and his horse. He felt the claws rip his skin as the world went black.

Jasmine had a bad feeling about the mist and was about to mention it to Zarcon when Mason screamed. It was quickly cut off. The horses were wild-eyed and hard to control. There was a strange smell in the air, like death but worse. The men rushed back to where Mason had been riding but couldn't find him.

Voltar was growling and barking, and his hackles were raised, but there was nothing to attack. Gradually the mist cleared, and they found Mason's body—or what was left of it. There was blood all around but no tracks. Mason's body was in pieces just off the trail. His horse was beside what was left of him. It was slashed and bloody. The horse screamed once and lay still. It was as if there was some kind of poison at work.

Some of the men gagged at the sight and smell of what had happened to Mason. Greta and Jasmine moved away to allow the men to take care of things. Seeing the danger they were all in, Zarcon started an incantation to protect them from whatever was out there. It was designed to encircle them all and not allow anything through. It was powerful enough to possibly alert the witches, but Zarcon knew he must protect all who were with him. He sent out a tendril of magic to try to locate what had attacked them, but there was only a small trace that quickly faded.

Jasmine said, "What could have attacked us and not left any signs? Look at Voltar. He can't find it either. Zarcon, could you detect anything?"

Zarcon was very worried. "I only felt a very slight amount of magic a while back, and it is quickly fading. I can find nothing even with using magic that would tell me something about it. I'm afraid I haven't heard of anything like it. There are many stories, but none of them make sense in this situation. It didn't even leave tracks— only that horrid smell. I have taken precautions to protect us from another attack, but it may alert the witches of our whereabouts." Zarcon turned to the men. "Did any of you see anything at all?"

One of the men said, "I think I saw what looked like red eyes in the mist just before it attacked Mason, but I'm not sure. It happened so quickly that I almost fell off my horse."

Another man said he thought he saw claws coming for him, but they stopped when Voltar started barking at it. The claws looked sharp and were about six inches long. They were at the end of long, thick, scaly limbs. The limbs were green or black. The rest was covered by the thick mist. The mist had enveloped Mason just before he screamed.

Neither Voltar nor the horses would go near what was left of Mason. Everyone was terrified that whatever it was might come back. They were grateful that Zarcon had used his magic to protect them. The mist was gone, but some of the smell remained. Jaron and Terrence dug a grave for Mason's remains, and the rest of the men collected what was left of him. They gathered what they could find, put it in the grave, and buried it. They also dug a grave for the poor horse and buried it as well. They knew they needed to hurry. It was starting to get dark, and there was still no shelter to be found. Zarcon was shaken by the suddenness of the attack and the brutality of it. He knew of no creature that could do such a thing. What could it be?

Jaron came up to the group and said, "I think I have heard of something recently that has been attacking farm animals and some of the farmers in this area. I just didn't believe the stories. They spoke of something that attacks from a thick mist and doesn't leave a trace. I'm sorry I didn't mention it. I just couldn't believe it could possibly be true."

Zarcon grabbed Jaron's collar and put his face next to his. "What are you saying? That you heard of this and decided not to warn us? Is there anything else you have kept to yourself that we should all know?" He released Jaron with a slight shove. "Jaron, this is not something that you can shrug off just because you do not believe it could be true. We must be prepared for anything in these hills. There are too many unknown creatures, let alone the ones we hear about, to let any of it go without at least some warning. Think, Jaron, what else did you hear?" Zarcon was trembling with anger and fear. Jaron had never seen him so upset. Zarcon's reaction brought terror to the hearts of them all. If Zarcon could be so terrified, there must be a reason.

Jaron was staggered by Zarcon's attack. He had never seen him like this. He said, "Zarcon, you know the tales told in small towns and villages. Most are meant to scare unwary travelers, but they mean nothing. I made the mistake of assuming this was another one of those. I did ask questions, but no one seemed to know any more about it. I'm sorry. That's all I know." Jaron felt close to tears, thinking that he may have warned them and prevented Mason's death.

Zarcon seemed to come to himself at that and said, "I'm sorry, Jaron. I don't know what happened to me. I'm not myself just now. This attack has left me trembling like the old man that I am. I cannot recall ever feeling so helpless and old." Zarcon looked around at the others and saw the fear in their eyes. "I'm sorry." He turned away and sat on a large rock.

Greta came to his side and put her hand on his shoulder in an effort to comfort him to some small degree. They were all upset and fearful. No one spoke for several minutes. They just paused and seemed to hold their breath. Finally, Terrence said, "I've been thinking about this for a bit now. I don't know about the rest of you, but I think we're dealing with the same creature that attacked that wolf a few days ago. It makes sense to me. What do the rest of you think?"

Zarcon looked up suddenly and made the same connection. It could not be a coincidence that both times the creature caused deep wounds such as they had not seen before. "Terrence, I'm sure you are right! I hadn't put it together like that, but you must be right! It's the only thing that makes any sense. At least we know what we're up against to some degree."

Greta, Jasmine, Jaron, and Lantz looked at each other and nodded. It made sense to them as well. It was not exactly comforting, but it did explain what had happened to the wolf. The puzzle remained. What was this creature—and how could they possibly defend themselves against it?

Terrence said, "Well, it looks like we may have solved some of the mystery here, but I'm not willing to sit here and wait for it to come back. What say we all pack up and get out of this cursed place?" Terrence helped Zarcon to his feet while the others gathered up any belongings that had fallen off the packhorses in their terror. They finished packing and mounted up to leave. The horses were still a bit restive but were compliant as they were mounted.

It was a solemn group that left the site of Mason's death. No one spoke above a whisper. Even Voltar sensed the mood of the group and stayed near Zarcon's horse while they began their travels once more.

The loss of Mason was a serious blow to them all. He had been a well-liked hard worker.

Gradually the sun began to shine through the few clouds as they rode. The mood of the group lightened a little, and Terrence set the pace a bit faster so they could leave their fear behind them. It would put some distance between them and what had happened to Mason.

For the first time, they set their horses to a gallop. It was ride swiftly or be left behind. Voltar ran along with Zarcon and kept up easily. The group was feeling the strain of the past few hours, and they knew they must ride hard to reach any place of relative safety.

As they rode, Jasmine and Terrence were looking for anything that might provide a safe haven for the night in case of another attack. They were worried that if the witches felt Zarcon's use of magic, they would most likely send the wolves after them.

They had been riding hard for a while when Jasmine called out to Zarcon to stop. "I see what looks like a cave in the mountain ahead. Maybe it will be large enough for all of us to spend the night."

"You have a good eye, Jasmine." Zarcon sent one of the soldiers to investigate. After a few minutes, the man returned with the news that the cave was large enough for the party and the horses. This was good news indeed. They were all frightened to one degree or another and the thought that they might have had to sleep out in the open was truly frightening.

As they rode up the hill to the cave, they could see that there was a large opening at the mouth and a smaller room for them to sleep in. The area at the opening was large enough to protect the horses. They tethered the horses and foraged for some grass to feed them. After the horses were settled, they started a small fire. Fortunately there was a small opening at the roof of the cave that would allow the smoke to escape. They kept the fire small to prevent any sign of their occupation of the cave from showing as night came on. Now they could settle in and sleep in relative peace and safety. They ate the jerky and bread with cheese. There was still some water from the stream earlier that day. They hoped they would find more water in the morning. Voltar hunted a rabbit for himself and ate it just outside the cave mouth. He settled down at the mouth of the cave to help keep guard through the night.

Terrence set watches for the night and finally settled down near the fire. They had lost a comrade that day and they all felt the loss. That they had been attacked with so many humans around did not add to any sense of peace. They spoke in low murmurs of the day's events until all was finally quiet, and they slept as best they could. The next morning came early as Zarcon urged them all to awaken and be off. There was still a fair amount of ground to cover, and the threat of more trouble brought them to their weary feet. Many were sore, and all were somewhat fearful. They loaded the horses and cleared away the remains of their camp. They scattered the remains of the fire to ensure that no one would recognize the camp if they came looking for the group. Zarcon was also concerned that the magic he had used to protect them from further attack would alert the witches to where they were, but it couldn't be helped.

They reluctantly left the cave and its relative safety. They continued west toward the mountains. It was still several days before they would reach those mountains. So they kept going. Occasionally they would pass fellow travelers, but in this area, so remote from villages and towns, people kept to themselves. Most wouldn't look them in the eye. Gradually they were getting closer to the more populated areas of the land. Small farms could be seen as they traveled. A few farm animals were also in evidence. Voltar barked at some of them as they passed.

They finally stopped for the night at a small forested area that looked like it had been used for camping many times before. The soldiers picketed the horses and let them eat the plentiful grass. There was also a creek nearby, which was the main reason they stopped there.

Each person in the group did his or her part to prepare the evening meal and set up the bedding. They had a fire to cook on and to warm them for the night ahead. They kept it low, however, to avoid drawing too much attention in the night.

The night passed quietly. They did hear a large animal roaring in the night, but it was miles away. It made the hair on the backs of their necks rise. There was a soft mist on the ground, but it was not nearly as thick as that which had brought death to Mason.

They woke to a misty morning haze. The sun was barely filtering through a low-lying fog on the forest floor. They saddled their horses and loaded the pack animals for the day's journey after eating a quick breakfast of jerky, cheese, some of the hard bread, and water. The creek provided water to fill their canteens for the day. It was with some trepidation that they set off for another day of travel. Fortunately, this day passed without incident. Birds were chirping in the trees, and a squirrel would occasionally warn them away with his chatter.

The next few days passed relatively peacefully. The group began to feel somewhat rested after the episode with the mist, though they still kept a wary eye on any movement in the forest that might not be natural. All still feared the mist might return. In the backs of their minds was the additional concern regarding the witches' wolves and when they might attack.

The weather remained cool with some morning mist close to the ground that melted away with the rising sun. There were more people traveling on the road as they progressed. They passed a village now and then, but they slept in the forest at night to avoid any undue attention being drawn to their passage. It was feared that the witches would have spies in the taverns along the way to report their passing. It was known that the witches did such things. There were too many poor peasants willing to do the witches' bidding for the money. It was also healthier for them to do as they were told. The witches were not known for their mercy.

The group had not forgotten that the assassin, Black Hawk, was looking for them. It would do no good to have him get word of their passing since they did not know what he wanted. All these thoughts made for a sleepless night.

A Journey For Witches

The planning was completed for the journey the witches were about to take. They would take ten men with them, along with their coach and cook wagon. There was no sense in making the travel more difficult than it had to be or any sooner than it had to be. The men chosen to come with them were called in to discuss the plans the witches had made. The men the witches employed were large and strong. They shared the witches' talent for cruelty. These men also feared the witches and the power they held. They knew it was to their advantage to be quick to obey any whim the witches might have.

When people saw the men, they knew the witches were not far behind. The roads often became fairly vacant when they approached a village. The men enjoyed the power that being with the witches gave them. No one dared to cross them if they desired to live long. The leader of the men, Cardeegan, was especially cruel. The others followed him with precision. He had a scar on his left cheek that legend has it was put there during the Wolf Wars by none other than Donavan. The scar made his already hard and cruel face even worse to look upon. It ran from his left eyebrow to the corner of his mouth, curving it up into a perpetual smirk. The knife wound had also severed the nerves there, and the left side of his face sagged. Cardeegan had a special hatred for Donovan. He had sought revenge since that day.

When Zora told the men what their journey involved and that Donovan may be part of the revenge they would be seeking, Cardeegan was especially pleased and looked forward to the many things he would like to do to him. Zora promised him first crack at finishing Donavan off. Cardeegan's expression became very frightening. It was difficult to determine if he was smiling or frowning. The glint in his eyes caused those men close to him to back away a step or two.

The witches' men were given the responsibility of preparing the pack animals and cook wagon with whatever food would be needed as well as tents for their shelter as the travel became more primitive. Zora gave them two days to prepare all that was needed. No excuses would be allowed, and Cardeegan knew it. As soon as the meeting with the witches was over, he ordered the men to be quick about all that was necessary, assigning each man part of the preparations. They hurried out of the room to go about their business.

As the men left, Zora looked at her sister witches. Sometimes she did wish that she were tall and beautiful like Anesthia, but fate had chosen to give Zora the power the others coveted instead. Zora grew up in a home where her parents either ignored her or persecuted her for being so ugly and fat. Her mother paid little attention to Zora as a child. Her mother had more important things to attend to, and they did not include the frivolous demands of a child. Whenever Zora did something that particularly annoyed or angered her mother, she would get a whipping or worse. One day, Zora's mother was particularly angry and spanked little Zora so hard that she could not sit for several days.

In her little heart, a cold hatred began to develop. Without nurturing of any kind, she began to loathe other humans. She felt no compassion or empathy for any other person. She became a very bitter and angry child. It was then that Zora discovered her talent for magic. The black magic was the one she chose to study. She had begun developing her talent long before most children could lace their shoes. It came naturally to her.

She found her power quite by accident one morning when her nursemaid, Lila, had tried to wake her. Zora preferred to sleep late even when very young. She preferred the night hours. Lila had startled her in addition to trying to get her up before she was ready. Zora was angry and half-afraid of her nursemaid. She reacted by imagining what it would be like for Lila to die. Suddenly, Lila crumpled to the floor unconscious. Zora started screaming. Her mother came running into her room. When she saw Lila on the floor, she shook her to try to revive her. Lila finally came around, but she couldn't speak. Her eyes were filled with terror, and she clung to Zora's mother.

"What have you done, Zora? What have you done?" Zora's mother's eyes were wide with shock. "Tell me what happened here!"

Zora looked at her mother and smiled. She would tell no one what she had done. It was her little secret. There were no witches in Zora's family until then, and no one knew how to handle what Zora had done. Her mother was afraid to mention it to anyone else for fear there would be repercussions she was not able to deal with. People in the area might want to hurt her little Zora. Witches were greatly feared, and fear bred cruelty. Her mother didn't care so much that they might hurt Zora as that they might lose face in the community.

It was about a month later that Lila had finally been able to talk, but she had no recollection of what had happened—only that she had been very frightened at the time and afraid she was going to die. Once Lila was able to get around and resume her duties, she never would go in to wake Zora. She always sent in one of the lesser maids. They only went in when they could hear Zora up and moving around. No one wanted to be cursed as Lila had been that fateful morning. Yes, everyone was calling it a curse. Zora's mother could do nothing about the rumors. Oh, she had threatened the servants not to talk about the incident, but ultimately, that was something she could not control.

Zora was excited by her newfound power. She had the servants right where she wanted them. They would flinch if she looked at them. They would cower if she acted like she was heading in their direction. She grew more and more confident as time went by.

When she got older and could venture from the castle, Zora began practicing on the animals in the forest. She would sneak out late at night when everyone else was sleeping. She would find a squirrel in the tree close to the castle and think about the squirrel falling out of the tree … and it would. She could pick up the squirrel and look it over to see what had happened to it. Sometimes the squirrel would die, but sometimes it would wake up suddenly and scratch or bite her as it ran off. She was learning how to control her power, so it didn't really matter. A few scratches were nothing compared to what she was learning. She worked on her spells from then on.

A year later, Zora was still working on her concentration. She was getting better and could do many more things to the squirrels and other small creatures than she had at first imagined. She would torture them to see how long they would survive. Then she tried using her power to keep them alive even longer. It was becoming addictive to her.

Finally, she became somewhat bored with the experiments with small animals. However, she still enjoyed watching the life flow out of them at her will. As she grew older, she decided to try her power on something bigger. The episode with her nursemaid had scared her in a way, but now she felt that she could control it better. There was an old dog, Lester, in the castle yard that would hang around the stables. Zora decided to try to get the dog to go to sleep.

While everyone was busy with chores, Zora went out to the stable to find the old dog. She called him to her. He looked at her and whined.

Zora called to him to come again, but Lester put his tail between his legs and whined again. Zora was becoming angry in her evil heart. She thought about the dog being dead, and she meant it. The dog whined once, fell over on his side, and died. Zora was glad. The old thing was just a nuisance anyway.

Zora knew she could kill with a thought. She smiled to herself as she hurried back to the castle. No one must know what she had just discovered. What she did not know was that one of the stable boys had seen her with the old dog. When he ran over to it and discovered that it was dead, he cried. He had loved that old dog. The boy, Donavan, would find a way to get Zora for this. There must be something he could do. Zora was becoming so cruel. Maybe he could teach her a lesson.

Unlike Zora, Donavan had some history of magic in his family. He had known for a while that he had some ability. There were signs that he could use a word and focus his attention and move things. So he began to ask questions of his mother about magic and how to use it in self-defense. She was surprised at his questions, but she humored him, not knowing why he was so curious. Finally, in frustration, and because Donavan wouldn't leave her alone, she went into the cellar and came back with a book that had been in the family for generations. It was the family Book of Spells. Donavan's family had only used the white magic and never to control or harm others. The book was dedicated to those kinds of spells.

Donavan began reading the book every moment he was alone. He would practice many of the spells, but the one that seemed to be his strongest was the one that seemed to block the spells of others. He hadn't known it worked until Zora came to him one morning and asked him to go with her for a horseback ride. Donavan had too much to do to go anywhere with her. He said, "No. I have much to do this day and cannot leave just now."

She quickly became enraged and puckered up her mouth to speak some incantation. Donavan, fearing that she might do to him what she had done to the dog, responded with the spell he had learned. Zora sent the spell to Donavan, hoping to at least disable him for a time. She got a funny look on her face when nothing happened to Donavan. She tried harder this time. Still nothing happened. Her face grew very red indeed. She ran into the castle and told her mother to send Donavan away because he was a bad boy and wouldn't do what she told him to do.

Zora's mother, fearing her own daughter's anger, agreed. Donavan was sent home to his mother. He and his family lived in Riza, the neighboring town, in a small cottage by the river. Donavan's father earned a living as a fisherman and wheelwright. Donavan's wages from the castle allowed them to purchase some extras. Now that Donavan was no longer bringing in the extra money, they would have to be more careful with the finances. Donavan was still young and needed a job desperately. He was told the town blacksmith, Jonas, was looking for help.

Donavan went to see the blacksmith to ask if he could work for him. He was willing to do almost anything. The people of the town knew he was a good worker. Jonas hired him to help clean up the place and keep his fires going. Donavan was willing and worked hard. The smith continued to give him more responsibility as time went on. Donavan began to work the forge and hammer the metal for horseshoes and other things. He remained short for his age, but he became very strong with broad shoulders.

A few years passed. Things seemed to be going well for Donavan and his parents, but the word eventually got around about him upsetting Zora. Zora found out where the boy had gone after she had him sent away. She was outraged that he was still around. Jonas heard rumors in the tavern one night. One of the stable hands working for Zora's family told him that Zora wanted Donavan so she could destroy him. Jonas came to Donavan the next morning to warn him about Zora and her anger.

Donavan did not want to put Jonas or his family in any danger. He left town, and that is how Donavan came to be in the army. He had to leave his family and travel to the king's city, Harling. He found the army barracks, and after asking around, he found Sergeant Murphy. Sergeant Murphy was a tall and stocky man of few words. He had a handlebar mustache that nearly reached his chin.

Donavan was nervous but stood his ground and asked Sergeant Murphy about signing on. Sergeant Murphy was more than happy to sign him up. He saw that Donavan was not tall, but he was very strong and willing. That was the main thing. Sergeant Murphy was impressed with him. He decided right then to sign him up. Donavan was in the military from that moment on. After that, he never had contact with Zora again. It would be many years before Zora would have a hand in destroying his family and home. Zora never forgot Donavan's treachery and use of magic against her. She was frightened that anyone would have the power to block one of her spells. Her fear fired her resentment and desire for revenge. She would bide her time, but her day to ruin Donavan would come.

Now, years later, she thought of Donavan and feared that he might join Zarcon in his plans, whatever they might be. She had heard that Donavan had sworn to stay out of human affairs, and she was glad, but what if he changed his mind? She would have to worry about that later. For now, she must prepare to leave with her sister witches. The servants had packed the witches' belongings, and the horses and carriage were made ready to leave. The witches left their castle, but Magg had been chosen to stay behind to care for the castle and go to them if needed.

The witches decided to head for the Backlash Mountains. It seemed like a good place to start looking for Zarcon. That was the last place Donavan had been seen. The wolves would follow them as they traveled. Their servants would take care of the horses and their baggage. Cardeegan would lead the way with his men. They had a cook who traveled in his own wagon with the supplies. Once they got to the mountains, they would have to give all that up and ride horses. There was no sense in doing that any sooner than absolutely necessary. The witches enjoyed flaunting their wealth to anyone who would look. They were a little bit worried about things now that the orb was in the hands of Zarcon and Jasmine, but they were very much assured that they would get it back. It was just a matter of time. One thing did concern them, and that was the fact that their magic did not seem as strong without the orb. They chose not to acknowledge that uncomfortable fact thinking they would have the orb back quickly enough.

They stayed in their carriage as long as the roads were passable. The first day out, they were on the main thoroughfare between their own Rimeron Valley and the city of Koorim. There were many caravans and travelers. Even so, they stood out among the rest with their large coach and Cardeegan and his men leading the way. The witches enjoyed watching the people stop and look as they rode by. However, as time passed, the novelty of traveling outside the castle began to wear thin.

Myshella grouched one too many times at Anesthia, and Zora jumped on her for it. "Leave it alone! You must behave yourselves, all of you. We can't afford petty squabbling now. Don't you see that? I will not tolerate it. There is much too much at stake here! Save it for some other time. Let's get to an inn for the night in some kind of peace, shall we?"

Myshella was not happy with Zora for rebuking her in front of the others. She hated the smirk on their faces. She would get even soon. They would not forget this. Besides, she had a right to be touchy.

Anesthia was snoring in her sleep and kept resting her head on Myshella's shoulder. Everyone knew how she hated to be touched! It was disgusting!

Koorim was one of the larger towns of the area, but the buildings and shops were in poor condition. The paint was peeling on most of the shops and other buildings. Only a few had been maintained with any care. There was something depressing about it that bothered Zora, but she could not name what it was. The people dressed shabbily and rarely smiled as they passed each other. The women wore long dresses, either brown or black, that hung on them like sacks. They wore floppy hats that covered their hair and shaded them from the sun. The men wore baggy black or gray coveralls that hung from their shoulders. Their white shirts were a dirty gray. It was odd to see the people of the town dressed almost in uniforms that were so similar in style and color. The whole town felt drab and sad.

Zora was beginning to be affected by the apparent lack of joy in the town and tried to put it out of her mind. As they drove through Koorim, the men were looking for a place the witches could stay for the night. They finally found an inn that was acceptable. Cardeegan and his men would stay in a place not far from there. It was a place for travelers, mostly men, who needed to spend one night with a stable in the back for their horses and carriage. It was called Charlie's and was large with many single rooms to rent. Cardeegan rented the rooms he and his men would need for the night and saw that the horses were taken care of and the carriage was put away where it would be safe. He went inside to be with his men while they ate a simple meal before going to their rooms for the night.

The inn the witches chose to stay at was the Wayfarer. Though the paint was peeling and the roof was in need of some repair, they could see it was the best place in town. It wasn't up to the standard Zora and the other witches had become accustomed to, but it would do. They walked into the inn, and all eyes turned in their direction. Heleren smiled sweetly at them all. The men could hardly take their eyes off her until one of the men recognized her and told the others about her and the things she had done. The witches were feared by all and hated by most.

The innkeeper hurried over to them as soon as he realized who they were. He was tall and thin with a hooknose and thinning hair. His voice was thin and whiny, and he had a lisp. He had a thin mustache and yellowing teeth. He said, "Fenrod at your thervith, dear ladieth. I have the betht food and finetht roomth in town. How may I take care of you?" He favored them with a raised eyebrow and a nasty smirk. He sprayed spittle when he talked and was difficult to understand. The witches did not miss his meaning, however, or the smirk on his face. 'This was a man in big trouble; he was just too dumb to know it.

Zora frowned at him and said, "Kind sir, we would have some of that fine food and two of your finest rooms for the night. If you value your health, you will keep to yourself beyond that." Zora sent a sliver of power into the man to warn him. It was enough to jolt him but not enough to kill him.

Fenrod jumped and grabbed at his chest. "Ahh, that hurtth. What did you do to me?"

Zora looked him in the eye and said, "I don't know what you're talking about, but if I had done something, it would surely be to give you a hint of what will happen to you if you give us any trouble at all! Do you understand?"

Fenrod cringed and quickly said, "Yeth, milady, motht athsuredly. You'll have no trouble of any kind from me." He was shaking as he returned to the bar. Whatever the witch had done to him had hurt and terrified him. He realized that he was lucky to be alive.

The witches went to one of the tables in the corner. Everyone pointedly looked the other way. There was no point in asking for trouble after what had just happened to poor Fenrod, though nobody who knew him really liked him.

Fenrod brought out their meals very quickly and asked if there was anything else they were in need of. They told him no and proceeded to eat their dinners. Nothing was said during the meal. By silent agreement, the witches did not want anyone nearby to hear what they were planning. The witches ate and then asked to be taken to their rooms. They went upstairs and were shown to their rooms by Agnes, the barmaid. Fenrod was too fearful to go near the witches again.

The rooms were at least clean. The witches settled in for the night. Zora and Anesthia had one room. Heleren and Myshella had another.

During the night it began to rain. At first there was a slight sprinkle but the intensity increased until the witches thought the world was going to end. The racket on the roof was deafening. The rain continued through the night and most of the next day. The witches were depressed at having to wait another day in this horrible, miserable town.

Zora sent word to Cardeegan that they would be spending another day there.

The witches decided to confer in Zora's room to decide when they might be able to leave.

Zora thought a minute and said, "There is no sense in leaving until the rain stops and the roads dry out a bit."

Myshella was upset at that and cried out, "What? And let the thieves get another day on us?"

Zora tried to calm her down and said, "It would be too dangerous to leave now with the roads being too wet and slippery. There is no sense in taking unnecessary risks at this point. We will catch Zarcon and his band very soon. Besides, there is no doubt that their group would have to stop as well. So let's take advantage of the opportunity to rest another day."

The other witches reluctantly agreed to her instructions. Though there was a great deal of inner grumblings. They dared not challenge Zora at this time. Myshella felt humiliated once again. She would surely get revenge before this journey was over.

Fenrod was sure to serve the witches needs quickly and without incident. He was still terrified of them and wanted to see their backs as soon as possible. It upset him that the rain kept them there another day. Time seemed to drag on and on.

The rain trailed off as evening closed in. Zora decided that they could leave in the morning. The night passed without incident. The next day, the witches were up early. They ate breakfast in the common room with the other travelers. All was quiet. They called for their carriage and horses. Cardeegan and his men came and loaded up their baggage, and they were off. They continued to make good time for several days. There were small towns with inns all along the way where they could spend the night. It was apparent that word of their passage went before them as the inns were always ready and waiting in case the witches should stop there as they traveled through. None of the other innkeepers acted out of line either. Zora's attitude was that sometimes it paid to use her power over others to get what she wanted.

It was getting stuffy and close inside the coach after so many days on the road. The witches were on edge from traveling in such close proximity. Suddenly, as they were gazing out the window of the coach, Zora jerked around and looked at Anesthia with astonishment. "Someone has just used magic and a lot of it! It must be Zarcon! Oh, this is wonderful! Now we will find which way they are going and send the wolves to find them. I'm so excited, Anesthia. We have them!" Zora was laughing as they crested a hill.

Anesthia thought Zora was being a bit premature with her joy, but she tried to share it at any rate. It never paid to question Zora.

The wolves stayed just off the road so that they would not be seen—but could be called when needed. It wouldn't be good to have the wolves frightening people along the way. It would raise the alarm before the witches were ready to do so. It made no sense to announce their passage to Zarcon too early. He and his band could be anywhere, but now she had a pretty good idea of where that actually was.

Zora called to the driver to stop the carriage. Cardeegan helped her out of the carriage. She concentrated and called the wolves to her. The big gray male came to her quickly and left the pack in the forest. She sent him the image of Zarcon and where she thought they might be. The burst of magic had made an impression on her that was like a compass to the whereabouts of its use. The big gray wolf ran to the others, and they took off for the hills where Zarcon and his group were sure to be.

The witches continued on their trek, staying in inns when they could and using their supplies and cook wagon when they could not. The men were getting restive with so little to do. Tempers began to flare, and Cardeegan had a difficult time keeping his men in line. Since they all feared him, he would simply give them a look to settle them down. If he had to do more than raise his voice a bit, the man who incurred his wrath would pay dearly.

One night, a man by the name of Rafe was taunting another of Cardeegan's men, Josepe. Rafe was calling him names and shoving him. Anger was building between the two men. Cardeegan raised his voice and told Rafe to stop before there was any more trouble, but Rafe kept taunting and shoving Josepe. Rafe was dead before he knew what hit him. He had a large knife in his back as he fell forward into the fire.

All was silent, and no one moved. Cardeegan grabbed Rafe by his foot and yanked him out of the fire. He ordered the others to bury him quickly. It was a great lesson for the other men and not one they would soon forget. Cardeegan had no more problems after that. There were no complaints either.

Josepe was grateful for Cardeegan's interference—even though it would mean trouble for him when Cardeegan wasn't around. Rafe had been after him since they left the witches' castle. He had been careful to avoid Cardeegan's observation. Josepe figured Rafe was much drunker than he appeared. Now there was one less man to help with the witches.

7

Black Hawk

Black Hawk was a man feared by all who knew him. He was very tall and thin with thinning hair. He had a thin mustache and yellowing teeth—not attractive by any measure. He always wore black, and his nose was shaped somewhat like the beak of a hawk, hence the name. His eyes were very cold and told the story of the emptiness within. He had spent the greater part of his life killing for hire. He had killed so many men and women that he had lost count. The one thing he knew for sure was that he was very efficient and never missed. He was paid handsomely for his services. Many leaders hired him to eliminate potential threats to their power or influence. Now he was on the hunt for one Zarcon, the wizard. He had never been hired to kill a wizard and found the opportunity intriguing. He had never heard of someone killing a wizard before. This was the chance of a lifetime. He would be known the world over as the one who could do such a thing. He smiled at the thought. He also had a large, sleek black cat, known as a werecat, who could also assume the shape of a beautiful young black woman at will. The cat was called Beauty. He found the combination irresistible. The cat followed him wherever he went and was very helpful in so many ways.

Black Hawk was currently working for the prince of Landpur. Prince Curzon was hungry for power and wanted to eliminate Zarcon because he feared his power and that he might try to deter him from taking the throne from his mother. He knew Zarcon would never allow him to rule as he desired, so he had to eliminate the risk of having someone who might resist his desires, or try to stop him from having his way with the realm he wished to rule.

Black Hawk cared nothing about the affairs of the world as long as he continued to work and collect his pay. He really had no loyalty or concern for others of his race. He thought only about the job he was given and how quickly he could complete it and move on to the next one. He was truly dangerous.

His grandmother raised him, and she was old and very cruel. He was known as Jeremy then, but no one knew his real name after he left his grandmother dead one day. She had beaten him cruelly with her horsewhip once too often, and he had grabbed it from her and beat her to death with it. He left the small village he grew up in and never looked back. No one had tried to help him as he grew up under the terrible hand of his grandmother, so he had no fond memories there. His heart had hardened within him. Indeed, he felt no pain or longing for human companionship. It had brought him nothing but pain his entire life.

When he killed his grandmother, he had a fantastic sense of power and a kind of joy he had never experienced before. When he first started killing for money, he got the same thrill each time. After so many years, the killing was routine, and he had gradually become unconcerned about the work he did. It was just a living, though very lucrative.

His skills were many when it came to taking human life. He had trained with masters of many of the killing arts. He was also able to use the skills he learned in combinations that no one else had thought of. He was a quick learner as well, but the thought of killing Zarcon was something new for him. He hungered for the opportunity to kill the great man and have the world live in fear of him because none could escape him and live.

He rode through the villages and towns, seeking Zarcon's whereabouts and quietly asking after him. He could find no trace. No one seemed to know where he had gone. There were tales that he was seeking a man by the name of Donavan, but Black Hawk had never heard of the man and knew of no way to find him. He kept searching, hoping that someday soon he would get a lucky break and Zarcon would be his to destroy.

He worked his way methodically through the land, looking for anyone who might have some knowledge of Zarcon's whereabouts. He stopped at an inn in Moroville and listened to the parrot just long enough to want to kill it. He refrained, but it was difficult. He ate a meal there and stayed the night, hoping to hear of Zarcon's passing, but he heard nothing. He finally asked the innkeeper about Zarcon as he was leaving the next day—but still nothing. He was becoming frustrated and discouraged, yet he knew it was just a matter of time before he would find the man. It might even be entertaining to find out who he traveled with and eliminate some of them just for the fun of it. At least he hoped he would find some entertainment from it. That commodity was becoming harder and harder to find. His life was empty and meaningless, and he knew it, but he was at a loss to understand why.

He had heard rumors that Zarcon might be traveling with a young woman by the name of Jasmine. He wondered about that and what the implications might be. There was also some news that the witches sought the blue orb that was said to have been found again. Black Hawk had his suspicions that Zarcon might have come into possession of it. That might explain why he was traveling with Jasmine. He would find out for himself soon enough. The thought that he might also get the blue orb was intriguing as well.

Wolves Attack

Zarcon's group was traveling west and getting closer to the mountain where Donavan lived. It was getting late in the evening, and they still hadn't found anything that looked safe enough. They kept going for another hour until one of the scouts finally found a small box canyon with cliffs on three sides with a narrow entrance. It was about a hundred yards from the trail. Zarcon and Terrence decided it would be wise to spend the night within the canyon walls.

Zarcon said, "This looks like the safest place we could hope to find in this area. There is much to be done before we can rest."

Terrence directed the men to cut through the underbrush that blocked the entrance into the canyon. It was thick with the scrub brush common to the mountains. It was a lot of work, but they knew it would be worth it if the wolves attacked. Once the area was opened, they cleared more of the brush so they would be able to have a small fire and sleep in relative safety. They also knew that Voltar would warn them if the witches' wolves came near.

They made camp and started their fire once the immediate area was cleared. There were large pine trees and small bushes near the cliff walls. It looked as if the area had been used as a camp before. The area in the middle of the canyon was relatively clear with just a few smaller scrubby shrubs that had to be removed as they were too close together to allow for their bedding. They were able to clear some space for their bedrolls without much trouble. There were also some large boulders scattered around that must have fallen from the canyon walls. A few of them were close to the entrance and would make it easier to defend if the need arose.

Jaron decided to explore the canyon farther back from the entrance. He walked to the wall of the canyon and followed it around. Close to the back, he found a small spring that was fresh and clear. He called Terrence to come see what he had found.

Terrence joined him and smiled at the news that there was fresh water as well as shelter for the group. He was able to relax a bit. He had been concerned that they might run out of water before they could leave the seclusion of the canyon. He said, "Good work, Jaron. I'll let the others know what you have found." He left to join Zarcon and the others. It was good news indeed.

When he told Zarcon and the others about the water, they were greatly relieved. The water situation was getting pretty grim. Now there was one less thing to be concerned about—at least for the time being.

Jaron continued searching for anything that might be of use to the others. He found a relatively clear area to hobble the horses for the night. It was safely away from the entrance and would give the horses plenty of fodder and a place to rest with plentiful grass near the stream that ran from the spring he had found. As the day drew into night, he would bring water to them before bedding them down.

The group settled in for the night after eating a meager meal of jerky with some berries they found on small bushes. They also had a little of the hard bread left. It didn't taste very good, but it was filling. There was plenty of water from the spring. Before calling it a night and collapsing in their bedrolls, they were able to wash up a bit. They slept near the fire for heat and comfort.

Terrence took the first watch and kept guard near the narrow opening to the canyon. All was quiet as they drifted off to sleep.

Terrence turned guard duty over to Lantz, one of the soldiers, and went to his bedroll to catch a few hours of sleep.

As the early morning light began to brighten the west walls of the canyon, Voltar began to snarl. He got up and moved quietly toward Lantz. Lantz looked out into the brightening day, and after a few moments, he shouted, "I hear wolves howling. It sounds like they are about a mile away." Voltar started barking to wake up the others.

Zarcon came running. "Everyone, bring your weapons and help Lantz protect the entrance."

Jasmine ran with him and said, "I'm so glad we are here and not out in the open. At least we can protect ourselves much better here." She drew her short sword in preparation for what was coming. The others agreed as they made themselves ready for the attack. Some of the soldiers grabbed their bows and arrows and climbed on top of the boulders close to the entrance to shoot the wolves as they came through—if they could get past Voltar and Lantz. They could not be sure how many of them were coming. They could only wait.

Gradually, they could hear the wolves coming closer. The wolves were making a lot of noise, howling and barking as they approached. The noise got louder when they realized they had Zarcon's group cornered in the canyon. They arrived at the entrance to the canyon and started milling around and whining. It was apparent that they were trying to decide how to attack.

Finally, one of the large males jumped through the brush and tried to attack Voltar, but Voltar saw him coming and attacked the wolf before he could get a good grip. They wrestled, snapped, and growled. Both of them were trying to get to the other's neck. The big male bit

Voltar's hindquarters and drew blood. Voltar was limping and whined once from the pain. The wound seemed to enrage Voltar, and he leaped at the wolf and was just able to get on the wolf's back and grip the back of his neck with his teeth. Voltar shook him until he broke the wolf's neck. When the wolf quit moving, Voltar released him. The other wolves started howling at the loss of the male and charged the entrance as one.

Two of them got through the defenses at the entrance, but the soldiers on the rocks were able to kill them with their arrows. However, another one of the wolves jumped on one of the boulders, surprising the soldier. Jeremia had shot one of the wolves as it ran through the entrance. He thought he was safe for a moment when the wolf attacked. Before any of the others could help, the wolf knocked him off the boulder and killed him. There was no time to respond. He screamed once before he died, but nothing could be done. The fight raged on.

Jasmine was able to kill one of the females as she lunged for her. Jasmine stabbed her in the chest with her short sword. The wolf fell on Jasmine. Jasmine was able to push the body off when the wolf stopped moving. Terrence was going to help Jasmine when he saw another wolf heading straight for him. The wolf had broken through their defenses and was wounded and angry. Terrence stood in shock. He saw the yellow eyes of the wolf looking at him with anger and hate. He couldn't seem to make his body move to protect himself. The wolf leaped at him. Terrence was strong, but the young wolf was stronger. The fact that he was wounded made him full of rage. He bit Terrence on the arm and was about to bite him on the neck. Terrence groaned, thinking that his life would end that way.

Just as it looked like the end of his life was a certainty, he saw movement out of the corner of his eye. Voltar ran forward and jumped on the back of the wolf. He grabbed the wolf's neck and bit through his spinal cord, killing him instantly. Terrence was in shock, but Jasmine ran up and checked him over. She said, "Greta, hurry. Terrence has been wounded and needs bandaging quickly. He's bleeding pretty badly."

Greta came quickly and saw the blood all over Jasmine and Terrence. She wondered who was hurt worse. Jasmine reassured her that the blood was not hers. Greta did what she could to clean and bandage Terrence's wounded arm.

The wolves were in disarray. They were greatly diminished as a pack. What was left of the pack, led by the big gray wolf, ran back out the canyon entrance and ran for cover in the forest, whining and licking their wounds. Those that were not killed were wounded in the fighting. Some had arrows in them and others had knife wounds or bites from Voltar. The big gray wolf had an arrow stuck in his shoulder. He was limping as he ran, which made him very dangerous. They hoped they would not have contact with him again anytime soon, but it was a vain hope—and they knew it. The witches would not give up that easily. They just hoped that the wolves would be gone for some time while they mended.

Zarcon called the group together to check on wounds and any care that was needed. That was when they realized that Jeremia was dead. His body was badly mangled. The wolf that attacked him had died when another soldier on the boulder shot him, but it was too late for Jeremia. The group grew very somber. Zarcon asked two of the men to bury him. The soil in the canyon was fairly soft. The grave was dug, and Jeremia's body was placed inside. When the grave was filled in, Zarcon said, "We have lost another brave man today. I am greatly saddened by his sacrifice for the rest of us. We will discuss what we need to do later. I do not have the strength just now. Jeremia was a good man, and I, for one, will miss him."

Terrence said, "Yes, another good man is gone. Let's not let his loss be for nothing. We have suffered on this journey. We must carry on."

The rest of the group agreed, but it did not help with the loss of such a young soldier. He was liked and did his part willingly. All of them would miss him.

Zarcon checked on Terrence. His arm was in bad shape. As for the rest of the group, there were a few scratches and cuts, mainly from the underbrush. Those wounds could be easily bandaged.

As the men were burying Jeremia and counting the survivors, Jasmine realized that Jaron was not with them. She decided to check on the horses to see if he was watching over them. She heard some scuffling and growling and ran to see what was happening.

Jaron had stayed back to protect the horses. One lone wolf had actually broken through their defenses and had approached the horses while the others were unaware. Jaron saw the wolf sneaking up on them just in time to draw his sword. The wolf was a large black female. She came at him in a crouch and jumped on him. Jaron was knocked to the ground, and the wind was knocked out of him. He struggled for breath as he held the wolf away from his throat. His sword was too long to do him any good. The wolf kept snapping at him and biting his arm. Jaron rolled over and was able to get his knife out of his waistband to cut the wolf's throat. Blood poured over his face and hands as the wolf continued to struggle. Jaron was finally able to ram the blade of his knife up through the wolf's jaw and into her brain. When she finally stopped struggling, Jaron was able to roll away from the wolf, catch his breath, and check his wounds. His arm was bleeding badly. The bites were deep and jagged. He was losing a fair amount of blood.

Jasmine crouched beside him and checked his wounds. "Jaron, are you all right? This looks pretty bad. Let me get some bandaging for it. I'll be right back."

Jaron nearly fainted from relief that Jasmine was going to help him. He was going into shock and didn't quite feel the pain yet.

Jasmine called to Greta again to come help. She gathered some bandaging and her canteen. Greta hurried behind to help. They both rushed back to Jaron to see what needed to be done. Jasmine used her canteen to clean the wounds. Wolf bites were dangerous. She could see that the bites were deep and needed special care. Greta stayed with Jaron and tried to calm him to keep him from going any further into shock.

Jasmine went back to find Zarcon. She found him working on Terrence's arm. She told Zarcon what had happened to Jaron and asked him to come when he could. Jasmine went back to Jaron and asked Greta how he was doing. Greta looked very worried and shook her head. Jaron's arm had been chewed up badly. His neck was also bleeding. The wolf had been able to graze his neck as they fought. She put a pressure bandage on his neck to try to stop it as best she could.

A few moments later, Zarcon walked up to them and bent over to see Jaron's wounds. He said, "Jaron, this doesn't look good. I will have to use a small amount of magic to help it heal and to cleanse the wounds. There will be some pain involved. I'm sorry, but it is necessary in order to do the job right. Are you up for that? We don't want you to have any infection from those bites."

Jaron was nearly unconscious from the loss of blood and the pain. He nodded his head very carefully. He knew things were looking grave and was willing to do whatever was needed to get better.

Greta found some herbs in the canyon that would help with the pain. She set to brewing them in the kettle over the fire to be ready when Zarcon had done all he could."

Zarcon was very concerned about how deep the wounds were. He closed his eyes and placed his hands on either side of the wounds. He spoke a special healing incantation that would also help calm and comfort Jaron. Zarcon could see that he was going deeper into shock. Jagged wounds like these are hard to heal and take longer to do so.

With Zarcon's direction, Jasmine was able to wrap the wounds and tie off the bandages. They were tight enough to help stop the flow of blood but not cut off the circulation. Jasmine would check the bandaging frequently to make sure all was well with Jaron. The wounds on his neck were a special problem. Zarcon took extra care to heal them so they would stop bleeding. It was very draining on Zarcon. He would need a day or two to recover from using so much healing magic. He knew they didn't have that kind of time.

The rest of the group came to see what was going on and became very concerned about Jaron when they realized he had been fighting a wolf alone. Greta sat beside him to add her calming influence. She could see that he was in shock. She continued to work with him. She gave him sips of the tea she had made to help with the pain.

After some time, Jaron began to calm down, and his breathing gradually returned to a more normal rate. His color started to come back. He had been so pale and sweaty. He finally opened his eyes and was embarrassed to be the center of so much attention. All he could do was give a weak smile and say, "I thank you for your concern and care. I think I might live."

Jasmine spoke quietly, "Jaron, you had better live. That's all I can say." There were tears shining in her eyes, and she had to swallow her emotions. She hadn't realized how attached she had gotten to these men who were willing to sacrifice their lives to help her with the orb. She realized how precious each one of them was to her.

By silent agreement, no one spoke of the death of Jeremia. Jaron was just barely coming out of shock and would need some time before he would be given that kind of news.

Terrence came closer to see for himself if Jaron was okay. He said, "Jaron, I can see that you have saved the horses from serious injury or worse. You have done well. You two, Lantz and Jaban, come and carry Jaron to his bedroll and help him get comfortable. We won't be going anywhere for a while. He needs to rest and mend for a bit. We'll discuss plans for leaving later."

Zarcon agreed that Jaron needed to rest for a few days, but they really didn't have a few days to spare. After Jaron was settled, Zarcon gathered the group to discuss what they needed to do. Jaron needed to rest at least overnight. They all agreed to that. Zarcon said, "I propose to see how Jaron is doing tomorrow morning. I have used a bit of magic to help him heal and have given him what comfort I can. I would propose that we make a travois for him. That way, we can keep moving. Hopefully he will not be jostled too much as we do. What do you say, Jaron? How do you feel about that? Do you think you can manage if we try it?"

What Zarcon did not say was that he needed the rest as well. The strain of the fight and the magic he had to use to heal both Terrence and Jaron had drained him alarmingly. In addition, the loss of Jeremia hurt his heart in a way he had not expected. He was getting to old for this, and it scared him.

Jaron felt a bit nauseated. "I think I'll be all right. My arms are not so sore now. My neck is stiff and sore, but I think it's healing fairly rapidly. I will do my best to keep it from opening up again as we travel. I know we need to be leaving here soon. I'm pretty sure I'll be fine." He was not really sure, but he knew they needed to keep moving—or the wolves might come back for revenge.

Zarcon knew his words for what they were: lies to keep up his spirits. He knew Jaron was brave and would not hold the group back no matter his own health. Zarcon would check on him regularly to make sure he wasn't just being brave. He was concerned about Terrence's welfare. His arm was badly chewed up.

They all agreed with Zarcon that they needed to leave the area soon. They also knew the wolves would be back if they didn't. They prepared to spend one more night in the box canyon. The day went by swiftly with the worry and care they needed to give each other, especially Jaron and Terrence. As the day drew to a close, they lit the fire, had a meager meal, and slept near the fire. They knew the horses were fine—thanks to Jaron. They were all so very grateful for his quick thinking and sacrifice to save the horses.

Jasmine and Greta had been taking turns watching Jaron through the night. They were concerned that he seemed to be developing a fever and sweating profusely. The redness around his wounds was also cause for concern.

Just after midnight, the women went to Zarcon with their concerns. An infection was setting in, and there was nothing to stop the infection from spreading. Zarcon hurried to see if he could do anything to help. He had used his magic, but it was obvious that it wasn't enough. There seemed to be more at work than he thought at first. Zarcon laid his hands on Jaron's head to see if he could detect what was troubling him. There must have been something in the wolf's bite that was toxic, but he couldn't figure out what it was. He was afraid he didn't have a lot of time to do so. Jaron was fading rapidly. By morning, the wounds smelled bad. Both his arms were infected. Jaron had also started having nightmares. He kept tossing and turning and crying quietly in his sleep.

As the sun came up, Zarcon knelt by Jaron and sent a tendril of magic into him. What he discovered frightened him, and he quickly withdrew. The organism causing the infection had started to follow the magic back to Zarcon to invade his body as well. There was nothing he could do. He looked at the two women and shook his head in sorrow. "I don't dare use anymore magic. There is something inside Jaron that tried to attack me. The wolves, at least the one that attacked Jaron, have something in their bite that is very aggressive to using magic. I assume that the only reason I could help last night was because it hadn't gotten hold of Jaron at that time. It has taken over now, and I dare not try again. I really don't think it would help at any rate."

Jasmine and Greta looked at Zarcon in disbelief.

Greta whispered, "How could this be? We can't just let him die. Can I do anything? Please say I can help."

Zarcon shook his head again. "I am too afraid that the organism would attack you as well. Then you would be lost to me. I can't bear the thought of losing both of you." His voice shook with emotion he could not contain. He cleared his throat and reached for Greta's hand. He held it to his heart and tried not to weep for Jaron. Jaron was beloved by all who knew him.

Jaron's body suddenly became rigid. He was having a convulsion. He screamed and tore at his bandages. The rest of the group woke quickly and ran to Jaron to see what the matter was. Jaron seemed to be in great pain. They watched helplessly as he cried out and went still. He never regained consciousness. He seemed to slip away quickly after that. Jasmine sat down beside him and held his head in her lap as he relaxed and breathed his last breath.

All were weeping openly at his loss. It was too much.

The group stood as if in shock at the loss of Jaron. He had been a major part of the group from the beginning. What were they to do now that he was gone? Jasmine took his loss especially hard. She knew that if she had kept the orb to herself and not involved these wonderful people, Jaron would still be alive. The guilt was tearing her apart. She couldn't stop crying. So much had happened to them. She had kept her faith in the journey until then. How could she ask the rest of them to risk their lives on something that now seemed so futile? The witches would win. She knew it. In the dark places of her soul, a voice whispered, "See? You are nothing. The witches will win the orb back, and you will die slowly and painfully—just as Jaron has done. Give up now and save the others." She was in despair.

Finally, she said, "This is too much. I can't ask the rest of you to go on with me. I will carry on by myself and do what I can. You can all go back to your homes and families and forget this ever happened. I am not willing to risk one more life for this quest. I can't do it." She sobbed and couldn't stop.

Greta quickly knelt beside Jasmine and took her in her arms. She poured all the comfort she could into Jasmine. Greta could not bear watching her in such despair. They were all feeling much the same. Should they go on? Could they not? What could they do now?

Zarcon felt the tension and despair they were all feeling. The group was dwindling, and he felt helpless against the attacks. He called to Terrence so he could be reassured that he was doing well. Terrence came to him and showed him that his wounds were healing. It was hoped that it was just the one wolf that was infected. That was one sign of hope at least.

Micah finally voiced what the rest of the group was thinking. "I understand Jasmine's feelings—I really do—but I want to know how we can go on like this. We don't even know for sure why we are on this quest. What is it that is so important that we have lost such good men in the process of it? I'm not sure I want to go on."

Two of the men agreed, nodding their heads and voicing their agreement.

Terrence frowned at this. He was concerned, but he did not like that his men were on the verge of leaving. They could not afford to lose any more men—no matter the reason. He pulled Zarcon aside and said, "Zarcon, could you please give the men something to go on? They are just as invested in the success of this quest as any of us are, but they need to have more reason to continue. The loss of Jaron has affected us too much to let it go. You see how Jasmine is now. She needs help and so do the men."

Zarcon looked at Terrence and could see that he was right. It was either give the men more information or disband the group and hope for the best on their own. He gathered his thoughts, trying to decide how much to tell them. Finally he said, "The reason we are on this quest is to keep the witches from getting the blue orb back. Tell me if you have never heard of it." The men had all heard stories of it and the power it represented. This got their attention.

Zarcon continued, "Jasmine has succeeded in getting the orb away from them, and our quest is to see that they do not get it back."

The men gasped at that. There was some discussion starting about how Jasmine could have accomplished such a thing.

Zarcon raised his hands. "I'm not going to tell you how it was done. Just know that it was. We are going to find Donavan and try to convince him to join us on this quest because he has some valuable magic that would help us accomplish our goal of keeping the orb out of the witches' hands." He looked around the group.

One hand went up, and Micah said, "I guess I'm in. I can't bear the thought of those witches having that kind of power. They would destroy all we hold dear."

There was general agreement with that remark. It was agreed that they would continue. They realized that too much was at stake not to.

Jasmine had been listening to the discussion. She said, "You don't understand. I cannot allow you to come with me. There has been enough loss of life already. I can't bear to have that on my conscience any more than it already is. Please let me go on alone. I can handle it from here." She started crying softly. She couldn't let go of Jaron. She stayed where she was, held his head, and wept. Greta stayed with her and kept trying to calm her.

Zarcon quietly asked Terrence to delegate two or three of the men to take Jaron's body and wrap it in his blankets for burial. He bent down to Jasmine, and as the men took Jaron away, he pulled her into his arms and held her until she quieted and regained control of her emotions. "Jasmine, it looks like we're going to continue on this wretched quest whether you like it or not. You know none of us can do this alone. We certainly will not allow you to do so—even as capable as you are. We will bury our dead and continue on. It is all we can do. As you said, there has been too much loss already. That is precisely why we must continue. We can't let this all be for nothing. You heard the men. It is their choice to continue as well."

Jasmine felt humbled by these men who would sacrifice so much for the quest they faced together. For the first time, she felt that, together, they just might succeed. She turned away from Zarcon and said, "Thank you, all. I will never forget this moment. You have renewed my faith in all of you."

Micah said, "Well, we couldn't let you go on alone. That orb would represent the end of us all if it got back to the witches. I, for one, am in this to the end."

The others quickly agreed.

Jaron and Jeremiah were buried near the back wall and covered with stones to protect their graves.

Terrence said, "We bury two brave soldiers today. They were heroes to the quest, and we honor their memory. We will not forget them."

And so it was with heavy hearts that they filled their canteens at the spring they named Jaron Springs and broke camp. They loaded up the horses and pack animals and left the relative safety of the box canyon. They finally headed out and continued to follow the trail as it wound through the forest. They were still exhausted from the fear and terror of the battle with the wolves and grief for the loss of two good men, but they knew they had to get going. The witches were undoubtedly closing in.

They were making pretty good progress when they came into the small town of Merrido. The group stopped at the inn and had a big meal. They rested the horses and had them fed as well. After their meal, they headed for the local mercantile. There were supplies to be bought and loaded on the packhorses. They had been getting very low at that point in their travels. It was good to have the supplies they would need and to take a break, if only for a few hours. They mounted up and headed out of Merrido by early afternoon.

They rode a few more miles and finally reached a crossroads that would lead them to the mountain on which Donavan lived. It was getting late, so they found a spot off the road that was somewhat secluded among some trees. The men set up camp, and a fire was started to cook their evening meal. Micah was doing the cooking and made some stew using the vegetables they had purchased in Merrido. They also had some ale to go with it. The stew was great after the long day, and the ale helped wash it down. Watches were set for the night as the rest of the group settled in for the night. Terrence wanted to start fresh in the morning. They were much too tired to attempt the mountain this night.

The sun came up and found them just stirring from their bedrolls. They had slept a bit late. Micah had gotten the fire going again and was cooking flatbread on a skillet for breakfast. They had also purchased a few precious eggs for their morning meal. The air smelled fresh as the sun began to warm the day. Once breakfast was finished and cleaned up, they started repacking their supplies and bedding.

As soon as all was made ready, they started out for the mountain and found that the way they must go was more a track than a road. They would have to ride single file from there on. They noticed no one as they turned and headed southwest. The trail began an incline, and the going became rougher as they progressed. The air grew cooler the higher they climbed. The forest grew thicker as well. They were grateful for the cloaks they wore. Winter was still a few weeks away, but the weather was already turning chill at this elevation.

The group was subdued as they continued to ride. They stopped once for a meal and to rest the horses. There was some grass and another small stream to provide water for all. As they climbed back on the horses, clouds began to roll in from the west. It smelled of rain. It was asking too much for the rain to stay away while they traveled, especially this time of year. They could only hope it would be short-lived.

The group continued in a southwesterly direction as the trail wound through the hills and brush. The forest was not as dense on the mountain as it had been. It made the ride easier in some respects, but it did not provide the same cover as they had had. Zarcon noted that they were getting closer to Donavan's cabin. They would be there in another day if all went well. The rain could change everything.

It started as just a sprinkle. They stopped for a moment to dig their rain gear out of their packs just in case. They had been ready to stop for a quick meal when it suddenly started raining a bit harder. The wind picked up, and the horses were getting skittish.

Zarcon decided they had better forget about a meal for now and push on until they could find some kind of shelter. The trail was becoming a bit slick. Zarcon asked Jasmine, who was riding directly behind him, if she could see anything in the area that might provide some shelter.

Jasmine told him that she had been looking for the past half hour and hadn't seen anything.

The wind started howling, and as they climbed, it became louder. They had to yell to be heard over the sound of the rain and wind.

Voltar was whining, and the horses were sliding in the mud. It was imperative that they find some sort of shelter very soon.

Just then, one of the men at the front of the line shouted that he saw something over on his right. It looked like an overhang from the rocks above. He was told to go check it out. He returned moments later with the news that it would provide enough shelter for them to rest and eat. They all started for the overhang and made it just as the rain became a torrent. The wind blew spatters of rain into their shelter periodically, but it was good enough shelter for them to be able to eat their usual jerky, cheese, and hard bread. They were able to fill their canteens from a small rivulet that poured off the lip of the overhang. They knew then that they would have to wait this one out—at least until it let up a bit. With the trail becoming muddy and the horses getting skittish because of the wind, it would be tough to make any safe headway.

It was getting close to sundown when the rain finally let up and the wind died down. They really couldn't stay where they were for the night. There just wasn't enough room, and it was getting wet. So they mounted up to try to make it to a better shelter for the night. The sun made a sorry showing through some of the cloud cover. At least it was enough to see where they were going.

Zarcon let Jasmine take the lead since she had better eyesight under these conditions. They sent one of the men, Yasima, ahead to scout as well. The going was slow because the trail was slick in places. Finally, just when they thought they might have to sleep on the wet ground, Yasima came back and told them that he had found an old farmhouse off the trail a bit that they could spend the night in. There was also a barn in back of the house for the horses. They made their way to the farmhouse. The group took their horses to the barn and removed their saddles and tack to bed them down for the night. Two of the men brushed the horses down and checked their feet for any signs of problems. They were concerned that the horses might have picked up a rock, but they were fine and ready to spend a relatively dry night in the barn.

The farmhouse proved to have been abandoned for some time. The roof leaked in places and was still dripping as they worked their way through the rooms. There was a large room just inside the door that would do nicely for the night. It was relatively dry.

A search of all the rooms was made to be sure no one was living there. The rooms were empty except for a few scraps of old furniture and what might have been curtains at one time hanging in ragged strips at the openings that were once windows. There were glass fragments in the sills.

There was nothing else to suggest who might have lived here. The men started a small fire in the fireplace and they all ate a small meal of jerky and hard bread. They were too tired to fix anything more and went to their bedrolls for the night.

Neither Jasmine nor Zarcon slept well that night. They had too much to worry about. Jasmine had a nightmare about some creature that would devour humans and leave only the bones. It was chasing her and gave her such a scare that she nearly screamed. She woke with a start, looked around, and tried to place where in the world she was. The sound of soft breathing calmed her, and she finally slipped back into a fitful slumber.

Zarcon couldn't sleep after all and went outside to talk with the soldier on guard duty. It turned out to be Lantz. "Have you seen anything tonight?"

Lantz frowned. "No, and I thought I would for some reason. There is something strange about that farmhouse. I can't put a finger on it, but it gave me a chill."

Zarcon was thoughtful for a moment. "It seems almost that something is living here, or near here, that is not natural. I also caught the scent of something similar to the creature that took Mason. Did you smell anything?"

"I did detect something in the air a bit ago, but I couldn't tell where it was coming from."

"Well, I have been worried and couldn't sleep. We will make a thorough search in the morning. Keep this between you and me."

"That I will, sir."

Zarcon told Lantz to go on to bed. "I know I won't sleep much anyway." Zarcon sat near the wall and pulled his knees to his chest. He wrapped his cloak around him and pondered what might have happened to the inhabitants of this farm. None of his speculations comforted him at all. Voltar had followed him out of the house and dozed beside him.

During the night, Zarcon heard some strange noises, but nothing came near the farmhouse. There was some distant movement and hissing. He remained wary throughout his watch. Voltar whined and growled, but he did not move to chase it down. One of the soldiers, Jake, came to relieve him just after midnight. Zarcon told him what he had heard and asked him to be alert to any danger. He went back to his bedroll in the farmhouse and relaxed until it was time for the rest of the group to get going. The sun was just beginning to rise when he got up. He was still tired, but that couldn't be helped. It had been a long night with little sleep.

Suddenly, there was a terrible scream. Everyone jumped at the sound and ran out of the farmhouse, yelling to one another, to see what had happened. They found Jake writhing in pain on the ground. He was badly cut on his face, and his legs were shredded. He was bleeding badly.

Zarcon ran to Jake and knelt by his side. He held the man's head and said, "What happened, Jake?"

Jake said, "I saw mist forming on the ground just over there by the pine tree. It grew thicker as I watched … I could see red eyes just as long sharp claws came out of the mist and tore at my legs and body … I ducked under one of the trees … so I could see what it was … and still try to hide … suddenly it came at me … it was slashing with its claws. I had my shield up … and tried to get at it with … my sword, but it was … too big and fast. It cut me badly. I think it went away when it heard you all running and shouting. It looked like something out of a nightmare. It must have some sort of poison in its claws … I can't breathe, and my skin burns where it cut me." Jake fell unconscious.

Zarcon realized that the claws of the creature must have poisoned Jake. His shield had protected him somewhat, but the claws had still gotten to his legs. Jake's face was also badly cut in several places. Zarcon continued to check Jake over and realized that the cuts over Jake's body were most likely fatal. He could do nothing but help him by easing the pain. He looked up at the others gathered around them. He said, "All of you, spread out around the farmhouse and check the barn. Make sure the horses are well. If you see anything, shout a warning. We'll all come running."

Greta joined him beside Jake while the others searched the grounds. Voltar stayed with Zarcon and kept watch over his master. Terrence also stayed with Zarcon. It frightened him that the creature could have come earlier while Zarcon was on watch. He vowed he would not let Zarcon have another watch alone. These times were much too dangerous for that.

Jasmine was reeling from the injury of yet another one of their group so soon after the losses of Jeremiah and Jaron. She asked one of the men, Erik, to go with her to search around the house. She had seen the cuts on Jake and was frightened of what had caused such terrible wounds. They circled the farmhouse and came back to Jake, Zarcon, Terrence, and Greta.

Greta was offering what comfort and support she could give him with her magic. There wasn't much else she could do. The man was dying, and though Zarcon was a powerful wizard, he had no power against something this deadly.

Jasmine said, "Zarcon, can you help Jake? Will he live?" Zarcon just shook his head.

Jasmine was horrified that another of the men would likely die. She was having a hard time coping with so much loss. She finally said, "Is there anything I can do to help? I feel so helpless. Eric and I have searched the grounds around the farmhouse, but we haven't seen anything. What would you like us to do now?"

Before Zarcon could answer, another man shouted to come quickly. Jasmine and Erik ran to him. The man was pointing at some mist on the ground on the side of the barn. They could just see it around the corner. As they looked, they caught a glimpse of what appeared to be red eyes looking at them from the mist.

Zarcon came up and said, "It looks like the creature Jake described. It is also very likely the creature that killed Mason. Everyone, stay well away. We don't really know what we're dealing with here. This explains the noises I heard in the night. If it is the creature in the mist, it explains the terrible cuts on Jake. Look at those claws!" As they watched, the creature extended its claws for a moment, then the mist seemed to dissipate, and it was gone.

Zarcon had a terrible thought and ran into the stable to check on the men and horses. The horses had been jittery with the smell of Jake's blood, but the men were calming them. All was well. Micah was with them. He said, "The horses went wild with the sound of screaming and the smell of blood. We are just getting them to calm down."

Zarcon was grateful to the men for their good work with the horses. It could have been very bad if they had not acted so quickly. He said, "Thank you for taking such good care of them. I think it would be good if we had a meeting, all of us, to discuss our next course of action. I don't want to stay here any longer than we must." There was a general agreement to that. All felt the strain and wanted to once again put distance between themselves and what had happened here.

They went back to see how Jake was doing. He was slowly dying. Some of the men offered to carry him into the farmhouse. Greta said he might be more comfortable there.

They gently carried him into the farmhouse and laid him on his bedroll. He wasn't in much pain at this point. He was just cold from the loss of blood. They covered him with his cloak, and Greta held his hand. He drifted off as if he was going to sleep. He died quietly.

Yasima and Micah went to the barn to look for something to dig a grave with. They found an old shovel and took turns digging. The ground was still soft from the recent rain, and they dug the grave deep enough that no predator could get to Jake's body. When they finished, they went back into the farmhouse, picked up Jake, and gently carried him to his grave wrapped in his cloak. They gently lowered him into the grave.

Yasima and Micah began to fill the hole in as Greta and Zarcon and the others looked on.

Zarcon said, "We will miss Jake. He was a good soldier and an even better man. May the gods welcome him home."

Jasmine was crying again. "Zarcon, I just can't bear this. Another man is gone, and we haven't even found Donavan yet. How will we ever beat the witches at this rate? How will we survive? I'm in despair."

Zarcon pulled Jasmine into his arms and tried to comfort her. "Jasmine, we knew this would be a dangerous undertaking before we left my castle. We must carry on. The only alternative is to go back, and if we do that, we might as well give the witches the orb and tell them how sorry we are to have inconvenienced them. How long do you think any of us would live if we did that?"

"I know we must go on. I just hate losing so many good men. We must succeed. I know that. It's just so much harder than I imagined."

The two of them walked back to the farmhouse with the others as the two soldiers filled in Jake's grave. After filling in the grave, they found some large stones and placed them on top to protect it. It was a sad day. The men were anxious to leave now that Jake was laid to rest.

As soon as the horses were made ready and the packhorses were loaded, Zarcon ordered everyone to saddle up. It was time to leave. There was no way to know if the creature would come back. No one had to be coaxed. They hurried to do as Zarcon asked. Many of the horses were already saddled. Jake's horse would be used as a spare. Zarcon was becoming more concerned that their numbers were dwindling and, as Jasmine pointed out, they hadn't even found Donavan yet.

They left the farmhouse with relief. They made good time throughout the day. The weather had cleared, and it was getting warmer. The sunshine seemed to put the lie to the thought of danger from creatures in the mist and wolves. Perhaps if Jake were still with them, they could pretend nothing ugly had happened, but Jake was no longer with them, and they knew that there were things going on that they didn't understand.

As Zarcon's group continued to head west, Zarcon said, "By now, you know that we are headed for the Backlash Mountains. Donavan lives on the other side of this canyon and on top of the plateau on the other side. We should be there by tomorrow night." The others had heard about the Backlash Mountains. They were known for the odd assortment of wildlife that lived there. There had been many reports of strange animals lurking in the shadows.

No one dared protest. This is why they were on this journey. They would see it through.

Jasmine began to feel like they were being watched. She had keen eyesight, and every once in a while, she would catch a glimpse of a fleeting shadow. She rode up close to Zarcon and asked if he had noticed.

He said, "I have been watching something moving in the shadows for some time now. I can't tell if it be man or beast. What do you make of it, Jasmine?"

"I am hoping it is a man, but I fear that it may be an animal—maybe a large wolf or hound. If it were a hound or a wolf, Voltar would have warned us, wouldn't he?"

"I would think that he would give notice of anything that could be dangerous to the group. Let's keep an eye out. If anything changes, we'll deal with it."

It was not that much farther to Donavan's cabin, and they kept hoping all would be well until they got there. Zarcon warned the men that there might be something in the area. "Be sharp, and watch for anything you don't recognize. You know the stories of this area. We must be careful. Voltar will warn us of anything dangerous."

They traveled for another hour. Suddenly a strange, many- legged creature with a misshapen head and large, bulbous eyes jumped in front of Terrence and Zarcon as they rode along the trail. It screeched at them as if warning them away and scurried into the brush at the side of the track.

Zarcon and Terrence were startled. They didn't even have time to react.

Jasmine, riding close behind Zarcon, said, "What in all creation was that?"

Voltar hadn't even barked. Apparently he didn't smell the creature or detect its passing. He finally howled and started after it, but he turned back after a few moments with a look of disquiet on his face, having lost the trail.

The others in the group came forward with questions. "What happened?" "Was that what I thought it was?" "I never thought those things were real!" "Is it gone?" "Is anyone hurt?"

Zarcon tried to quiet them and said, "I'm not sure what that was. It must be one of the rare creatures that live in this forest. Voltar didn't even detect it before it appeared in front of us. He lost the trail of it right away as well. Let's just be grateful it didn't have any desire to attack. I can't take much more of these surprises. Let's keep moving. We have some distance before we get to Donavan's cabin."

All agreed with that, and the group moved on. Every once in a while, they heard strange cries from the forest. It was a bit unnerving, but since nothing else came close enough to see or attack them, they became less frightened by the noises. Gradually, the trail started to descend the mountain. As they came to a flatter area with a small spring, they decided to stop for the night. It was growing darker, and it would not be good to try to travel through this forest after dark. The trail was far too narrow and twisted for that.

Witches Simplify

The witches were on their way once more. Gradually the road became narrower and rougher as the witches and their group approached one of the small towns in the area. There were few travelers now, and the witches were looking conspicuous in their large carriage with all the baggage and cook wagon. This would normally not have been a concern, but as they were trying to get to Zarcon and his cohorts before they realized they were coming, it was time to simplify.

After several days in travel, the witches decided they would leave the coach and cook wagon and three of the men in the small town of Merrido to guard the cook wagon back home. They sought a man in town who was known to have good horses. He was found in his stable in the center of town. He was a tall man with strong, broad shoulders. He wore a goatee and had a thick head of black hair. He was handsome and slender.

His name was Reynoldo, and he had heard a few days before that the witches were coming through Merrido. News traveled fast in small towns and the areas around them. The witches were a spectacle that no one could miss. So it was that he was prepared, at least mentally, for their coming.

Reynoldo knew the witches preferred black horses, and he happened to have five very strong ones.

Zora walked into his business as though she owned the place. "We are in need of five of your best horses, and we prefer black. Can you help us?"

Reynoldo said, "I just happen to have five of the most beautiful black horses you will find anywhere. I will show them to you, and you can tell me if they meet your expectations."

Zora took one look at his beauties and knew she had to have them, but she didn't want him to know how desperately she wanted them. She said, "Well, they look good enough. Are they strong? Will they do well climbing the Backlash Mountains?"

"These are the strongest horses you will find. They will take on anything you can give them."

Zora could tell by looking at the horses that they were sound and would have a lot of stamina. She was excited to own them. She said, "How much do you ask for these horses? I cannot pay more than they are worth. They aren't exactly what we are looking for, but I think they will do."

Reynoldo knew she was trying to bargain at this point. He also knew she had the upper hand. If he asked more than she was willing to pay, she could cause him much grief. Reynoldo was more than anxious to be rid of the witches; he gave them a bargain price to hurry things along. He was relieved to see their backs and still have his own skin when they were done. He regretted having to sell his beautiful blacks, but life was more precious to him. Reynoldo had one of his ranch hands saddle the horses for the witches. He really did want them out of his life as quickly and painlessly as possible.

The witches didn't much like riding, but they were able enough. These horses would serve nicely until they no longer needed them. Zora loved the look of the horses, but she would use them until they no longer served her purpose. There were plenty of horses to be had whenever she needed them. She also thought she was quite the dealer when she secured these beauties at such a price, and to get the riding gear thrown in was very gratifying. She didn't realize it was so Reynoldo could be rid of them. And if she had known, she wouldn't have cared.

Heleren had been admiring Reynoldo while Zora was bargaining with him. She decided in the depths of her wicked heart that she would return to Merrido once they had the orb and have some pleasure with him. It excited her to think about what she would do to him.

The wolves had been gone for some time and returned as they were ready to leave Merrido. When the pack met the witches, the big gray wolf communicated his loss to Zora. His mate and others of the pack had been killed in the fight with Zarcon and his group. He had sustained a wound to the shoulder that still caused him to limp. He whined, hoping Zora would help him. Zora was disgusted that the wolves had failed to stop Zarcon, but she hoped they had at least caused them some harm. The message from the big gray wolf was so confusing. She could only guess what had really happened. She reluctantly held the leader's head in her hands and did a quick healing of his shoulder. She had a difficult time with healing spells; they were not exactly her specialty, but she knew she needed the big gray wolf at least for now. He could lead them to Zarcon and the orb.

The other witches gathered around Zora and asked what had happened.

"The pack has failed to stop Zarcon. I'm not sure if they even caused any serious harm. The impressions I get are too confusing to make any sense of them. One or two of the men may have been hurt; one might have been killed. That is all. Four or five of the wolves are dead, including the big gray's mate. This really is disturbing to me. How could Zarcon and his band of thieves do such damage to my beautiful pack? I will make them pay dearly for what they have done." She smiled her most evil smile at the thought of what exactly she would do to them. The other witches agreed that they would enjoy nothing as much as revenge on Zarcon and his band.

Zora sent the wolves out into the countryside to follow them as they started on their way to find Donavan's cabin. The wolves would stay close enough to know when the witches stopped for the night and where they were going. They would also stay far enough away not to arouse people in the area too much.

It had taken the witches several days to get this far. It would probably be another week or so before they were able to climb the Backlash Mountains and search for Donavan's cabin. No one in the town seemed to know exactly where the cabin was. Some said north, and some said south. This was frustrating in the extreme, but no amount of threats or punishment would clear things up for them. The people of the town seemed to have made an agreement not to speak of Donavan or where he was living. They had to follow their instincts and hope they could find the group of traitors soon. They had a feeling that time was running short.

As the witches and their small band headed out of Merrido, they looked an evil sight: Cardeegan, his men, and the five witches all on black horses with black cloaks flying. There were also pack mules for each of the men to guide. It was all the more frightening as darkness descended on the town. They made it as far as the crossroads and made camp in the same area Zarcon and his group had stayed. There was a full moon that night so they could set up the tents easily enough. Cardeegan's men set out a small meal, and then they all went to their bedrolls for the night.

Morning came, and there was flatbread and ham for breakfast. The meal was cleared away, and they packed the tents and bedrolls and headed out. They kept to the trail for the better part of that day.

The going was slower since the trail was so narrow and winding. The sun climbed higher, and they knew they would have to stop soon to eat and rest the horses. There was a small clearing that would serve the purpose. There was jerky and hardtack for a quick meal. The witches tried not to complain.

They mounted back up and headed up the trail. They continued on until the sun began to set. It was getting dark. The forest seemed to be closing in on them. Cardeegan began to look for a place to camp for the night. Finally, they came upon a meadow with a small stream. They decided this would be as good a place as any to camp. They ordered the men to start a fire and put up their tents. They obeyed without question. They had a cold meal, and when the tents were up and the bedrolls were readied, they went in to sleep. The men slept on the ground around the campfire. The wolves were scouting the perimeter as the witches slept. No creatures would disturb the witches' slumber.

As dawn was breaking, the witches and their men were up and making ready to leave. All were tired from the previous day's travel, but no one dared risk losing time sleeping later. There was too much ground to cover and too much at stake. They had lost enough time in Merrido.

They ate another cold meal and ate the last of it in the saddle. They filled their water skins and mounted up. It would be a long day. They would be making only necessary stops to eat and rest. The wolves were growing restless. There was anxiety in the air, and the witches grew increasingly agitated.

They started up the trail once more. One of the men was the lead scout. He had gotten about half a mile ahead of the group. They had been riding for about three hours when the man screamed. The witches sent two men to find out what had happened. They reached the other man just in time to see a thick mist dissolving around the man's legs. It was plain to see that the man was dead. He didn't have a head, and the rest of him was bloody and torn. The man's horse had run off. They would likely never see it again. The two men rode hard back to the witches to report what they had seen.

Cardeegan and the others went to the site and looked for clues for what could have happened. They only found the body of the man—no tracks or other signs of struggle. The only clue was the terrible smell that lingered near the body. Cardeegan was angry that such a thing could happen to one of his men. He felt impotent as he had not felt before. He didn't like the feeling, and it made him angry.

Zora was shocked. She didn't think anything would dare attack them with the wolves so close. She called to the wolves to find out what they knew. The leader came running. He sent her images of what appeared to be a strange mist with red eyes and claws taking the man off his horse and taking off his head. The wolves would not attack such a thing—not even in defense of the witches. Zora knew this to be true, but it did not make her feel any better. She said, "How could there be such a thing here? We haven't seen anything like it for a hundred years."

The other witches were shocked as well. The killing mist had been thought a thing of myth and legend. No one believed it to be real until then.

They started speaking at once. "What does this mean?" "What do we do now?" "Do we have any power against something like this?" "Do you think Zarcon created it as an illusion to scare us?" Heleren asked the last question, but all the witches were nervous.

Zora put up her hands to try to calm her sister witches. "This was no illusion. Can't you see the man has no head? Heleren, you simply must close your mouth. Stupid is coming out. Obviously, we carry on just as before. We will just have to be more vigilant than we have been. We have been relying on the wolves to protect us. We know now that we have been foolish. These mountains hide more than the usual woodland creatures. We will have two men ride ahead now. We will also use our powers to create a warning shield so that nothing will surprise us again. Work with me now."

The other three witches formed a circle with Zora. She began to chant the ancient spell. A haze rose up from the middle of their circle. It fanned out until it covered their party and the horses. Then it spread out for fifty feet around them. "That should do it," Zora said as the spell was completed. The others felt better with the warning spell in place, especially the men. The wolves went back to scouting. They were nervous about the mist and what it meant. Now they would also be much more alert.

Zora ordered Cardeegan to get the man buried so they could keep moving. Cardeegan in turn ordered two of his men to do the job. The ground was soft here, so digging the grave was not so bad. Once the dead man was pushed into the grave, the men threw dirt over him and moved to their horses.

The group moved on into the forest. The trees became thicker, and the trail was harder to follow. Zora began to wonder if they had taken a wrong turn. The problem was that there was only one trail. Maybe they should stop somewhere and regroup. Maybe the wolves could find a better trail to follow somewhere close. Zora sent the mental image to the leader of the pack. Hopefully he would find something soon.

The party continued on. It started to get dark. They looked for a likely place to camp for the night. The ground was fairly rocky. It was becoming difficult to see. The moon had not risen yet. Finally they found a relatively flat area on the side of the trail. Two men put up the tents again, while two others got the fire going and some food cooking. They had shot five rabbits as they were traveling and roasted them on a spit over the fire. One of the men had found some edible plants along the way to supplement their diet.

While the men were busy, the witches held a meeting a short distance away so that none of the men could hear.

Anesthia said, "Zora, what do you see for us from here? What about tomorrow? How much farther do you think we'll have to go to find the cabin? I'm really getting tired of these horses."

Heleren said, "Anesthia, how can Zora know any of that? How can any of us know? It is what it is. We will keep going until we find those horrible people, and then we will have some fun. Once we have the orb, the world will be ours. You know all that. Quite complaining and help us think of a solution to our current situation."

Zora held up her hands once more to calm them. "Now, sisters, arguing and complaining will not help the situation. I've sent the wolves to find a better trail if there is one close by. They are also being very vigilant in looking for whatever it was that attacked us from the mist. Maybe they will even find Zarcon and the others. That would be a happy thought. We will spend the night here and wait for the wolves to report, hopefully by morning. In the meantime, let's try to get some sleep. Think of ways to get our revenge on Zarcon's little group—that should bring sweet dreams."

The witches ate heartily of the rabbit and herbs the men had provided. They went to their tents and settled in for the night.

The men cleaned up the mess from dinner and laid out their bedrolls. None of them spoke. They communicated by gestures and looks. They could not afford to have the witches know their thoughts. They had seen what happened to anyone who had the courage to try to stand up to the witches and their demands. One other thing kept them from voicing their feelings. It was known that at least one of the men was very close to one of the witches, but no one knew which for sure. Everything that went on was being reported to her. Trust was not something any one had for the other. It was just better to keep quiet; life would probably be at least a little longer that way.

Just before dawn, the wolves began to howl. The big gray wolf ran into camp with his tail tucked between his legs. Zora ran out of her tent with her blanket wrapped around her to see what had happened. The gray wolf had been sending unsettling images to her for the past ten minutes. She had awakened just long enough to get the blanket around her when he came running into camp. There were images of a thick mist and a beast coming at the pack with long teeth and terrible claws. There was blood everywhere. The wolf pack scattered, but one of the females was caught and gutted before any of them could react.

The big gray wolf had never shown fear before. It was unnerving to see him so now. What had happened? It must have been the killing mist that had caught the wolves unawares. How could it have been so sneaky to approach a whole pack of wolves without warning? The wolf before her was trembling with fear. It was now in doubt whether the pack would be able to regroup. She sent images to the wolf to gather the pack once more, but he was in no state of mind to obey. She would have to wait until he could calm down. Her own alarm was growing as the wolf refused to calm.

Zora called the other witches to get up and come to her. They hurriedly threw their own blankets around them and stumbled out of their tents. As they saw the wolf, they started to ask questions, "What is it, Zora?" "What is wrong with your wolf?" "He looks terrified." "Where are the other wolves?"

Zora spoke softly to try to calm everyone, including herself. "It appears that something has attacked the pack. I'm not sure what it was, but I think it was the same thing that attacked us earlier. Something hit them before they could defend themselves. It may be that the mist is far more dangerous than we at first thought." Gasps from the others were heard. They started searching the night in fear. "I am hoping our leader here can gather the wolves to him again, but there is so much fear, I doubt they will come. One of the females was gutted by whatever it was. I can sense grief along with the fear."

"We must decide now if we will continue to search for Zarcon's miserable band or leave off our search and wait until we hear of them somewhere else. What do you say? What do you choose to do? Would you go on or go back for now?"

The witches looked at one another. It had cost them so much to come this far. Should they abandon it all and just wait?

Anesthia said, "I would go on. We must be close to our goal now. We have lost much already, but there is much to gain. Don't forget that the orb is also close now. I can feel its power pulling at me. What if we abandon our search now and they escape with the orb? I cannot allow that to happen. Can you?"

"What do you say, Heleren?"

"I would also go on. All that this journey has cost us will be for naught if we turn back now."

"What about you, Myshella? Would you also go on?"

"I understand what you are all saying. If we go back, we may lose this chance to get the orb back. But what if we die trying? What if this killing mist gets us all before we even see the orb again? What then? We will have lost it all—and for what? I would not tell anyone what to do. I am saying that I am very afraid to go on under these circumstances."

All the witches were silent at that.

Zora said, "Maybe we had better think about this a bit more. Let's go back to bed for a few more hours. When we get more rest, maybe we'll be able to come up with a decision that will meet all our needs."

The witches went back to their bedrolls and tried to get some more sleep. The wolf stayed by the embers of the fire throughout the remainder of the night. He whined periodically in his sleep.

The men looked at one another in fear. It was terrible to have one's fate in the hands of those who didn't care what happened to any of them, but they all knew they were stuck—no matter what the decision was. Cardeegan could make their lives even worse if he chose to. It was apparent that he was already angry and was looking for someone to vent it on.

As dawn brightened the horizon, the men fixed a somber meal and waited for the witches to appear. The horses were restive. The wolf had left sometime during the night. No one had heard him leave. The witches came grumbling out of their tents. This did not bode well. They ate their breakfast without a word and went into Zora's tent to discuss what they would do.

No one was happy. It could hardly be expected. The men kept watch just outside the perimeter of the camp. They had overheard some of what the witches talked about during the night. They were concerned that even the witches were afraid. They had not known them to show any sign of fear before. Everything was different now, but the men could only hope that things got better as time went by.

Once inside the tent, Zora said, "Now, tell me how you feel this morning. What do you think we should do? I have decided how I feel, but I want you all to tell me what you are thinking. Heleren, you speak first."

Heleren frowned at having to voice her opinion first, but she said, "I still want to go on. As I said last night, we have lost much already. For me, at least, there is no point in going back."

Anesthia said, "As I told you last night, I feel the pull of the orb. I can't help but feel it is close now. I am also afraid of the unknown. We may die, but didn't we know that when we took on this venture? Was that not part of the bargain from the very first? Did we not agree at the time that the orb was worth whatever the cost? Surely some of us will survive to use the orb! Even if only one of us survives, that one will rule the world! Is that not worth any price?"

Myshella had thought long and hard throughout the night. In the end, her lust for power outweighed her fear. She said, "I have come to agree with Anesthia. If indeed the orb is so close, we must press on. Who knows when we will be this close again? We just can't take the chance of losing the orb when it is so close. We knew it wouldn't be easy. The mist has added another level of danger we had not planned for, but that is the risk when we go out into the wild. Let's move ahead and do whatever it takes to get that orb back. We have tasted its power. Who can resist it now? Another thing that concerns me is that my magic is weaker the longer the orb is gone from us. I don't like to speak of it, but it is great cause of concern. If by some wild chance Zarcon and his band are able to destroy the orb, will we have any power left?"

Zora said, "Myshella, I would rather not speak of the loss of magic right now. We have so much else to concern us. However, since you brought it up, I have felt a decrease in my magic without the orb. That is another reason we must have it back! Now that we have decided to go on, let's prepare to leave as soon as we may." Zora was angry that Myshella would mention something so personal at a time like this. She came out of the tent and yelled, "Cardeegan, have the men pack up the gear. Let's be off quickly! The morning is growing late, and we have some distance to cover before nightfall."

The men quickly moved to pack, put out the fire, and take down the tents. It was only a matter of minutes before the horses were ready to leave. The witches mounted up and headed south toward the top of the Backlash Mountains. No one spoke as they moved along. The wolves had not been seen. It was hoped that they would show up soon. The witches had been depending on the wolves to provide a warning system for them in case of trouble. They didn't realize how much they depended on them until now. They also hoped that the wolves were on the trail of Zarcon and his band of thieves.

No one spoke as they rode out of camp. The level of anxiety had increased markedly. The witches could only hold onto the hope that one or two of them would survive this wretched journey. Each now lived in the fear that she might not be one of them.

Donavan at Last

Zarcon had the men build a large fire. The fire would provide the warmth they needed, and it would keep the worst of the creatures of the night away. It might also provide a beacon to let Donavan know they were in the area. Watches were set for the night. Their provisions were getting low, but there was enough for a small meal before calling it a night. Terrence took the first watch. There was little sleep that night. If all went well, they would be to Donavan's cabin by tomorrow evening. So much depended on a good outcome with the man that there began to be more tension as time passed.

Jasmine was still uneasy about their follower. She had hoped it was the creature that jumped out at them, but there was still something out there that was following them. She had been unable to identify exactly what—or who—it was, but since Zarcon showed no special concern, she decided to let it go and try to get a good night's sleep for once.

Greta had been sleeping next to Jasmine since the journey began. She looked at Jasmine and wondered how she could be so calm. Greta felt all wound up. She decided to get up and go talk to Zarcon. He was sitting back from the fire, leaning up against one of the trees with Voltar close beside him. He was looking out at the forest.

Greta wondered if he ever slept. "How are you doing?" she asked. Zarcon looked over at her. "I'm just tired. This has been a hard day and a long journey. So much has happened in these few weeks on the trail. How are you doing? It can't have been easy for you either."

Greta sat down beside Zarcon and laid her head on his shoulder. "I'm tired too. I'll be glad when we find Donavan. Do you suppose you can convince him to come with us?"

"I certainly hope so. We need him desperately. Without him, we don't have much chance of success. He's a tough one. I don't think he would let himself get soft, especially living here in the Backlash Mountains. You know, I also look forward to seeing him again. He was once a good friend of mine."

"Well, then let's hope we find him in a good mood. So much is riding on his help that I am nervous about what he might say. I hope the friendship you share will make a difference in the outcome. I feel better knowing that you have been friends."

They sat in silence for a few moments, watching the night.

Greta said, "I will try to sleep now. Good night, Zarcon." Greta smiled at him, took his hand, and kissed his palm. She got up and went back to her bedroll next to Jasmine. She fell asleep quickly. The talk with Zarcon made her feel so much better. His voice could be so soothing.

The group was able to sleep through the night.

At dawn, Zarcon woke them and said it was time to get moving if they wanted to get to Donavan's cabin before it got dark. They crossed the valley at the foot of the mountain. It was very quiet and peaceful. The sun was bright and warm. There were fewer trees, and what vegetation there was grew in marshy areas as they crossed the valley. They crossed a stream now and then. They had to walk the horses carefully. They couldn't afford an injured animal, not with their goal in sight.

They rode in silence for most of the day. Each lost in his or her own thoughts. Time passed, and they were able to start up the trail to the other side of the canyon as it got close to sundown. It was good that Zarcon knew the whereabouts of the trail; otherwise, it might have been missed. It was somewhat secluded from view by the cattails and snake grass nearby. The trail rose ahead in a gradual incline. They continued up the trail just as the sun was setting. As they crested the top, there appeared to be a meadow just ahead and off the trail to the left.

There was a small light through the trees. They continued on, drawing closer to the light. It finally began to show the outline of a cabin. They slowed, and Zarcon yelled, "Hello, the house. Donavan! We seek your aid."

The door to the cabin opened, and a man was standing in the open doorway with his hands on his hips. "What on earth brings you here, Zarcon? You're lucky I've been following you. You made so much noise I was able to recognize you before I set my wildcat on you."

"So, you are here! It is good to see you, Donavan. May we come forward and meet with you tonight?"

"I guess I have no choice. It is getting darker by the minute. Come on in. There is a barn in the back for the horses. Have your men take them there while we talk."

Donavan had prepared a meal for them. There was roast lamb, potatoes from his garden, carrots, and flatbread. Since he had been following them, he knew they were running out of food and would be hungry. He hadn't wanted to let them know he was there until he got a feel for what they were about and what kind of people they were. Zarcon followed Donavan into his cabin and introduced the group to Donavan as they entered. He was surprised that Jasmine was with Zarcon. She had not been happy with him the last time they had met.

Donavan was very muscular. He had dark, curly hair and bright green eyes. He thought Jasmine was pretty, but he knew that she was strong-willed. He wanted to get to know her better. However, he wasn't sure he liked this group of men and women. They were disturbing in their intensity. He could tell they were involved in something dangerous. He was interested to learn what Zarcon had to say. He could not fathom what could have brought him so far from home, and he feared what that might mean to him now that he had a relatively quiet life up in the mountains.

Donavan allowed them to get their food and settle in a bit. He wanted some time to watch them and see how they related to one another before anything was said about their journey and its implications.

Zarcon, for his part, let everyone get settled in the room before he tried to tell Donavan anything about their mission. Finally, when everyone had eaten what they wanted, Donavan told the men to go ahead and make their beds on the floor. He would sleep in the loft. Zarcon, Jasmine, and Greta were welcome to join him. Donavan could see that they were all very tired, so he refused to talk of anything important that night. There would be plenty of time for talking in the morning.

Zarcon was reconciled to wait one more day to discuss his problems with Donavan. Maybe it was for the best that they wait. He was exhausted and was afraid he might not be able to make his case clearly in his current state. Besides, there was no sense losing another night's sleep if they didn't have to. Donavan had two rooms in the loft that would serve as a place to sleep. Jasmine and Greta took one of the rooms, and Donavan and Zarcon took the other. The rooms were surprisingly large. There were two big beds in each of the rooms. Donavan explained to the three of them that he had built the cabin for his family. He didn't have the heart to leave. His family had been killed just before they were to move there. Now he was alone and liked it that way.

At the reminder of his family, Zarcon and the others felt like intruders in so many ways. If they hadn't needed his help so desperately, they might have reconsidered their plan. As it was, they did need him, and it would be worth the sorrow they felt if they could get him to come with them to help defeat the witches and their evil schemes.

Jasmine was thinking about the orb and what that might mean to Donavan if he saw it. Could that be enough to sway him to their cause? If the witches got their hands on it again, would it result in the potential enslavement or destruction of all they held dear? So many lives were at risk. It frightened Jasmine to think of the possibilities. She must help Zarcon convince Donavan of the danger—or all might be lost.

Zarcon looked Donavan in the eye and said, "We have had a rough journey. Have you seen any creatures in some sort of mist in this area? We saw two. They attacked us twice and killed two of our men. One attacked us on the trail and killed Mason. We came upon a farm that has been empty for many years and spent the night there. This creature, whatever it is, attacked us again while we were there and killed Jake. Things are getting very dangerous in the land lately. Have you noticed any of it?"

Donavan said, "I've heard rumors from men passing through the area, but I've not seen anything myself. This is cause for concern, but I don't believe that is why you are here."

Zarcon hesitated. He said, "It is likely part of what is going on. We are pretty sure of that. What we wish to discuss with you is of utmost importance. Think about the things I have just told you. Then we will grant your wish and discuss what we came here for in the morning. We are all tired from the journey and need our rest in order to properly address the issue at hand. I bid you all a good night." Zarcon nodded to Jasmine and Greta as he and Donovan entered their room.

Greta and Jasmine wished them a good night, walked to their room, and shut the door.

"Donavan is in a lot of pain, isn't he?" asked Jasmine.

"He certainly has reason to be. I only hope that he will help us. Perhaps the journey and trials ahead will help take his mind off his grief, if only for a while."

Greta and Jasmine undressed and climbed into their beds. They talked for a bit longer about their hopes for tomorrow, blew out the candle on the small table in the room, and went to sleep.

The men in the room below were quietly preparing for bed. Voltar stayed with them near the door for the night. They talked softly, then, one by one went to sleep. Micah was the last and blew out the candle on a shelf. He had taken care of the horses with the help of a couple of the other soldiers. With Jaron gone, he had spoken with Cardeegan about taking over some of Jaron's duties. Micah knew something about horses, not as much as Jaron, but he could help. Cardeegan consented and appreciated the offer.

The barn in back of the cabin was small but adequate for the horses they had. Tomorrow, the horses could eat the plentiful grass that grew in the area. Micah was relieved that this part of their mission was finished, but what would they face in the future? No sense worrying about that now. It was time to sleep.

Morning came with the sun shining through the windows of the cabin. It was a bright, clear morning, though a bit cool. They had all slept later than usual, a testament to how tired they were from all they had been through on this journey. Donavan was up and cooking something that smelled delicious. It was bacon, eggs, and fried vegetables that he grew in his garden. He also fried some bread dough in a pan. There was butter and honey for the fried bread and plenty of herbal tea. It was made of herbs and barley he grew. It tasted a little bit bitter, but no one complained. They just added more honey to it, and it was better. The warmth from the drink was what they needed after their long travels and cold nights on the trail.

Zarcon had risen with Donavan and taken Voltar with him. He was walking around the cabin to see what was in the area. It was quiet while everyone slept. No creatures seemed to be stirring near the cabin. There were a few birdcalls as the sun came up. It was so peaceful. Zarcon could understand that Donavan would want to stay here alone. It was beautiful. There were maple trees around the cabin, and a small creek was close by. Zarcon could hear it singing through the trees. It would probably be a pretty good bet that there were fish in that creek. Donavan also had a small corral for a few pigs and a coop for about a dozen chickens. Zarcon was impressed that Donavan was so capable of being self- sufficient. He hoped that somehow Donavan would be able to give it up for a few weeks.

Donavan called the travelers to come and eat. Everyone was so hungry for the kind of food that Donavan had prepared. They could hardly wait to sit down to breakfast. They ate heartily and thanked Donavan for the meal with much praise for his skills as a cook.

Greta and Micah helped clear away the dishes and cleaned up the mess.

Jasmine and Zarcon met with Donavan to discuss what they were up against. They went into a room that seemed to serve as Donavan's office, just off the main room, where it was quiet and somewhat private. There were windows facing the garden. There was also a desk and shelves for books. Donavan had gone through a lot of work to make his home comfortable.

Zarcon decided to get right to the issue that brought them there. He looked Donavan in the eye and said, "Donavan, you know we have come to ask a favor of you. Please hold your answer until we finish explaining what it is we seek to do."

Donavan was somewhat alarmed at that and said, "I will try, but you know how I feel about war or anything related to it."

"Yes, but please let me tell you what is going on. The witches are up to their old tricks. I don't know how they got it, but they had the blue orb for a time."

Donavan gasped.

"They no longer have it, however, thanks to Jasmine."

Donavan looked at Jasmine with new respect. He had never heard of anyone able to take anything from the witches and survive.

Jasmine said, "I managed to get it from their castle while they were otherwise occupied, but the witches set their wolves on me. I barely made it to Zarcon's castle in one piece. You can imagine how the witches feel about that. We left Zarcon's castle soon afterward. We were hoping to move before they could decide what to do about it. I think we have managed to stay ahead of them so far, but we can't count on that much longer. They are out looking for me and the orb—of that we can be certain. The wolves did track me to Zarcon's castle, of course, and we suspect the witches used some kind of scrying to see where the wolves went because they stayed around the castle for about two days, sniffing around. They seemed to find what they were after because they left with a howl and didn't come back.

"That's the main reason we left so soon. Zarcon used magic on the trail to try to protect us from a strange creature that comes out of some sort of mist and kills with poisonous claws, as Zarcon mentioned last night. We have to assume the witches detected it. The wolves attacked us three days later. They were definitely the witches' pack. I'd know that big gray male anywhere. We happened to have spent the night in a box canyon—or the wolves would have caused much more damage. As it was, we suffered greatly, but so did the pack. We were able to kill four or five of them before they took off. Two of the men were killed. Terrence had his arm chewed up pretty badly, but he's doing fine now—thanks to Zarcon's magic. The wolves have left us alone since then, but we cannot count on that lasting. Now you know some of what we're up against."

Zarcon said, "I know you've heard about the blue orb and the power it possesses. It is a reality. The witches have used the orb to get money and power over the people unfortunate enough to live near them. I believe they were just getting the hang of it. I greatly fear what they will do with it if they get it back. I also need to tell you that the witches have used the Black Wind to destroy my castle. You know what that means, don't you? I am betting that Zora is drunk on the power she has gained with the aid of the orb. I would also bet that she is going insane with it. She is more dangerous than ever before. We must keep the orb from her at all costs. I suspect that, even though they no longer possess the orb, having had it may increase their powers. Having lost it, their powers may be diminished. If that is so, we have more reason to fear their rage. If we are to succeed, we need your powers desperately. You have the power to block the witches' spells, and we will help you find other powers you may possess if you come with us."

Donavan was appalled to think of Jasmine running from the wolves and then being attacked by them again. He was also concerned that the blue orb was a reality and that the witches had possessed it for a time. He had heard the tales of the orb, and if only half of what he had heard was true, he was terrified. He was thoughtful for a moment and then said he needed some time to think it over. He hated the witches as much as anyone, with more reason than most, but he was also tired of the fight. He couldn't imagine going through another battle like he'd been in the last time he left his home. He'd lost more than he could tolerate as it was. He could see how desperate they were and could understand their needs. He just needed time to decide if he could leave what he had built here, not knowing if he would ever return. He was impressed with all Zarcon's group had accomplished, but he needed to decide if he could be a part of it or not.

Zarcon and Jasmine agreed to let him think about it for the rest of the day. They could use the day to prepare for the rest of their journey—whether Donavan came with them or not. They had been prepared to give Donavan some time. It just meant that they would have to wait a little longer to know whether he would help them or not. So much depended on Donavan's magic. Jasmine was almost desperate to know his answer. She was not the most patient woman.

In the meantime, Greta and Micah had finished cleaning the kitchen and hearth. They were busy putting away the bedding and packing their belongings for the day when Jasmine and Zarcon came down the stairs. The looks on their faces told Greta that there was no answer from Donavan yet. It was troubling to have to wait, but you couldn't rush a man like Donavan. He needed time to view the issue from all sides. They just hoped it would work out to their favor.

Greta was anxious to talk to Zarcon about what was said. He beckoned for her to come with him as he left the cabin with Voltar at his heels. She followed him with some anxiety. They left the cabin and walked a short distance before Greta said, "What happened with Donavan? How did you feel about him? Do you think he will come with us? What will we do if he doesn't?"

Zarcon raised his hands to calm her. His voice held sorrow as he said, "Greta, I don't know the answers. We told him briefly what we needed from him and why. He looked troubled, but who wouldn't? All I can say is I'm grateful he was at least willing to listen. I won't put a spell on him to get him to come with us. The decision must be his to make on his own. As for what we will do if he chooses not to come … that is what concerns me most. We will just have to think of something or someone to help us. I'm getting too old to deal with all of this without more help. Greta, think positively. If you don't, it will make matters worse."

Zarcon knew that Greta could alter people's moods. She could have a calming influence if she only felt that way herself. Zarcon needed her help too.

Greta knew what he meant by his remark. She took a deep breath to calm herself so that she could have that influence on the others.

Zarcon smiled when he saw her do that. He knew she would do her best, and that was all he could ask of anyone. He hugged her softly to calm himself as well. They walked on through the trees that bordered the cabin and stopped by the creek to relax for a moment before they had to go back. They found a large rock that they could both sit on and listened to the stream for a few moments before they had to get back to work. Zarcon kept his arm around Greta to keep her warm. The morning was just a bit chilly.

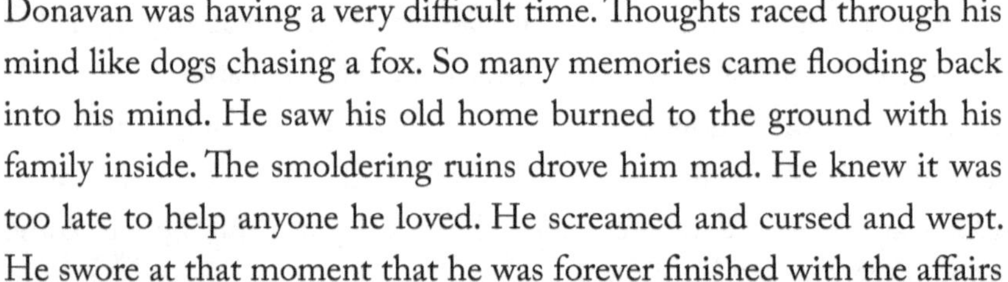

Donavan was having a very difficult time. Thoughts raced through his mind like dogs chasing a fox. So many memories came flooding back into his mind. He saw his old home burned to the ground with his family inside. The smoldering ruins drove him mad. He knew it was too late to help anyone he loved. He screamed and cursed and wept. He swore at that moment that he was forever finished with the affairs of this world. If he had not gone off to fight the war, his family might still be alive.

Other thoughts reminded him of all the lives that had been saved because of his magic. Where was sanity at a time like this? He had grown to hate the word *duty*, but if he was needed now— and if he could really make a difference—what was his life worth? Could he really tell these people, especially Zarcon, to go on their way—that he didn't want to get involved? It was almost more than he could bear. As he wiped his face, trying to focus his thoughts, he felt the moisture of tears he had not known he was shedding. *Oh, life! Why is it so complicated?* He knew what he must do—like it or not.

The afternoon was fading into evening when Donavan finally came down the stairs to meet with the others. They were all waiting in various attitudes of unease as he descended. Zarcon tried to read Donavan's expression, but he failed. Greta sent all the calming energy she had out into the room. People started to relax a little.

Donavan even seemed to slow his pace down the stairs. It was apparent that he was weighed down by his decision. There was no sparkle in his eyes. He moved as if in a trance. Finally, when he reached the bottom of the stairs, he said, "I have made my decision."

Zarcon said, "Is there anything I can do to help you. You look so troubled, my friend."

Donavan looked back at Zarcon and smiled. "I want you to know that this has been the hardest damn decision I have ever had to make. I told you those many years ago that I did not want to be involved in the affairs of men ever again. I have been content here. It is peaceful and beautiful, if a bit wild, but it has given my heart time to heal. However, I am tired of spending all my days alone. After much deliberation, I have decided that I will come with you. I need something to help me forget the pain. I need a purpose for my life. This seems a crazy undertaking, but if I can help you stop the witches, I'm in."

Suddenly the whole room erupted in shouts and laughter. Voltar began to bark at the noise. Greta and Zarcon were smiling. Greta grabbed Donavan and gave him a hug. Zarcon slapped him on the back.

Jasmine watched the display with mixed emotions. She was very glad that Donavan was going to come with them, but she was also anxious about him. He was a very attractive man, and she could sense a physical pull toward him. He was like a magnet to her. How would she deal with that day after day?

Zarcon had not realized how much the rest of the party was counting on Donavan's help until they burst into such a joyous response. Maybe they had a chance now. Maybe they could stop the witches. Time and careful planning would tell. Between his own and Donavan's power and the blue orb, they could possibly come up with a plan. Hope finally began to enter his heart. He had not realized until then how much he had depended on Donavan's help.

Now they could take the time to plan their next step. They would start in the morning. They agreed to rest another night before heading out of the mountains. There was relative safety there, but it wouldn't last. Sooner or later, the witches would figure out where they were and attack.

Dinner was a simple meal of roast chicken, more vegetables from the garden, herbal tea, and roasted apples. As soon as everyone had eaten their fill, the mess was cleared away. It was time to get out the bedrolls and settle down for the night. It was a much happier evening than any of the group had spent in many long nights. It was with gratitude that the lamps were blown out for the night.

Zarcon and his group were sitting around the table near the fire the next morning, after breakfast had been eaten and cleared away, discussing where to go from there. Now that Donavan had decided to aid them in their quest to stop the witches, there was much to discuss.

Zarcon said, "I propose that we take the blue orb to Landpur. It's a quiet place with plenty of places to hide. We could stay there until we decide what to do with the orb. There are people there who know me and would be willing to help us. That is where I found my horses. The witches won't be expecting us to go there. What do you think?"

The others looked around for someone to have an opinion. Donavan said, "I've been to Landpur when I was in the army. It is a pleasant place. The people are gracious. We could probably stay there for a while. It would be good to rest and plan. Maybe we could even find out what the witches are up to while we are there. Then we can decide how to respond."

Jasmine said, "I agree. Landpur is a nice place, but it is out of the way. It is actually near where I grew up, so I know it well. I don't believe the witches would expect us to go there."

"Greta, what do you think?" asked Zarcon.

Greta was nervous. She had a feeling that something bad would happen if they went to Landpur, but she couldn't say why she felt that way. She said, "I would like to have a vote from all who still want to come with us. Would that be acceptable?"

Zarcon looked at her for a moment, trying to discern what was going on in her mind, but he could get no clue from her expression. He said, "I see no harm in that. All in favor of going on to Landpur, raise your hands."

For some strange reason, none of the men raised their hands. All had an odd expression on their faces.

Zarcon was puzzled. He asked, "What is the reason for this? Have we missed something here?"

Seeing that no one else wanted to respond, Micah stepped forward and said, "Pardon, sir, but just before we left the castle, a messenger said that Landpur was in a state of revolution. There was a rumor about the old queen being replaced by her son. Prince Curzon wanted to change things in a way that the people did not agree with. Apparently, he wanted to take away many of the people's rights that they had enjoyed under the old queen."

Zarcon asked, "How bad is it … and why was I not told of this development?"

Terrence had been quiet because he had been busy with helping the men and Zarcon with other things. Now that he was directly involved in the decision, he decided to speak up. He said, "With all the rushing to leave, it was forgotten until now. It didn't seem that important at the time. We were all concentrating on leaving and getting away from the witches. Going to Landpur was the furthest thing from any of our minds."

Zarcon was stunned. How could this have escaped him? Why hadn't anyone chosen to tell him any of this? So what now? He said, "If that is true, then we had better decide on another place to go. There is a place I have not been, but I have heard of it. It is Synkana. We would have farther to travel, but from all reports, it is a beautiful place with many races and freedoms for the people. I don't think the witches would expect us to go there. What is the vote now?"

All hands went up with renewed excitement. "Synkana it is then."

Greta was so relieved. She had to wipe the tears from her eyes. Zarcon noticed the emotion and decided to talk to her as soon as he could. This was a mystery he must uncover. Greta always seemed to surprise him. There was so much more to her than he had ever imagined.

Since it was late, Terrence advised leaving at dawn. It was readily agreed, and the men moved off to their various activities to prepare for their journey. There was much to do.

Zarcon called Greta over to him. "Please walk with me. I have need of conversation with you."

Greta moved out the door with him. She was a bit nervous. She knew he would ask her about Landpur. They walked near the creek that flowed by the cabin with Voltar close behind. Zarcon said, "Greta, I noticed that you wiped tears from your eyes when the decision was made to travel to Synkana instead of to Landpur. Would you mind telling me why that was?"

Greta thought for a moment, not sure how to begin. "As soon as you said you wanted to travel to Landpur, I had the most terrible feeling that something bad would happen to our party if we did. I have heard rumors about Queen Mira's son. Curzon is very cruel and would rule the land with an iron fist. He craves power and control over all who are within his reach—much like the witches. He would change everything that Queen Mira has spent her life creating for her people. I fear that we will be brought under his power if we go there. He would take the blue orb one way or another and would likely use it much as the witches plan to do. We cannot take that risk. We have not spoken of the power of the orb. I know that it is very powerful, especially if it falls into the wrong hands, but would you tell me more about it? I wish to know why it is worth the risk of death to keep it."

Zarcon was thoughtful. Greta needed to know at least some of the facts about the orb. He just needed to figure out how much to tell her. Even knowledge of the orb could be dangerous to the hearer. He motioned for her to join him on one of the large flat rocks near the creek. They sat together.

Zarcon gathered his thoughts and decided how much of the story he should tell Greta. He gave her a weak smile and said, "Legend says that the orb was created long ago by an ancient wizard whose name, it is said, was Xyrene. It has been said that he was the most powerful wizard to appear for many lifetimes. It is also suspected that he created the orb as a legacy of his power. He had an apprentice who took the orb after Xyrene's death, but he died shortly after that. The orb was said to have been placed in the apprentice's tomb. Time passed, and the city and castle turned to dust. The orb disappeared for many centuries, and no more thought was given to it. It became the thing of legend.

"One day, the orb was found by a farmer as he was looking for one of his animals. He was actually in the area where the orb was last seen. No one usually went there because it was said to be haunted. He found a strange stone encrusted with layers of dirt and grime. He was able to clean it somewhat and found a blue stone. Upon closer inspection, he could see swirls of mist and strange symbols. He didn't know what it was so he took it to the wizard, Zenniten. Zenniten polished the stone and discovered that it was the blue orb, which was thought to be a legend. It was he that discovered that if you could stop the spell used, it would save the user from certain death. He paid the price of its use. He became a selfish and embittered man. He was also said to be very jealous of the orb in his possession. One day he cursed his servant, thinking he was trying to steal the orb. The curse was especially vile, and something dangerous stirred within the orb. Blue fire shot out from the orb and leveled everything. It is a barren land now. It used to be very fertile and green. The orb disappeared again after that and was thought to be gone from the world. We know that the orb is no longer a legend. It is a reality and one we must be extremely wary of.

"One thing is known: the orb seems to take the thoughts of a person with magic and use them against them if caution is not used. That is why no one touches it now. The witches kept it in a velvet bag most of the time. Zora is thought to have used it sparingly to get what she wanted. Jasmine has mentioned that she saw a blue light in Zora's bedroom window occasionally. They were trying to unlock its secrets when Jasmine took it from them. Fortunately, no real harm was done.

"Speaking of the witches, no one really knows how they came to have it in the first place. Some say they found it in the old ruins of a castle. It might have been Zenniten's castle. It was in the area where the witches last resided. That's another thing. How the witches got the castle they are in now is a mystery. They were poor until they found that orb. So, the orb may have other powers we can only guess at.

"So, what shall we do with it? I honestly don't know. We must keep it out of the hands of the witches. I have no doubt that they will try to use it to destroy much more than this small group. The whole world is in danger if they ever get it back. You have had a taste of their lust for power. Tell me what you think."

Greta was stunned by the story. She was also shocked that it could hold such power. Fear of what the witches could do with it was almost more than she could face. She said, "If the witches ever get their hands on the orb, I hope I am long gone from this land."

They both smiled, and they both felt the same way. They knew that things must be worked out so that either the orb was destroyed or hidden where no one would find it again. They continued to sit on the rock and talk about small things before going back to the cabin. The topic of the orb was wearing them both down. There was so much at stake for their small group that it was nearly overwhelming.

Meanwhile, Jasmine was talking with Donavan. "Is it that far to travel to Synkana? I've never been there. I've heard so many stories about it."

Donavan was surprised that Jasmine had not been there. He had thought she would have traveled to all the lands. He said, "I was only there for a few months while in the army. I was stationed there for guard duty. They had a small uprising of the native tribes. We just protected the army base until everything was settled again. I know that it is very beautiful there. The people are from everywhere. They are very friendly. It will make it easier for us to hide there. There are so many people coming and going that no one will notice our little band. We just have to be careful that we don't tell anyone why we're there. We need to talk to Zarcon about our cover story when we get there."

Jasmine said, "It is so good of you to come with us on this journey. We are in for some hard times, I'm sure. Tell me about your childhood … if you don't mind. I hope I'm not prying. I just want to know more about you … if it isn't too painful."

"Let's go out to the barn and check on the horses while we talk. I want to make sure all is well out there." Donavan was nervous around Jasmine. She was pretty and petite. He knew that she was capable of taking care of herself, and she was stronger than she looked. He was almost intimidated by her strength. If he was going to talk to her about his past, he wanted to be away from the others.

The two of them walked out into the yard behind the cabin and headed toward the barn. As they walked, Donavan said, "I wanted to get away from the others so we could talk in private. I don't talk about my past with many others. It's difficult for me to explain where I came from and where I have been. I spent my youth in the town not far from the castle the witch, Zora, grew up in. Her family owned the castle. I will just say that we had a run-in, and I had to leave my family. I went to work for a smith in a town not far from there, thinking I would be safe. After a few years, Zora heard where I was. I had to leave again. She has a very long memory and is set on revenge—no matter how long she has to wait.

"So, I joined the army to get away from Zora. I found that I actually enjoyed the life. I learned a lot and found strength I didn't know I had. I found a woman, Zerina. I loved her very much. We had two beautiful children—a boy and a girl. We were so happy. My family traveled with me to the various posts I was sent to. When the Wolf Wars broke out, I decided to find a more permanent home for my family. I got them settled into a home I built near a small river with plenty of land for farming and cattle. My wife was very capable. She had grown up on a farm and knew how to take care of one. I went off to war.

"Zora was fighting with the wolves and found out where my family was hidden. She sent the wolves to do her dirty work. She burned the house to the ground, and the wolves stopped my family from escaping. So, I have more than one score to settle with that witch! I will not hide from her any longer. It's time to stop them and end all this fear and anger. I hope you can understand my feelings a little better now."

Jasmine was touched that he would share all that with her. She felt connected to him now—more than she had felt before. "Donavan,

I never knew. I'm so sorry. You have much more to repay the witches than I do. I'm so grateful to hear your story."

Donavan was relieved to finally have it all out in the open. He was glad that he had shared that small part of his life with Jasmine. She was so easy to talk to. He liked her eyes. They were so open and kind. "Jasmine, what about your life? I haven't heard anything about where you came from or how you know Zarcon. Would you mind sharing a little bit of yourself with me? I am really curious about how you got the orb from the witches. It has never happened that anyone survived to tell the tale."

They both laughed.

Jasmine was pleased that he was so interested in her life. It had been a long time since anyone had gotten close enough to ask those questions. She hesitated because she wasn't sure where to start. "Well, I will tell you about some of my life. And I will explain a bit more about how I got the orb from the witches. I grew up in the Jade Mountains. There are actually a lot of dwarf mines there. I'm not sure if that is why my people are so short, but it could be. I am small even for my people. I grew up with four brothers. I had to become tough at a very young age just to survive their teasing and roughhousing. They taught me many things about self-defense as I grew up. It was difficult at the time, but as I look back, I'm actually grateful. I don't think I would have survived on my own if I had not learned the fighting skills my brothers taught me. They were worried about me being so small.

"I was orphaned at the age of sixteen. My parents were killed in an avalanche that year. The snow had been extremely heavy, and it came roaring down out of the mountain during one of those freak hot spells in May. I decided to set out on my own. My brothers weren't happy about it, but I wanted to live my life my way. As you know, it's a big world. I wanted to see more of it. I was foolish, but I didn't know what I was getting into. Who could know?

"I traveled to Landpur first. It was east of my home and seemed like a good place to start. I fell in love with the silks they produce there. The people were also wonderful. I left because I wanted to see more of the world and the people with their different cultures. I was ready to move on.

"I headed for Kaphur to see what I could see. Did you know they grow grapes there and make the most delicious wine? It is right on the ocean and so beautiful, but the people aren't very friendly. I got into trouble a couple of times with some men who thought they could do whatever they wanted to me because I was alone and small. They learned the errors in their thinking pretty quickly. They came at me one at a time, and I was able to render three of them either unconscious or incapacitated. The other two took off. I never saw them again, but I decided that it wasn't any fun anymore. I left and never looked back.

"From Kaphur, I joined a caravan headed for the Tamarind Valley. It took a couple of weeks to get there. The wagon master was kind. He allowed me to help him with the cooking to earn my way. I stayed in a wagon with one of the women traveling to meet her husband in Darpor. She was lonely and welcomed my company during the trip. Her name was Lillian. She was wealthy and had traveled to Kaphur to help her husband sell some of his silks to the merchants in Kaphur. She had servants with her, and some of them were men sent to guard her and their property. I was grateful that she took a liking to me. I enjoyed her company and the relative safety of the caravan. The trip was uneventful. We traveled over the Azure Mountains to get to the Tamarind Valley. Darpor was very interesting once we got there. Have you ever been there? It is truly beautiful."

"I haven't seen it, but I have heard tales of the beauty there. Is it true that the women wear pants and flowing robes over them?"

"Yes, that is true. The colors they use are amazing. I never did discover how they did it. Anyway, as we traveled, I learned so much about life from Lillian. She had been married for many years and told me all about her life. She was given a lot of responsibility for her husband's business, but she got no credit for her hard work. Her husband never appreciated all that she did. He was always praising others—but never her. She was very unhappy. I think she would have left with me, but she didn't want to give up her position in the city with all her friends and family. At that point, I swore I would not marry and have that kind of life.

"I met the witches while I was there. Well, I should say, I saw them a few times in the marketplace. They were easy to spot. They all wore shabby black gowns and stayed together most of the time. I was standing next to one of them when they started talking about something they had just found. They whispered about it being of great value to them. They said it would give them more power than they could ever have any other way. I was intrigued. I carefully followed them to their lodgings. Once I knew where they lived, I decided I needed to find out more about their secret. They were staying in a relatively small home in Darpor. It was strange. At night, when I would go to watch them, sometimes there would be a strange blue light coming from one of the upper-story windows. I think they were trying to figure out what the blue orb would do. At the time, I had no idea what it was, of course, but it made the hair stand up on my arms and the back of my neck. I could feel some kind of power even then.

"It wasn't long afterward that they moved into their castle in the Rimeron Valley. I don't know how they did it, but the blue orb had to be involved. I checked around Darpor and asked questions, especially when I found out where they had gone. Someone seemed to think they had found the ancient blue orb. They were frightened to tell me. Others would tell me more of what the blue orb was supposed to have done in the old days. I knew then that, if even half of what was told was true, the witches could not have that blue orb.

"I found their castle. When the witches left it one day to go on some errand, I sneaked into the castle. I found that Zora's sister, Magg, had been left behind to guard the orb. I watched her activities for a few days and found that she slept every day at the same time. While she slept, I sneaked in the front door, which was not locked. It was amazing that the witch was so sure no one would come in. I went upstairs and was able to get into Zora's bedroom by using certain tools I have."

Donavan smiled.

"I found the orb in a box under Zora's bed. I guess she thought that was a great place to hide something valuable. There was a small lock on the box that held the orb, but I was able to open that as well. I grabbed the orb out of the box. Fortunately, there wasn't a spell on it either. The orb was wrapped in a velvet sack. I was pretty safe carrying it.

"As I was running out of the castle, Magg woke up and saw me leaving. She screamed as I left the castle with the orb. She knew what I had done. I had hoped that her sister witches were far away, but I was wrong. They were coming up over the hill to the castle. I took one of the guards' horses and rode off in the other direction. It took them a while to figure out what to do. By that time, it was getting late. They sent their wolves after me. I had a small lead on them and was able to keep ahead of the wolves … just barely. Fortunately, I had some jerky and hardtack in my backpack so I could eat a little as I rode. After riding and resting for two days, I was running out of strength, as was my horse. The wolves were relentless. They would rest for a bit and then be right back after me. "It was a very dark night, and the rain was coming down in torrents. The wolves were closing in on me. I only knew that Zarcon's castle was in the area. If I were to be safe, I would have to find it soon. I barely made it to Zarcon's castle before the wolves got me. I've never been so terrified in my life. The horse I had taken was tiring and couldn't go much farther. It was strange. It was almost like his castle was raised out of the ground just when I needed it most. I don't know if that's true, but it sure seemed like it. And that is how I came to be here with Zarcon's help."

Donavan was amazed that she had done so much in such a short period of time. He suspected there was a lot more to her story, but he would wait until she was ready to tell him the rest of it. He knew that she had a reputation for being dangerous. She hadn't really explained that yet. He thought maybe she needed to trust him before she would tell him everything. He said, "Jasmine, you are amazing. Where did you learn all those tricks—and to be able to steal from the witches? I have never heard of anyone being able to do that. There is much more to you than I could have guessed."

Jasmine answered, "Donavan, there is still much to tell, but there is not much time to tell it. Be content with what I have told you … at least for now. Maybe I will tell you the rest someday. We'll see, won't we?" She smiled at him, hoping he would understand her need for privacy.

He said, "I will look forward to that time, Jasmine. Count on it. If we survive this quest, I will hear it all from you."

Jasmine was impressed with this man. He seemed genuine enough. Time would tell her if that were so as well. She would not give up her secrets so easily, but for now, Donavan was good company—and that was all she asked of anyone.

Just then, Zarcon and Greta came through the door. There was a look of quiet contentment on their faces as they entered. They must have come to an agreement about something. It was good to see.

Zarcon said, "Is everything being made ready for our departure tomorrow morning? Is there anything we can do to help?"

Terrence looked up from cleaning his sword and said, "All is moving along nicely. We are almost ready. We have just a few more things to pack and weapons to clean and sharpen. Micah is helping start our dinner. If one of you wouldn't mind helping, we'll have it ready in no time."

Jasmine and Greta moved to help. Neither one of them had things to occupy them at the moment. Micah was fixing some roast pig along with some potatoes that he dug out of the garden. Donavan went out and pulled up some carrots and onions to go with the potatoes. The women washed the vegetables in a bucket of fresh water. They slow-cooked them in a pot over the fire. In an hour, all was ready. They set the plates out on the table, and everyone lined up to fill them. The food was delicious. It was good to have another full meal before they had to set out in the morning. It would probably be a while before they had another good one.

There was much talk and laughter around the room as everyone ate. They drank Donavan's ale or fresh water from the creek. Gradually, the mood shifted. Some grew tired and headed for their bedrolls. Zarcon and Donavan escorted the women up to their room for the night. They all said good night and went to bed.

Jasmine smiled at Greta. She wanted so badly to ask her what had happened with Zarcon.

Greta could tell something had happened between her and Donavan. It was very intriguing. Greta said, "Jasmine, how did your day go? Did you get a chance to talk with Donavan?"

Jasmine answered, "Yes, we spoke for a while. He is very interesting. And you know, he actually listened to me and wanted to know more about me. It was nice, but it was also unnerving."

"How so?"

"No man has ever taken the time to want to know more about me. They are usually too busy talking about themselves. You know how it is."

Greta laughed. She did indeed. "You know, that's what I like about Zarcon. He actually respects my opinion and will even take my advice sometimes. It's pretty amazing."

"Well, right now, I'm more interested in Donavan than I ever wanted to be. This is not the time to be involved with someone. Too much is at stake, don't you think?"

"I have a philosophy about things like that. To me, the more dangerous the outlook, the more we need each other to get through it. Wouldn't it be nice to lean on someone else for once, if only for a while? No one is promised tomorrow. Enjoy these few moments of quiet and companionship. Don't judge or analyze them too closely."

"Maybe you're right. I've kept myself to myself for far too long. I'll try to be more trusting. It's just hard when I've not really had any practice. I only trust Zarcon and you right now. Maybe I could let Donavan in for a while."

"You can try. I think it would be a good thing for both of you."

"Well, we'd better call it a night. It's going to be morning soon enough. Good night." Jasmine needed to think about her relationship with Donavan if they were to have one when all this was over with.

"Good night." Greta smiled as she blew out the candle on the dresser near her bed. Time would tell where all this would lead. In the meantime, it was going to be very interesting indeed. For Jasmine and Donavan, she hoped that something good would come out of their current trials.

The Witches Have a Rough Night

The trail the witches were on became a little clearer as they progressed through the trees. The wolves had not found an alternate trail because of last night's problems. They were disappointed that the wolves had not found another trail, but it was obvious that they had to stay with the trail they were on anyway. The forest to either side of the trail promised nothing but hardship. The trees were so close together that it would be almost impossible to travel between them.

As the day wore on, they all began looking for a spot to stop and spend the night. They were running low on water and needed to find a brook or stream to refill their water skins.

Just as the sun was setting, they came upon a small clearing that opened up into a meadow just ahead. In the meadow was a small farmhouse. The group approached the farm and called to the house, "Hello, the farm. We come in peace." There was no answer. As the group moved closer, it suddenly became very quiet. No birds called, and no animals moved.

They tied the horses to a rail in front of the house. As they entered the farmhouse, they noticed that it had been occupied not long ago. There was dried blood on the floor. Zora smiled and said, "Perhaps

Zarcon and his merry band were here not long ago. I think we may be on the right track after all. A bonus might be that one or more of their group suffered an untimely end. What do you think, ladies?"

Heleren looked at the blood on the floor and got an uneasy feeling about it. "What do you think happened here, Zora? It makes me very nervous to see so much blood here. I hope it was a wound that was caused by a fight among them. That would make me very happy. The thought that we are not far behind them now is also cause for rejoicing. We truly are close to our target." She still didn't feel good about any of this. It was so very odd that they would find blood like this. *What if there is much more to this than we see?*

Just as the group was feeling somewhat excited that they might be getting closer to Zarcon, the night grew darker. As they lit the fire in the fireplace, the horses suddenly became restless out front, stamping and whickering.

Zora told the men to go see what was causing the alarm. The men were hesitant to check, but they were more afraid not to obey. Cardeegan assigned two of the men to go out front to see if anything was wrong.

Those inside heard the screams and ran to the front door to see what was happening. One of the men was gone. The other one was in a state of shock. He stared ahead as tears ran down his face.

Zora shook him, "What happened here? Where is your companion?"

The man looked at Zora as though he had never seen her before. He started screaming again.

Zora slapped him across the face. "Tell me what happened! Get control of yourself, man! What happened here?"

He finally looked around and seemed to come to himself. He said, "It was in the mist ... it was ... in the mist." Then he clutched his chest and fell over. He was dead.

Zora was shocked. "This man was scared to death! What on earth would cause such a thing?"

The group stared in horror at the scene. Then they noticed the smell. It was overpowering. Myshella gagged, and one of the men vomited. The men were so much more fearful. They looked at each other as if they were hoping to get some kind of strength or courage from each other. All shifted about nervously wondering what the witches would do next. They knew their lives would depend on their decision.

Anesthia, in hysterics, cried, "What do we do now? This is too much. How can we go on when we don't know what we're facing? What if it attacks one of us? One man gone and the other one scared to death? What has happened, Zora? Please explain this to me. I can't stand it!"

Zora slapped her. "You must get control of yourself! It is not helping anyone for you to lose control. We will deal with this. We must, but we must also regain the orb or all our plans will fail. You want to rule the world, don't you? We have planned this for a long time. We are so close. Think about it. We'll have everything we've ever wanted. You remember that, don't you?" Zora was almost crooning.

Anesthia sniffed, and Zora patted her hand. She said, "That's my girl. We'll be fine. You'll see. We'll get through this and be queens together. All of us." Zora looked at each of the other's and hoped they believed her.

Anesthia looked at Zora and Heleren. She drew herself up to her full height and said, "Yes, you're right, of course. We will come through this and be queens together. I am sorry I lost control for a moment. I am fine now." She trembled and pulled her cloak closer.

Zora looked around and growled, "Now let's calm down and figure out what to do next."

As the rest of the men searched the area, they found that there were no tracks. There was only a brief trail of what appeared to be heel marks where the man was dragged, but they ended suddenly. There were no other tracks to explain where the other man had gone or what had taken him. Strangely, none of the horses were injured or missing, though they were very skittish and wild-eyed.

It was lucky they had been tied before whatever it was struck. They would have been gone otherwise.

Zora and the others walked back into the farmhouse. Zora said, "We will spend the night here, but we will leave first thing in the morning. This place is disturbing. It may be that what attacked our man also attacked someone in Zarcon's group. One thing is for certain: we don't know what took the man or if the thing will be back. I am thinking it is the same thing that attacked our men on the trail a while ago." She told Cardeegan to have one or two of the men check the back of the house for a barn to put the horses in for the night. They would be safer in some form of shelter than out in the open.

Cardeegan sent two of his men out the front door. They left, looking in every direction for any sign of danger. Seeing none, they proceeded to gather the horse's reins and led them to the back of the house where they saw the barn and shut them inside after checking for any danger there. They hurried back to the house as quickly as possible without running and showing how afraid they really were.

Zora said, "Cardeegan, tell your men that you may all find a room in the farmhouse with us for the night. We can't afford to lose any more of you." That was certainly true since they had lost three of the men already. Things were looking awfully grim at that point, and the witches knew it.

They prepared for sleep, but no one was foolish enough to think they would actually sleep. They took care of their own bedrolls and ate jerky, cheese, and hard bread. There was a little water left in the water skins. They would definitely need to find water in the morning.

The night passed quietly for the group. The sun came up through dark clouds and mist. The rain started soon after sunrise. It was just slightly lighter as the sun came up fully. It was a drenching rain. There would be no travel that day. They would wait until the rain let up a bit before venturing out of doors. The mist made any travel dangerous, even more so with the monster somewhere out there. The men found a bucket to catch the water. That was about the only good thing about the day.

The witches were uncharacteristically quiet. Gloom had settled on them all.

Myshella began pacing from one end of the farmhouse to the other. She always had a hard time sitting still for any length of time, but she was making it very difficult for the others to think at all. Then she started complaining about their situation. "This can't be happening! We've traveled so far and suffered too much loss—and now it decides to rain! Who knows how many creatures are waiting out there to have us for a meal? We are running out of food. I'm getting cold! Why, oh why, did we leave home? Now we're all going to die! I can't stand it!"

Zora was disgusted with Myshella. She was the one who insisted on going on with the search. She practically screamed, "Myshella, stop it right now! You're just upsetting everyone else. We will find a way out of this, and we will get the orb back. We just have to stick together and figure out what to do."

Myshella looked at Zora in shock. No one had ever talked to her like that. "But, Zora, tell us what to do. We're too upset to think."

Zora really was disgusted now. "Listen to me. We're going to try to get some sleep tonight. We'll head out first thing tomorrow. With any luck, we'll find Donavan's cabin in the next few days. Hopefully, we will at least have some safety for the night. We may even find food there that we can share. If we're really lucky, we may find Zarcon's little band there as well, and we can settle this then. What do you think?

Are you feeling any better? Tonight, dream of what we will do when we meet up with Zarcon and that little thief, Jasmine."

The other witches smiled. Zora hoped it would at least be enough to get them through the night. She was worried that they did not all have the strength to do what needed to be done. Thinking and planning to do something was a far cry from actually doing it. So many unforeseen difficulties had plagued them on this journey. They were feeling the strain on their nerves and stamina. She sincerely hoped that what she had told them would actually happen soon. They didn't need any more death or terror.

The night passed slowly. Most in the group tossed and turned. A few times, they would cry out or moan in their sleep. The farmhouse seemed to engender nightmares and unease. The men slept in the room just off the main one where the witches were sleeping.

The men spent a sleepless night, watching for movement outside the house. They dared not venture out into the night, but they watched at the windows. It was not so much for the witches that they watched. It was for their own safety. None of the men felt any loyalty to the witches. They paid well, but they were truly heartless. None of them had shown any remorse at the death of the other men unless it was because there were three fewer men to carry their baggage and cook their meals.

Cardeegan could sense the restlessness in the men, but he didn't quite know how to deal with it since he felt much the same. He served the witches and even enjoyed cowing the men to his bidding, but that was where his sense of duty ended. This journey was not at all what he had expected. Now his men were dying, and he had no answers for why or how it had happened. The frustration was mounting for all of them.

Dawn came late. The sun was hidden by thick storm clouds. It was not raining, but it threatened to at any moment. The witches had to leave at any rate. They only had a small amount of jerky and cheese left for each of them. They must find food and water soon.

They packed up their bedrolls and saddled their horses. There was no time to wait for the men to do it all. Myshella grumbled, but she said nothing aloud. Finally, they were on their way. The trail was nothing more than a muddy track when they finally set out for the day.

Zora hoped that the rain would hold off long enough for them to make some progress. There was no knowing how far they would have to go before they would find Donavan's cabin or Zarcon and his group. They could only hope such a thing would happen before they had to spend much more time on this accursed journey. It would be good to be done with it and move on to more important matters. The world was waiting to be conquered.

The leaves dripped rain and soaked their cloaks. They were getting cold and miserable. They had a scare when they heard something rustling in the brush beside the trail. It turned out to be a rabbit. One of the men was able to shoot it with his bow before it could get away. At least they would have something to eat tonight. Maybe they could get another one before long.

The day dragged on. They finally found a small clearing to camp in for the night just as the sun began to set. The men killed five more rabbits for dinner as they traveled along. Fortunately, game was plentiful in the area. They skinned them and roasted them over the campfire. It was very tasty after so many nights with barely enough to eat.

The group settled down for the night, but they did not sleep well. The ground was still damp and cold in spite of the fire.

12

Time to Move On

The next morning came early for Zarcon and his group. The men had prepared breakfast for them all and let the women and Zarcon and Donavan rest a bit longer. When the four of them came down the stairs, they were surprised to see that breakfast was ready and the horses were saddled and mostly packed. The four ate quickly and cleaned up the rest of the mess. They were relieved to have things ready to go so quickly. Zarcon was especially grateful for the extra rest they had given him. He was finally getting his strength back. This had been a rough trip, and he was not used to the life they were living. However, he did feel that he was getting stronger for all the exercise he was getting.

Everyone in the group spoke in excited voices and hurriedly got things finalized to leave. Donavan felt a twinge of sadness as he mentally said goodbye to his home of the past four years. He truly did not know if he would be back, but there was much to look forward to. Jasmine was a mystery he wanted to solve. He hadn't had anything to look forward to for so long; it felt strange to him now.

Zarcon and the others left the cabin and headed out the opposite direction in which they had come. There was a small trail that led through the farm and garden and into the forest. They had to travel single file for a few miles. The sky was clouding up again. They hurried through the trees, ducking under the low limbs. Their horses were rested up, so they made good time. They kept a steady pace for three hours and finally found a wider area to stop and have something to eat. They ate hurriedly, sensing somehow that the witches were not far behind. They really needed to put as much distance between themselves and the cabin as possible—as quickly as possible. They all sensed the urgency and made no unnecessary noise or conversation, choosing to concentrate on the trail ahead.

The group traveled with mixed feelings and some misgivings for what might await them in the future. They still did not know what the witches were up to. They only knew that the Black Wind was loosed upon the world and that the wolves would very likely return to harass them.

It was cool here with the weather changing to fall, especially so high in the mountains. The horses were quiet, and they moved forward into the forest. The party followed the trail that wound beside the creek. They hoped the strange creatures of this forest would leave them alone. In the back of their minds was the fear that they may have to face the creature in the mist again. They had not really resolved how they were going to do that.

Zarcon called Donavan and Terrence over to him as they rode along. He said, "We need to prepare a plan of action in case we happen to come across the creature again. Any ideas?"

Terrence looked grim. He had heard tales of strange creatures when he was a child, but he had never thought he would have to deal with one of them. "That creature that attacked Jake was so terrifying. I'm not sure what we could do to stop it. Zarcon, do you have any magic that would help out? Can you give us some assistance?"

Zarcon hesitated. "I can use magic. The thing that worries me is that this creature may have some magic of its own. I couldn't detect any, but that is not to say with any certainty that it does not. If I were to try to cast a spell on it, it could backfire in some way that we would not be prepared for. I will think about that for a while. What do you think, Donavan?"

"I say we just run like rabbits. I have no desire to confront one of those creatures. Could we set a trap for it? When we set camp tonight, let's make some plans to protect ourselves. Maybe we won't need magic."

They agreed that maybe that would be the best course of action until they knew more about the creature. If they were lucky, they wouldn't have to deal with it at all, but they would plan for it in any case.

They took a few breaks as they rode through the forest. They ate cold food, mostly jerky with some bread and cheese that Donavan had stored. They still had the creek water to drink as they rode along. They were making good time as the day grew late. They finally found a small clearing to settle down in for the night. They set up watches and lit a small fire. The night was cold.

Zarcon, Terrence, and Donavan sat together and planned how to protect the camp at night. There were other animals that might attack in addition to the mysterious creature in the mist. They decided to set pointed tree limbs in the ground around the perimeter of the camp. They would also set out a warning system in case something really big approached the camp. Men would stand watch in pairs. No man would be out alone. They could not afford to lose any more men.

They went to their bedrolls and waited for their turn to stand watch. Zarcon would not have a turn this night. He would be able to sleep through the night. Of course, he didn't really sleep. He spent the night worrying.

They had done well for their first day of travel. They had gone more miles than they had hoped. All seemed quiet, which was unsettling in a way. There had been a few birds singing throughout the day, but it was not what they would have expected. Sometimes they felt that unfriendly eyes were watching them.

They kept going the next day. Zarcon was tiring, however, and needed to stop for a rest. They found a secluded spot off the trail where they could hide and rest themselves and the horses for an hour. Zarcon was feeling his age. There had been so much pressure on them throughout this journey that it had taken a toll on Zarcon. The others were feeling it too.

Jasmine was grateful for the break. She had been scouting ahead with Voltar for two hours. It was time for her to rest as well. Greta was concerned for Zarcon. He never revealed his condition unless he was really feeling it. She sat next to him and said, "Zarcon, are you going to be all right? I'm worried about you. You look pale tonight. Are you in pain? Is there anything I can do?"

Zarcon winced. "Is it that obvious? I had hoped no one would suspect. I have felt a little shaky for the last hour or two. In the last few minutes, I noticed that my balance was off a bit. I was afraid I might fall out of the saddle. I decided to call a halt to see if I could recover. I'm sure I'm just getting old, but would you stay close by in case it's more than that?"

"Of course."

Zarcon seemed to do better after a while. He got up and was talking with the others. Voltar came up to him and nuzzled his hand. Zarcon patted him on the head while he talked with the men. After half an hour of conversation, it was decided that it was time to move out. They still had some daylight to travel in. They mounted up and headed down the trail.

Greta took her place close to Zarcon and kept a wary eye on him. He rode tall in the saddle and seemed rested enough to carry on. They would stop soon anyway.

A few hours later, they were all getting hungry and decided to find a place to stop for the night. There was a clearing a hundred yards off the trail with plenty of cover in a grove of trees. Jasmine had spotted it as she was scouting ahead. Voltar had gone after a rabbit. When she followed him, she found the clearing. She hurried back to the others to tell them about it. They all joined her and started to set up camp just as the sun was setting. They decided it would be best not to have a fire. No sense making it easier for the witches to find them.

As they were setting up camp, one of the men shouted to Zarcon that he saw some mist forming just outside the camp perimeter. Zarcon, Donavan, and Terrence came running. Just then, Zarcon could see red eyes becoming visible in the mist. One of the creature's forelegs was extended to grab one of the men or Voltar. He panicked and drew on his magic to destroy the creature before it could harm anyone in the group. He moved his hands in a powerful incantation and let loose a ball of fire into the mist. It appeared that the creature burst into flames. It fell over as the mist dissipated around it. The smell was overwhelming. Many of them gagged, and a couple of the men vomited.

Zarcon and Terrence stepped closer to see what it was. They had to hold their kerchiefs to their noses to get closer to the repulsive creature. It was obvious that the creature was dead. It was charred almost beyond recognition. It had shriveled up and was blackened from the spell Zarcon had used, but they could tell that it was large enough to carry off a man or large animal. It had a large head with very long teeth, long front legs with claws that were several inches long, and a tail that had barbs on the end. It looked like it crawled on four legs, but how it made the mist that hid it was not obvious. There appeared to be tubes at the side of its neck that could possibly have served the purpose, but it was difficult to say for sure. The hide of the creature consisted of tough, dark green scales. No one wanted to touch it. They were so grateful that it was dead and hoped there were no more of the creatures around. They still remembered the one that had attacked them on the trail and at the deserted farmhouse. However, they could not know if they were one and the same or two more of the things.

Zarcon was upset about something and finally said, "I'm so sorry I've used the magic to destroy the creature. I guess I panicked. This will alert the witches to our whereabouts without a doubt. We must be more vigilant in watching for their wolves now. Zora will be able to pinpoint our location. I know that this creature would have killed one or more of us, but I still wish I could have used something besides magic to kill or destroy it."

Greta said, "Zarcon, you did the right thing. Who knows what would have happened to us if you had not stopped the thing when you did. I have a feeling the witches would have found us and sent the wolves after us sooner or later anyway. We are just grateful that you killed the monster when you did."

The others were in agreement with Greta and were very glad to not have to face the creature again.

Zarcon relaxed and decided that they must be more careful. The witches would surely be on their trail now. He did regret that much, but he was also grateful that the creature was dead.

They hurriedly buried the remains of the monster in a very deep hole. The smell lingered in the air. They decided to move down the trail another mile before they set up camp. There happened to be an even better clearing just ahead that offered more cover and was far enough away from the place the creature died that they could rest a bit easier. The smell was gone. They finished preparations for the night and settled down to sleep. No one slept much; many had nightmares of the creature they had buried and the wolves. All knew it was inevitable now that Zarcon had used his magic.

They awoke just before dawn and packed up the horses after eating a quick breakfast. It was cold because they hadn't had a fire. It would be another long day in the saddle. Zarcon seemed better this morning, even though using his magic had tired him greatly. He didn't complain of dizziness, thank the gods. Greta watched him closely for any signs of fatigue, but he seemed as ready to go as the rest of them were. It was decided that they would need to get out of the mountains as soon as possible. It would be difficult to fight the witches in the forest. There were too many obstacles. There was also the certainty that the witches would send their wolves after them. Fortunately, Voltar would warn them if any were in the vicinity.

Zarcon and Terrence discussed the fact that they would have to pick a place to fight the witches. That would require them to decide what kind of fight they wanted. They would have to rely somewhat on Donavan and Zarcon's magic. They thought that Donavan would need to practice his magic and find out what his powers really were. They might even have to push him a little to see what he could do. These thoughts were part of the puzzle Zarcon was trying to put together for the coming battle. He was also concerned that Donavan and Jasmine were becoming more and more open about their feelings for one another. It was obvious to Zarcon that their affection was becoming stronger as time went by. That could be a good thing or a distraction at a critical moment. He would have to talk with them both very soon. If only he were younger. All this emotional anxiety was wearing him down. Well, there really wasn't much he could do about it anyway. He just hoped it wouldn't compromise the mission in any way.

They rode mainly in silence. The only sounds were the birds singing in the trees and creatures scurrying in the forest. There was always the fear in the back of their minds that one of the creatures from the mist might come for them, especially since they had killed one of them. Who could know what that would mean for them?

Jasmine rode ahead as she had done and took Voltar with her. He was a good scout too. He was also good company as he trotted along beside her horse.

Donavan stayed with the group, taking up the rear. Micah rode just in front of him on the trail. Donavan was confused about Jasmine. They had talked about each other's lives and had made some progress in getting to know each other, but that was as far as it went. He felt that it was probably a good thing they were so busy right now. There would be time later to pursue any feelings they might have for each other if they managed to survive this crazy mission or war or whatever it was they were embarked upon.

As the day wore on, they stopped periodically to eat and rest. The land began to level out. There was much less slope to the trail, and the trees were thinning out a bit. They could now ride side by side. This meant that conversation was possible. Zarcon was talking to Greta about the upcoming battle and what it would possibly entail for them all. They would find a good place to rest and practice their skills in magic as well as the art of warfare. No one doubted the fight would be terrible.

13

Witches Find the Cabin

Zora's group came to a small valley and traversed it. It took the group most of the day to get there. The valley floor was somewhat marshy. So they led their horses across the driest parts of it. They decided to camp at the far side of the valley where it was dry with some trees for shelter. The night was long, but at least they were dry and warm. Their fire would also protect them from any of the strange animals in the area. At least that was what they were hoping. They could hear animal calls in the night. Some of them were strange and unnerving, but nothing attacked them as they slept. They could thank the fire for that. The wolves also kept them safe. The pack surrounded the group that night, keeping just out of sight. Zora could see the yellow eyes of the big gray male reflecting the fire. It gave her some comfort to know he was there.

As morning crept over the top of the mountain, Zora and her group woke late. They had slept better than they had for a long time. It was difficult to get moving again. They loaded up the horses and ate a quick breakfast of jerky and some cheese. There was a stream close by to fill their canteens and wash down the cold breakfast before they mounted up to leave.

Zora was leading the way when she found a trail leading up the mountain that was difficult to see. It was somewhat hidden by cattails from the wet ground nearby. They followed it up and around the mountain. It took all day to climb the trail, but as they reached the top, it opened up into a small meadow. As the sun was setting, they could make out a cabin in the middle. Donavan's cabin! No lights showed in the windows, but they didn't care. They hurried forward, jumped off their horses, and tried the door. It wasn't locked, so they hurried inside to see if they could start a fire. There was kindling on the hearth and dry logs stacked in the corner. It was as if the owner expected to be back momentarily.

One of the men rushed to start the fire, and another skinned the rabbits they had killed on the trail. Zora found a pot in the kitchen to cook the rabbits. Anesthia found the salt and some onions to throw in with the rabbits. Myshella found the garden in the back and brought in some carrots. They cut up the vegetables and added them to the pot of boiling water. When the rabbits were cleaned and ready to cook, Myshella cut them up so they would cook faster. It wasn't long before the aroma of rabbit stew was filling the air of the cabin.

The group made ready for the night as the rabbit stew cooked. Their bedrolls were laid out in the common room. No one wanted to be alone tonight. The stew was finally done, and they found bowls to fill and spoons for the stew. It was wonderful to have a warm meal in a nice warm cabin. It was so unlike the previous night's terror that they were on the verge of tears. Everything was going very nicely.

Myshella screamed, "They were here—and not very long ago either! Look at this! I found a piece of clothing that would belong to one of those women. We must be very close indeed! Zora, can we leave tomorrow and search for them?"

Zora was so weary she could hardly answer. "Myshella, we will stay here for only two days to rest and stock our supplies. Then we will be on our way. We will find them all and have our revenge, but for tonight, will you please just relax? I'm glad you found the proof you need that they were here. I knew it the moment we saw this place. It could only be Donavan's cabin, but we are all exhausted and need some peace so we can regain our strength. Can you do that, Myshella, for everyone's sake?"

Myshella was embarrassed that Zora would reprimand her again. It really was humiliating. She swallowed her pride and said, "I'm sorry, Zora. I was just excited to find real evidence that they were here. I know we're on the right track now so I can relax—and I will."

"Thank you, Myshella." Zora was relieved that Myshella had found the clothing, but she was much too tired to get excited about anything just now. The food they had eaten had revived her a little, but she knew they all needed rest.

The group settled in for the night after cleaning up the dinner mess. There was enough stew to feed them one more time. They had made plenty of it. They slept well because they were, at least for the time being, not worried about food or shelter or monsters. They would worry about the rest of their journey tomorrow and the next day.

The next day, they felt someone using powerful magic. They all knew it had to be Zarcon. They were elated to at least have an idea where he was. They conferred for a while and decided to send the wolves after them. Zora called the big gray male to her and sent a mental image of Zarcon and his approximate whereabouts to him. He howled and took off with his pack to find Zarcon and the others with him. This, at least, was something they knew how to do. The wolves would take care of Zarcon if they could.

Zora and the rest of the witches were rested and ready to head out after two days at the cabin. It took two days for the witches to finally feel rested enough to go on. In the two days they were there, they had eaten most of the food in the cabin. They took the rest with them.

The forest had been very quiet while they were there. The creek that flowed past was a wonderful source of fresh water and fish. The men were happy to catch the fish and cook them for breakfast. It was such a pleasant change from the jerky they had eaten for most of the trip.

They all slept soundly for the first time in days. They were rested and ready to travel. The witches were anxious to get on the road. They didn't have much farther to go. Myshella could almost smell the orb. Heleren was anxious to get to civilization where there were men to torment. She hadn't had any fun since they started this expedition. She was growing tired of the whole thing. It was not at all what she had expected.

They saddled up their horses and put the supplies on the extra horses still with them. As they prepared to leave, Zora wondered which way to go. They knew Zarcon's group hadn't gone the way they had come up. So, there had to be another way out of there. Zora instructed the men to look around for another way out. They scouted the perimeter of the cabin and the meadow. They searched for an hour or more, and they finally found the narrow track Zarcon's group had taken. The horses had left a trail that was plain to see once they found it. So many horses had widened the track and made it much more obvious. The men had just missed it a couple of times because there were bushes in the way. One of the men noticed a broken branch, and the rest was easy.

Zora said, "Well done, men. Let's get going. We've wasted enough daylight looking for this blasted trail. Come on, my sisters. Let's catch those thieves and have them for lunch if we can!"

The group left the meadow, yelling and laughing in excitement. They would catch up with the others very soon. Two days to rest up were costly, they all knew that, but it couldn't be helped. The important thing was that they were on their way.

Everything had dried out pretty well in the two days they were in the cabin. That was another very good thing. They took to the trail in single file and were making very good progress. The men had no trouble keeping to the track. It was plain to see. They actually had an easier time than Zarcon and his group because the trail was so well marked. They could gallop their horses for short distances when the trees thinned out a bit. They rested and ate at intervals, but they kept going. They traveled down the mountain for seven days. It was long, but it was not too difficult. The trail was easy to follow, and there were places to rest and camp for the night along the way.

They approached the end of the trail where it joined the main road after two more days. They camped as best they could as they traveled. The food was good, and they made very good time. At the main road, they had to decide where Zarcon and his party might have been headed. Heleren suggested that they might be on their way to Kaphur. Myshella thought it made more sense for them to head toward Landpur, but Anesthia was sure they were going to Synkana. She could feel the pull of the orb in that direction. Zora tended to agree with her. She could also feel the pull of the orb. So, the group decided to take the direct route instead of traveling with all the other people through all those little towns and villages. The other way was harder but so much faster. There was time to be made up, and off they went.

The road was easy at first. The main road led them through some smaller villages and into the Horned Hawk Mountains. They were not as high as the Backlash Mountains, but the road narrowed and became a track again as they climbed. As the towns and villages thinned out, the road became rougher. Still, it would save them many miles of travel and curious gazes of the people on the main road. The witches were well known in this area and would be marked if they stayed with the main road. They did not want to have word of their travel get to Zarcon and his party if they could help it. One good thing came of going this way: the wolves were back.

On the first night in the forest, they had a campfire going. The big gray wolf came to the edge of the fire's glow. Zora was startled at first, and then she realized what she was seeing. She called the big gray wolf to come, but he stayed where he was, just letting her know he was back. She could just make out three of his pack in the dark. This was good news indeed! She wanted to know what happened with Zarcon and his group, but it was late. She felt the need for rest, but she knew they would be prepared to attack Zarcon. Zora smiled at the thought. The others were smiling too when they realized what the sight of the wolves meant for their effort. Yes, now they could win! Gone was the somberness of the past few days. They knew the wolves could make all the difference in the coming battle. Zora didn't even need to know where the wolves had been or what they had done. She was just glad to have them with her once more. She was pretty sure they had made a dent in Zarcon's pride. It would be good to find out if the wolves had taken out any of his men.

That night, Zora plotted her attack. It would be sudden and fierce. She would show no mercy. Zarcon had stolen that which was most precious to her and her sister witches. She would show him what that meant! Oh, yes, vengeance would be sweet indeed. She slept soundly after that. After all, what difference did it make that Zarcon had Donavan to help him? She had her wolves, and that was plenty.

At dawn, Zora called the big gray male to her. She got a mental picture of what the wolves had done. This gave her hope as they started off again. There was a sense of jubilation now that the wolves were following just out of sight. It gave them all a sense of security. They had not seen or heard from the monsters of the Backlash Mountains, and all seemed right with the world. The sun seemed brighter, and life was once more full of promise. They would yet rule the world. It was just a matter of time now.

As they rode along, Zora practiced killing the woodland creatures with her thoughts. Sometimes she would kill them outright if they needed them for a meal. Sometimes she would take the time to stop and torture them just to see how long she could drag out their deaths.

Myshella enjoyed watching her. The wolves would eat those animals. Zora was definitely getting better at controlling her magic. Even though she could feel the power slipping away within her. She wanted to try it out on a human, preferably a man, but she needed all of the men with them. She would wait until an opportunity presented itself. Surely someone would come along—alone. She smiled at the thought. There was just a flicker of doubt, but she brushed it away.

The land rose and fell before them as they traveled the track to Synkana. There were a few farmhouses but not many villages this far off the main road. After three days on the trail, they came to a very small village, Kordiman, where they could spend the night under a roof. There was a small inn in the middle of the village. The men took the horses around to the back where there was a small stable to leave them. They paid a young man to feed and care for the horses for the time they would be there. Zora had given them money for that purpose as they reined in.

Zora led the group into the inn. It was small and dark with a bar on the left side of the door. A large man was drying his hands on a dirty rag behind the bar. "My name is Tory. I am the innkeeper here. What can I do for you ladies?" he said.

Zora said, "We are seeking a place to spend the night. Do you have rooms to let? We are also hungry and would like a meal for all of us tonight and in the morning. How much would you charge for that?"

The man finally saw who he was dealing with and realized it was the witches. He swallowed hard and stammered a bit. "Well, let me see here. We happen to have seven rooms, if you would like them all. I serve good, hearty meals. Normally, I would charge a hundred sovereigns for all of that."

Zora looked at him with narrowed eyes. He noticed and realized the error of his thinking. He continued, "But it has been slow lately, so I will give the rooms and meals to you for half that. Would that be fair, milady?"

Zora gave a half smile and a low chuckle. Using her favorite sarcastic voice, she said, "More than fair, kind sir. We shall be delighted to stay in your establishment for tonight. We shall leave early in the morning. I expect a full breakfast and to have our horses brought out and saddled before dawn. Is that possible?"

"Oh yes! We would be more than happy to accommodate you and your company in any way we can." The man was able to relax a little now that the money was settled. He didn't care that he would lose money on this deal. It was enough that he might survive the ordeal of having the witches staying overnight. He would be very careful to comply with their every command. That was the only way to survive.

The group settled into the tables in the common room. Tory wiped the tables off with his dirty rag and bowed and apologized as he did so. "So sorry about the mess. We just had a dinner rush, and I haven't had a chance to clean up yet." There were so few people in the bar that Zora knew better than to believe the man, but she let it go. They needed to eat and get some rest.

There were other people in the bar when they walked in, but now that the witches were settled into the chairs, they realized they were alone. The others had left one by one. They worried a bit that word would get out that they were around even in this little backwater. Well, they could do nothing about that. They just had to pay the price of fame.

The bar smelled of ale, sweat, and greasy dirt. It was not exactly appetizing, but it was all that was available. Zora gave serious thought to burning the place to the ground when they left, but she decided it would probably draw too much attention to their travels if they did. It was apparently already known that they were in the area. Oh, well. One could fantasize. It would have given her immense pleasure, but greater pleasures waited when they caught up with Zarcon. Some things were worth the wait.

When Tory brought their meal, he set it on the table. His kitchen helper set bowls and utensils before them. He also set a jug of ale on the table with mugs for each of his guests. The men sat off by themselves and were glad of it. The witches sat at the one larger table in the room.

Heleren was disappointed once again that there were no men left for her to torment. This was the most boring trip she had ever been on. Of course that applied to her special desires—not the trials they had faced.

Anesthia ate her meal in silence. She was so tired, she just wanted to eat and get to her room so she could sleep. Myshella felt much the same way.

Myshella said, "Zora, are you going to tell us your plans?" The others perked up at that. Finally someone had the nerve to ask the question that had tormented them all for days.

Zora blinked. She hadn't even realized she had kept her thoughts to herself this whole time. They had been so consumed with survival that she had only thought about what she would do about Zarcon as she was falling asleep. Now was the time to discuss what she had been thinking. "I'm grateful you brought it to my attention that I have kept my thoughts to myself as we have traveled. It has been so difficult for so long, hasn't it? Well, this is what I'm thinking we should do."

Zora then told them of her plans to use the magic they each possessed along with what the wolves could do to distract anyone in

Zarcon's party who would use magic against them. It was a simple plan, yet it was sure to succeed because of its simplicity. Sometimes the direct approach was the most effective. The others were pleased with the plan Zora presented. There were a few refinements suggested by Myshella, but other than that, it seemed a workable plan. They could implement it with little difficulty and probable success.

Tory jumped at the sudden laughter emanating from the witches' table. It wasn't just the sudden noise. It was the tone of hate and anger that overlaid it that was so unsettling. He bent his head down and continued to wipe out the dirty glasses with his dirty rag. He nearly ran from the room, but he didn't want to attract the witches' attention at a time like this. He really wanted to cower in the corner of the bar, but that would also draw unwanted attention. He tried to stay upright on his wobbly legs and keep his mind on his work.

The witches finished eating and left the common room. They felt much happier than they had in days. This was the beginning of the end for Zarcon and those who conspired with him. Good times were ahead, and they were eager to begin.

The witches slept soundly now that they had a plan to eliminate Zarcon and those foolish enough to be with him and Jasmine. It was good to know what they were going to do. Each of them gloried in their part in it. Myshella was looking forward to her part in taking care of Jasmine. She had asked for the special privilege. She smiled as she thought of the fun she would have. The others were having similar thoughts as they drifted off to sleep.

The witches were so excited to begin their journey that they were up and waiting for the men to get dressed. They hurried down to the common room. They could smell breakfast cooking as they entered. Tory had their plates set out with mugs of ale. As soon as he heard them coming down the stairs, he brought out the food. He had just finished cooking it. He was so glad he had gotten up early to get things going. He was so nervous and anxious for them to leave that he had been unable to sleep at all.

"I hope the meal meets with your satisfaction. I have more in the kitchen if you need it. I will be happy to take care of your needs this morning. Please let me know if there is more I can do." Tory hurried to the back of the bar once all was set on the tables. He didn't want to be any closer than necessary. He never knew about witches. He had heard that one of them could kill with a thought. He felt his skin crawl just thinking about the possibility. *Somebody ought to stop those witches. It just isn't right that there are such nasty people going about the countryside and scaring people like that.*

Tory didn't know it, but he wasn't the only person to feel that way. There were many who would love the opportunity to be a part of any effort to eliminate them. The witches had no idea the danger they were actually in. It was just their magic that kept people at bay. There was no love of the witches in any part of the country. The only reason they could rule at all was because of the magic power they held and the fear it created in the hearts of those who were unfortunate enough to come into contact with them. Even their own men would turn on them if given the opportunity. This was especially true when they saw the witches' lack of reaction to the deaths of the others. They reacted to it as a gross inconvenience— and nothing more.

It was known that the witches had no feelings for anything but their own desires and ends. The people were growing tired of their cruelty and sense of entitlement. It was hoped by many that they would meet an ignoble end. They just wanted to be there when it happened. They didn't necessarily want to be the ones to do it. So the witches continued to rule unmolested.

The witches finished their meals and prepared to leave the inn. The horses were tied to the hitching rail and waiting for them. Tory's stable boy knew about the witches and wanted no part of the rage they would direct at him if he didn't have the horses saddled and fed when they were ready to leave. He tied the horses and ran back to the shelter of the stable.

The witches and the men mounted their horses and rode off. The innkeeper hoped that it would be the last time he would ever see them. Just one night under his roof terrified him to the extent that he would have nightmares for many nights to come. The witches knew that Synkana was only about fifty miles ahead. They would be there in two or three days if they kept up a good pace. They had made twenty miles in the past couple of days. There was no reason they couldn't do it for two or three more, unless something unforeseen occurred, but they would worry about that if it happened. The wolves met them as they came to a crossroads just outside of town. They all looked healthy and strong. They had done some hunting in a more populous area. The witches hoped they hadn't taken too many of the farmers' sheep and cattle. They didn't want the people in the area to be too upset as they traveled through their farmlands. A well-thrown rock could be just as deadly as a sword if they didn't see it coming.

So they hurried on. The wolves kept pace with them just out of sight of the track. It was getting wider now that they were closer to villages on the way to Synkana. The farms were closer together, and wagons headed to the markets. They moved aside when they saw the witches approaching. The farmers would touch the rims of their hats in respect, but they never smiled or said a word to the witches or those with them. It was a cold greeting at best—and hostile at worst. The witches did not have time to deal with it. They would come back and take care of those people later.

Many of the men stared at the witches, especially at Heleren, but she had no time to enjoy herself. She would return—of that she was sure—and she would have some fun. She had missed out long enough. A few more days to take care of Zarcon and Jasmine, and then the fun would really begin. They would have the orb. She smiled at the thought.

They rode on. It was a beautiful sunny day. The road was dry and becoming more populated. It widened with each mile. People continued to back off the road as they approached. It was becoming unnerving, but the witches still had far to go before they could think of stopping for anything but a brief rest and food.

At dusk, they approached another small village. This one was larger than Kordiman—but not by much. There were two inns in town. The men asked villagers which would be the best one to spend the night. They were told the Tusk was clean and had good food. They proceeded to the Tusk. Outside the door of the inn, a very large tusk hung from a pole on the roof. It looked like the tusk of a large hoar beast. The men asked where it had come from, but no one knew.

As the witches entered the inn, the room grew very quiet. No one spoke.

The innkeeper frowned. He was not happy that the witches chose his inn. "What can I do for you ladies this evening?" he asked.

Zora looked him in the eye.

He quickly looked away. He had heard stories about looking witches in the eye.

She said, "We would have dinner and seven rooms for the night. We also require breakfast early in the morning and care for our horses. What is the cost?"

The innkeeper said, "I will charge you half my usual fee if you will promise to leave in the morning."

Zora was incensed. No one spoke to her that way. "I beg your pardon. What did you say?" Her voice shook with rage.

The innkeeper realized almost too late what he had done. He had insulted the witch. He quickly said, "Begging your pardon, I meant I will charge you half my usual fee because I have such respect for you all. I would be honored if you stayed as long as you wish." The man finished in a rush. By this time, he was sweating fiercely.

Zora said with a snarl, "That's what I thought you said. I will pay you in the morning when all meets our needs. I look forward to the beds and fine meals you will prepare for us. If you take good care of us and our horses, maybe I will allow this place to remain standing when we leave."

The innkeeper got the message. "I would be most grateful, milady." He bowed to Zora and the other witches.

"Yes, I'm sure you would." Zora smiled a bit tightly and moved to one of the larger tables in the room. Many of the patrons had left through the back door while she had been speaking with the proprietor. She was just as glad. The place had been quite crowded when they arrived. It was not so now. Those who stayed were apparently in the middle of their meals and wished to finish them before leaving.

The innkeeper brought out some food for the witches and the men. It turned out to be very good indeed. The stew was thick with lots of meat. The bread was crusty and tasted wonderful. The ale was mellow and quenched their thirst. They were happy about stopping there; whether the innkeeper was happy or not did not matter to them at all. They were all tired from the long ride. They ate and were shown to their rooms down the hall to the left of the common room. They slept two to a room again. Zora wanted to be alone with her thoughts.

They slept well and rose to the smell of breakfast cooking. They dressed hurriedly and made their way to the common room. The men were waiting and already eating. Zora sat at the table set aside for them. The innkeeper brought out their breakfast on steaming platters. It was large slabs of meat with buttered bread and cheese. They also had large mugs of ale. They ate heartily. Everything was so good. They were finally ready to go once they were filled. They rose from the table, and Zora paid the man for his services. "I thank you for the meals and rooms. We are pleased and will return when we can. We must be off now."

The innkeeper was glad to have them leave, but he was not glad to hear that they would return. He heartily hoped not. The witches had cost him by paying so little for their rooms, and his patrons had vacated the place as soon as they could. He hoped they would return. He was grateful that he had survived the ordeal. There were moments when he wondered if he would. He was finally able to breathe again. He went back inside to prepare for the rest of his guests and the meals for the evening.

The witches were happy as they rode away from the village. The food had been good, and their rooms had been adequate. They had slept well and eaten well. They would make good time today. The road was wide, and it was early enough that the farmers were not yet out. They galloped their horses for short distances to make up some time. Hopefully they would make another twenty miles before they had to stop for the night. That would put them within ten miles of Synkana the next day. They would arrive at midday and be able to ask around to see if Zarcon and his band of thieves had arrived. Anticipation was growing at the thought.

They rode all day again, only stopping to rest for short periods and to eat a few bites of jerky and drink some of the ale in the skins they carried. The travel was monotonous, but they were making very good time. They came to another village as the sun was setting. They had much the same experience they had the night before. The people continued to leave the inn when they arrived. The food and rooms were adequate. Again they felt rested and were on their way to Synkana as the sun was coming up. They only had ten more miles to go. They hoped to find Zarcon before evening—or at least to know if he and his company were in the city by then. If not, they would scout around and try to find out where they were. Surely someone would have noticed his nasty little band heading their way.

They rode out of the village early, and there were no obvious observers to their leave taking. The towns and villages certainly seemed quiet as they made their way through them. The witches were amazed that so few people seemed to be out and about no matter where they went. They couldn't credit it with the fear the people had for them. If they had known the extent of it, they would probably have smiled. They all wanted to rule the world with fear. It was something they each understood as a necessary component to the power they wished to wield with the orb, but fear can bring its own set of problems. They would surely find that out at some point in their struggle for supreme power. Well, time would tell.

As they neared Synkana, the roadway became more crowded. The people recognized them and moved out of their way as they approached. No one said anything. In fact, it seemed that they would all look the other way as the witches passed. None wanted to have attention focused on them. The witches were dangerous, and everyone knew it. As a result, the witches were able to travel through the crowds easily. The really good thing about it was that the witches were riding through the gates of Synkana before noon. They found an inn in the heart of the city that was finer than what they had been staying in along the way. The inn was called the Peregrine Feather. They had stayed there on a few occasions in happier times. The inn was known to be expensive and pleasant—more like the witches had been accustomed to before this trip.

The man at the front desk noticed them and welcomed them to the inn. "Ladies, it is such a pleasure to welcome you to our inn. We have not seen you for many months. Have you fared well? Have you been traveling long? What can I do for you today?" In his heart, he was dreading the fact that the witches had returned. He remembered how they had destroyed one of his rooms the last time. It was also suspected that they had killed one of the maids in some kind of rage. Nothing was ever proven, and no one pursued the matter out of fear of retribution. Nevertheless, he knew he had to earn their trust and keep them happy while they were there or be subjected to some form of evil.

It took a moment, but Zora finally recognized the man as Condi. They had spent a few nights there when the last time they were in Synkana. The man had been very accommodating then too. Zora said, "I remember you. Condi, isn't it? We had a wonderful time here the last time. We have traveled long and are in want of a bath and a good meal. We would also appreciate having our clothing cleaned and pressed. As I said, it has been a long and arduous journey. We are hoping to be finished with our business very soon, but we need a place to stay until it is finished. Would you have rooms for the four of us? Our men will be staying elsewhere, I'm afraid."

Condi smiled, though he felt far from happy to see the witches again. "We just happen to have rooms for each of you. A bath will be brought to your rooms directly. I will order meals brought to your rooms as well. Will you be staying long?"

Zora said, "Hopefully not more than a few days. We can't be sure at this point. I will keep you updated as time goes by. Is there a problem?"

"No, no, just wanting to be prepared for your needs, milady. You know we aim to please here at the Peregrine Feather. I will show you to your rooms myself. May we take your baggage up with us? I will have one of my men help you with that."

"That would be kind of you. We will be grateful for your service … as always."

Condi almost laughed. He knew what the witches' gratitude was worth, nothing, but he smiled instead and bowed his head to Zora in reply. She must never know how he really felt about having them there.

The rooms Condi showed them were very nice and very clean. The beds were feather with posters and curtains at the windows. It was beautiful indeed.

"This will do, Condi," Zora said.

A bath was brought up to her room soon after. A maid came in to help her undress. The maid, Santi, was shocked at how dirty Zora was and how badly she smelled. It was obvious that she had been on the road for many days. She helped Zora bathe and dress. There was clean clothing in her baggage. It was as if Zora were saving it for her arrival in Synkana, which was true.

It felt so good to finally be rid of the road dirt and grime. She felt almost herself again. All she needed was a good meal. In fact, the meal was being brought in as she was finishing up with dressing. She was very grateful, but she would not say so. "It's about time you brought my meal. I was about to call down to Condi and tell him how terrible the service is here, but I won't since you are here now. I am watching you all. Be aware."

The servants delivered the food and left the room. They were just grateful the witch hadn't yelled at them or put a curse on them or something worse. It had happened before when one of the maids was a little bit late getting a meal up to one of the witches. She was never seen again. No one knew what had happened—only that there was some yelling and then nothing. It had been a while before the maid was replaced. About a month after the witches left, the people's fears calmed enough that someone asked for the position. There were some bones found in the back of one of the closets later that may have belonged to the person, but no one would ever know for sure.

Zora and the other witches ate their meals and agreed that a short nap would be a good thing before they started looking for Zarcon. They wanted to keep to themselves for a few hours. They would find Zarcon very soon—of that they were certain.

Witches Closing In

After six days of travel down the mountain with nothing unusual happening, Zarcon and his group became just a little bit complacent. It was dangerous timing. The witches were closing in.

One night, as they were traveling through a dense thicket of trees, they heard the wolves howling. Voltar started barking, and the group became alert to the danger. They put the horses in the middle of them and circled with knives and swords drawn. They could hear the wolves getting closer. Suddenly the big gray male sprang at them from the trees. He took down one of the men and ripped his throat out before he could defend himself or even scream. The wolf jumped away as Terrence swung his sword at him. He managed to nick the wolf on the side, but he did no real damage. The other wolves attacked the group from different sides and tried to get to the horses. After a brief battle, the wolves gave up and ran off. The horses were too well guarded, and the men were too well armed.

The man killed by the big gray wolf was Jonathan, the youngest man with them. They mourned his death. He had been a kind and efficient soldier. They buried him, and Terrence said a few kind words about him. They all vowed to be more vigilant. It was too costly to be complacent and think the witches would leave them alone now that they were getting closer to civilization. They knew they were in extreme danger.

They decided to travel just a bit farther to put some distance between them and the event with the wolves. Zarcon felt that there was too much danger in staying in the same place. The wolves already knew where they were and might come back. They moved along until they found a meadow with a stream running through it. As they set up camp just before dark, they lit a fire. It was getting colder, and they needed to decide how to get to Synkana.

Donavan said, "There are two roads from the base of this mountain that will take us to Synkana. One is the more direct route. The other is more circuitous, but it is an easier road with more travelers. It is the main road through this part of the country. Do we want company—or is speed more important?"

Zarcon was thoughtful for a moment. "I would prefer to blend in with other travelers as much as possible. The witches would probably expect us to travel directly to wherever we go. Also, if the wolves are still following us, and we have no reason to think otherwise, our scent would be covered better with many others on the roadway. What do you say, Greta … Jasmine?"

Greta was in favor of more people on the roadway. She felt that it would be safer overall. Jasmine agreed. They had spent so many nights on the road as the only people for miles. It would be nice to have others around.

Jasmine said, "The only thing we have to be very careful of is to not draw attention to ourselves while we travel. If we look out of place or anything happens to cause notice, the word will spread quicker with more observers, agreed?"

Donavan said, "That is a great comment. We may need to break up into smaller groups for that very reason. We could meet up in the larger towns until we get to Synkana. Does that make sense?"

Zarcon said, "Very good ideas from you both. How do we want to break up? I would prefer to be with Greta and Micah. Terrence, you may go with Jasmine and Donavan. Take Lantz with you. The rest will travel close behind as one group. Does that sound fair? Does someone have another suggestion? I am open to comments from you all."

No one argued with that plan. So it was settled. They decided to get to bed early so they could get an early start. They set watches for the night and put out the fire to protect them from observation as much as possible.

The next morning, before dawn, they saddled up and headed out again. They ate as they rode. There was jerky and cheese with some water left in the skins. They had enough to get them to the first village. They rode out of the trees at about noon. They quickly separated into their groups and joined the main road. Donavan and his group led the way. He knew which way to go. He was the only one who knew the way from there.

There were others on the road as they rounded a turn. A large caravan was coming toward them. Donavan said, "Hail, have you supplies for some weary travelers? We are running low just now."

The wagon master sighed. "Well, sir, that depends on the color of your money … if indeed you have any."

"I have money. What supplies do you carry?"

"Let me see your money, and I will show you my supplies." The man was clearly suspicious of others. He probably had good reason.

Donavan took out his money belt and jingled the coins in it. It was considerably heavier than the man had expected. "Well, sir, come right on over here. I'll show you my wares."

Donavan watched to see that none of the guards on the man's wagon came forward to steal from him. None did. He walked up to the man and was shown to a wagon that held different kinds of dried meats and cheeses. He also had a barrel of ale to sell. Donavan bought enough of all of it to get his group to the next large town. They filled their water skins with ale. It would stay potable longer than plain water. Donavan paid the man after haggling with him over the price. The man gave them a reasonable deal. Donavan was surprised, but it may have been the presence of Terrence that intimidated the man into it.

Donavan, Jasmine, Terrence, and Lantz moved off with the supplies tied to an extra horse. Zarcon and the others were on their own from there on. Zarcon would be able to take care of his group, and the soldiers were accustomed to foraging for themselves. It might not be too bad. If they could just get to Synkana without meeting the witches or the wolves, life would be good.

Zarcon had told Donavan to try to use his magic. Jasmine could coach him. It would be interesting to say the least. Maybe they could really get something done together.

Donavan would really like to know if his powers were greater than just blocking other spells. He remembered that his mother had tried to work with him, but Zora had found him—and he had to leave. Zora was no end of grief to him. It would be good to have it settled for better or worse. He was tired of looking over his shoulder wherever he tried to settle. Those witches needed to be taken care of so they couldn't ruin anyone else's life. Of course, if they got the orb back, they would ruin everyone's life. That just could not happen.

Zarcon watched as Donavan purchased the supplies. He was grateful that Donavan had remembered to bring his money. That simplified life for his group. Zarcon and Greta had brought some of the money from the castle, so they would be fine too. The soldiers in the other group were also given some of the money Zarcon had with him. They needed to be paid for their efforts, so it was just as well that Zarcon had given them some of their pay now.

The separate groups moved on up the road at a rapid pace. They knew their luck might not hold up much longer in their efforts to stay ahead of the witches. They did not go fast enough to cause undue curiosity of the other travelers, but they needed to make good progress. Each group stopped to rest and eat at different intervals, each group taking a turn in the lead. They were able to stop at small villages most nights and stay at the local inns. When they would come to a crossroads, Donavan was able to let the others know which way was best as they stopped at a local inn. He kept all of them on track as they journeyed. They were making good time.

Zarcon's soldiers looked like a group of men traveling together looking for work. Donavan and Jasmine told anyone who asked that they were husband and wife traveling with her father, Terrence. It was a somewhat unlikely story since Terrence was so much bigger than Jasmine, but they said her mother had been very small. Most people didn't care enough to ask further questions, and one look from Terrence convinced the overly curious that it was not a good idea to pry.

Zarcon told anyone who asked that he was Greta's father and that they had a guard with them since he was old and needed help frequently with traveling. People didn't seem to want to know any more about that either. Their travels went relatively smoothly. They all kept to themselves. Conversations were discouraged. They would eat a meal and head directly to their rooms for the night. They got up early and left right after breakfast. The innkeepers were grateful for the short stay since it left the rooms open for new travelers who might come by.

Donavan was practicing his magic with Jasmine every day. They would practice early in the morning before they left camp and then again as soon as they made camp that evening. Jasmine would ask him to concentrate on starting a fire in the fire pit. That was pretty basic magic. He tried and tried, but nothing ever seemed to be happening.

One morning, Donavan felt that Jasmine was pushing him a little too hard. His anger started to rise. He said the words Jasmine had taught him with anger in his heart, and one of the trees burst into flame.

"Donavan, how did you do that? I don't know anyone who can do that!"

"I'm not really sure. I was angry and said the words. I'm sorry. Is that bad?"

"Bad? You have so much more power than you know. This is a major breakthrough. I can't wait to tell Zarcon. You could be a great wizard in your own right."

"Come on. It can't be that big a deal. What if I can't do it again?"

"Well, let's try it. This time, try to make it a smaller fire, okay? We don't want to let everyone for fifty miles around know what you're doing."

Donavan thought about what he had just done. He let a little anger enter his words, and he was able to start a rather large fire in the fire pit. "Well, that's encouraging. At least I'm not burning the whole forest to the ground. I guess it is pretty amazing, isn't it?" Donavan was getting really excited about his power. Maybe he really did have something he could use to help against the witches.

"Yes, it is, Donavan. Let's try something else now. How about changing the appearance of something? What if you could change the color of your horse or the color of that flower? Would you try?"

"What would be the purpose?"

"Some forms of magic are related. If you can manage one form, you can probably do the same to all forms that are related. Do you see?"

"Well, yes, I guess so. What are the words that go with it?"

She told him what to say to change the color of one of the many flowers that grew at the side of the road. He said the words, but nothing happened. "Concentrate, Donavan. Really mean the words as you say them."

He tried again. This time, one of the petals turned from yellow to violet.

"Try harder!"

He looked at the flower and spoke to it with feeling he didn't realize he had until that moment. It really felt different as he said the words. The flower turned violet and it grew to twice its normal size.

"Donavan, what have you done?"

"I just said the words you taught me."

"Yes, but I didn't think you would get this far so quickly. Donavan, aren't you excited? You have so much power!" She gave him a big hug.

He hugged her back, and they held each other for a while. It felt so good to be close. Neither of them wanted it to end.

Finally, Jasmine pulled away. She was kind of embarrassed by her show of feelings. She looked at Donavan and could see that he felt the same way. They both smiled and stammered for a minute or two. Terrence smiled to himself. He was concerned that they were growing closer at a very inconvenient time. There was much to do, and they all needed to be aware of what was going on around them—not distracted by anything.

Donavan said, "You know, I've wanted to do that for a long time. I can't explain it, Jasmine, but it just feels good to be with you. I'm glad we have each other for now, but I guess we'd better stick to business for a while longer, don't you think?"

"Okay, but as soon as this is over, we will spend some time together, right?"

"You bet!"

They both knew there might not be a time after for either of them, but hope would keep them going when all else failed. The feelings that were developing between them would have to wait. Besides, Terrence was embarrassed. The old warhorse hadn't even thought about loving someone in years. He just kept Zarcon's troops trained every day. There just wasn't time for much else. Maybe he would take the time when this was over.

Zarcon, Greta, and Micah were making good time. They were nearly a mile ahead of the others. Zarcon said, "Greta, have you ever wondered if you have magic? Have you ever tried to find out if you can influence other people's emotions? I have felt that you could if you tried."

Greta was thoughtful a moment. "You know, I've wondered that myself a time or two. It seems that if I'm upset, those around me become more upset. On the other hand, if I calm myself and try to project that to others, it seems to work. Is that what you're talking about?"

"That's exactly what I'm talking about. Would you be willing to extend that potential power? What if you could give others the courage they thought they lacked? What if you could get people to get involved in the fight against the witches before they realized what they were doing and had time to think better of it?"

Greta thought for a minute. "What you are asking might be taking away their right to choose. I'm not willing to do that."

Zarcon smiled. "I'm actually glad to hear it. Maybe we should just stop at the courage part of it. It could make a difference in the outcome of the battle we're facing."

"Well, all right … since you put it that way. How do I practice that kind of thing? Is it a spell or something I have to project to others? Can you help me do it?"

"I believe it's a projection you do already. You just haven't extended your power to other emotions yet. Let's try it on some of the forest animals. Would that be acceptable?"

"Sure."

"Okay. See the rabbit over there?"

"Yes, the one the cat is about to have for lunch?"

"That would be the one. See if you can project courage to the rabbit … enough that he will fight back."

Greta concentrated on sending courage to the rabbit. Suddenly, the rabbit was up on its hind legs. He leaped onto the cat's back and started biting it on the neck. The cat was so startled that it shook the rabbit off and ran away.

Zarcon and Greta started to laugh. "That was impressive. That rabbit's life will never be the same. I wonder if it will teach other rabbits how to fight back." They both chuckled at the thought.

"This is exciting. Maybe I will be able to help you in your fight against the witches after all. Let's keep practicing as we go. Can we?"

"We certainly shall. I believe you have some excellent potential. It will be very interesting to find out what it is."

They rode on in silence for a while. Micah had watched it all and was feeling the first stirrings of hope for this seemingly hopeless mission. Maybe they did have a chance against the witches.

The soldiers in the third group were having an easy time of it. They rode their horses and looked for pretty girls as they traveled. It wasn't difficult to pretend not to be soldiers. For the first time in a long time, they could flirt with any young women who happened to travel in their direction. When the parents became suspicious, they just moved on. The days passed quickly for them. They remembered to keep a wary eye out for the witches, but they hadn't seen anything to worry about. They were becoming complacent, which was a very dangerous attitude when danger could lurk around the next bend in the road.

Synkana was half a day's journey away when they stopped for the night at a larger town. Caprisio was fifteen miles south of Synkana. Zarcon had heard of a well-known inn called the Blue Falcon. It was a large inn, and it would be easier for the group to meet there and not draw undue attention to their activities. Many larger groups stayed at the inn because it was so large and was just outside Synkana.

Jasmine, Donavan, Terrence, and Lantz arrived at the Blue Falcon first. They sat at one of the vacant tables and ordered dinner. There were no curious stares or questions as they walked in. They blended in with the rest of the evening crowd. There was a good mix of races and accents here. Many merchants were passing through on their way to or from Synkana. Soldiers were also in evidence in those troubled times.

It was another hour before Zarcon's small group arrived. They had fallen behind a bit when Zarcon grew tired. Zarcon had packed his red robe long ago. He looked like an old man in the company of his daughter and her guardians. Any who knew him would not have been fooled. He seemed to emanate power if a person were to come closer or look longer. He did his best to mask that, but he was not totally successful. People would walk by, and if they touched him, an uncomfortable feeling would pass through them. Most people had no idea what it meant, which was fortunate.

The last group of men came in as night fell. The others were getting nervous that they were so long in coming. As agreed upon, the group went directly to the innkeeper and asked for six rooms to accommodate the rest of their group, which would be in later that night. They took a table and ordered their dinners. They sat quietly and ate their meals. They teased the serving girls a little, but they did not draw undue attention to themselves.

The ale began to flow freely as the evening wore on. Some of the patrons were becoming rowdy. It was time for the three groups to fade upstairs to their respective rooms. The men had rented one of the larger rooms that connected with two others. It was quick thinking on their part because in made it very easy for them to meet during the night. As the inn became noisier, they were able to get together without being noticed. They went into the rooms two or three at a time.

When all were present, they began to plan their approach to Synkana. They all agreed that the witches must have taken the other route to the city. It was apparent that they had not actually been followed on the road they had taken. That might possibly mean that the witches were already waiting for them in Synkana. They had to assume that was the case.

One of the soldiers had spent some time talking with some of the people in the inn that night. He had asked if anyone had seen or heard of a pack of wolves in the area. One of the farmers he spoke to mentioned that there was a rumor in the next town of a pack that was harassing the sheep and taking several from the herds. The others were not surprised. It only confirmed what they had suspected: the witches were definitely in the area. No one asked after the witches themselves. Zarcon knew they would have spies who would be alert to anyone asking about them.

Zarcon said, "I fear that our efforts to mislead the witches have failed. I can't explain why I feel that way, but there it is. If we march into Synkana, the witches will surely meet us. We must hide or destroy the orb. It cannot fall into the hands of the witches ever again. It is capable of great destruction as you all know, but no one has ever heard of a way to destroy it. Therefore, in coming to Synkana, there is a way to hide the orb. It will require great magical powers to do so. I do not possess such power of myself. I believe that if we can combine the powers of those of us here, we will find a way. I have thought long and hard about it on this journey. I am hoping we can trick the witches into helping us destroy it—or at the very least sending it to another dimension.

"First we must draw the witches out. I can do that without much effort. I just have to let it be known that I am here. Of course, they are also looking for Jasmine. I'm sure they suspect that Donavan is with us as well. So, we will keep them guessing as long as we can. Jasmine will maintain possession of the orb. It seems most quiet with her. I fear that anyone with major magical powers would fall to its lure. I have felt it myself as we have journeyed. It is very powerful. Jasmine has powers—but not the destructive kind. Her power comes from her ability to protect rather than to destroy.

"I would have the rest of you men find places on the roofs of the buildings close to the central square where it is expected that we will meet up with the witches. Have your bows and arrows ready to fire on the witches when we meet up with them. I am worried about the wolves. Voltar will help alert us to their presence. He is large enough to take on the lead male, but the rest of you must be prepared to defend him and us against the rest of the pack. We have no idea how many wolves are left after this much time. I will draw a layout of the city so we can take up defensive positions. I am hoping there will be enough people around that the witches will hesitate to use all their powers against us.

"Donavan, you will use your power to help protect Jasmine from any spells the witches might throw at her. Stay close. Greta, you will use your newfound power to give the people courage to fight. I am hoping it won't be necessary, but we must be ready in case it will help. If all else fails, we must make sure Jasmine gets away with the orb. We cannot allow the witches to have it back under any circumstances. Do you all understand how important that is?"

All present nodded.

Donavan said, "I have learned some new magic since last we were together. I believe I have more to offer than ever before. Perhaps we can discuss how my new skills could be used against the witches."

Jasmine said, "Yes, Zarcon. He is amazing! I know you will be impressed with the progress we have made."

"Donavan, I am very pleased to hear this bit of news. What is it you have learned?"

"I have mastered the art of starting fires. I can even cause an explosion if I'm angry enough. I'm sorry to say that I blew up a tree when I was practicing. Jasmine taught me how to control it. I can also change the appearance of things. I changed the color of a flower to start. As we traveled, I was able to change our appearance more and more. It came in handy when we saw someone I used to know from the Wolf Wars coming toward us. When I got through with my own appearance, my own mother wouldn't have recognized me."

"Zarcon, it's true. He can do all that. I've been so excited to tell you all about it. The amazing thing is that he never suspected he could do any of it. I believe he could become a great wizard, maybe even like you, Zarcon."

Zarcon smiled. "You know, I'm getting old. This expedition we've been on has taken a toll on me. If we survive this, I would very much like to train Donavan in the magic arts. There is much he could learn. I suspected he had the talent, but he was not in a condition to listen until now. Thank you so much, Jasmine, for helping him see his ability. This is marvelous news indeed."

The group spent the next two hours making plans for their defense against the witches. Zarcon drew a map of the city of Synkana. He positioned the soldiers in defensive positions on the roofs around the central square. He showed Donavan and Jasmine where to hide and where he and Greta would enter.

Terrence wasn't happy with that, but he knew better than to speak against Zarcon's plan. He gave a few suggestions, however, which Zarcon was at least willing to accept.

Micah was assigned to watch the horses and protect them from any harm that might come from the witches, their men, or the wolves.

"Well, does everyone understand what they are to do once we get to Synkana? The tricky part is going to be getting the witches to help us transport the orb to another dimension. We must not fail. Are there any questions?"

No one had any. The plan was simple, but it appeared to be effective. They would find out how effective it was in the next day or two. They decided it would be best to continue to travel in smaller groups so the witches would not get word of their arrival until they planned for them to.

Everyone went to their rooms for the night. They watched at the door to make sure no one was in the hallway before they left the main room or the two side rooms connected to it. They would need their rest for the coming battle. They decided not to set out too early in the morning. Since they were only a few miles from Synkana, they could get a little more rest before they had to leave the comfortable inn.

It was difficult to sleep. They began to realize that it was possible that not all of them would survive the next day. It was something they couldn't dwell on. It could incapacitate them, and it was sobering.

Jasmine and Donavan spoke of what they would need to do. They tried to avoid thinking about the possibility that one of them might not make it. They had come to realize that they shared more than just friendship during their travels. They dared not make any commitments, but they did realize how precious life is. They were trying to relax on Jasmine's bed.

Finally, as Donavan made ready to go to his room for the night, Jasmine said, "I can't bear to be alone tonight. Please stay with me. I need you to hold me while I sleep."

Donavan hesitated. He knew he would also be lonely if he went to his room. He held her close. It gave both of them great comfort, and they were able to sleep through the rest of the night.

They woke with the sun streaming through their window. They jumped out of bed, realizing it must be late. They went out into the hall to see where the others were.

The rest of the group had slept in as well. Zarcon, Greta, and Terrence were just leaving their rooms. The soldiers were finally emerging from each of the rooms they occupied. As they started down the hall to the dining area, they were all smiling. They had thought that no one would sleep.

Zarcon said, "Greta, your mischievous look wouldn't have anything to do with the fact that all of us slept late, would it? You couldn't possibly have been practicing, could you?"

Greta smiled. "Well, it worked, didn't it? I must say that it worked a little better than I had anticipated. I hope you don't mind." "Mind? I think it was a marvelous thing to do. Now we'll all be rested for what we must face today. I am very grateful for your foresight. Thank you, Greta." She smiled again.

They separated into smaller groups as they entered the dining hall. No one seemed to notice them. The dining hall was full. Each of the groups found a table and ordered breakfast. Their meal consisted of roast pork, fried potatoes, eggs, and a selection of local fruits. There was also a cool pitcher of juice available for each table. They all ate with gusto. There was no telling when they would have the time to eat like this again.

While they were eating, a hunter came in and talked about how scarce the game was in the area. He had noticed the tracks of several large wolves in the forest over the past week. He asked if anyone else had seen signs of them. One of the farmers said that some sheep were taken a few nights ago. There was some discussion about what could be done about the wolves. No one seemed to have an answer. The talk gradually dwindled and moved on to other topics.

Then, one by one, as they finished their meals, Zarcon and the others went back to their rooms to pack. It was even more important now that they didn't call attention to themselves. If the wolves were so close, it was time to move on and take care of business before any more damage would be done to the area. The witches must be stopped, and the only way to do that would be to get on with the battle.

The packing was done in moments. They gathered as groups at the stable, packed their horses, and left. They hoped that it looked like some people who had decided to leave at the same time. They tried to act calm and unhurried. As they looked around, no one seemed to be paying any special attention to them.

They didn't notice a man in black hiding in the stable and listening to every noise and word that was said. He was very curious about the group. He was being paid a very fine price to report anything unusual to his employer. He would surely report the group of people who seemed to be going the same way at the same time.

He counted the members of the group and concluded that the old man might be Zarcon. The small woman was in another group, but traveling at the same time might mean that she was Jasmine. If so, there was a good chance that she carried the thing his employer was after. He smiled to think that he might be so close to the blue orb. If what he suspected were true, there would be a fine reward in store for his information.

If Zarcon's group had noticed him, they would have been very fearful indeed. The man was an agent of the prince of Landpur. What Curzon would do with the information was not going to be healthy for any of them. The question would be whether Zarcon and his people could take care of the witches before this man could get word to Curzon, but Zarcon was unaware.

The man was from Landpur, and he was nicknamed Black Hawk. He always wore black to blend into the shadows. His allegiance was to the highest bidder, but he was currently working for Curzon. It was a temporary assignment. Black Hawk only had loyalty to himself and the gold he made with his formidable skills. He was highly trained in many weapons, including swords, crossbows, spears, and knives. He knew more ways to kill a person than anyone else. He could kill with his hands or feet. He had learned his arts through observation and from a master. He studied with Clement of Landpur for many years, learning all the ways a man could kill another. He learned his spying skills when he was a younger man and had to survive by stealing. He learned to climb almost anything and could open almost any lock. He could be in and out of a room before anyone knew he was there.

Black Hawk had decided that, if the information he carried were of real value, he would sell it to the highest bidder. He had a feeling that it would be worth much more than Curzon was paying. He would bide his time, watch these people, and see what he might learn of value to himself and someone with lots of money to give. Black Hawk also had his werecat to keep him company at night and as he traveled the lonely roads. The cat stayed close—but out of sight of any other travelers. She had more than once saved his life when an animal would have attacked him in the night. He was prepared for whatever Zarcon's group might deliver.

He saddled his horse and rode out behind Zarcon's group. He followed far enough behind that he would not draw attention to himself. He kept to the side of the road, near the shadows of the trees. The people who passed him were afraid to look at him. He was tall and very thin. He had sharp features and thin, cruel lips. His eyes were the worst part. No one could bear his silver-gray gaze for long. There was death in that gaze.

Zarcon was glad they were on their way. They would finally have the situation resolved one way or the other within the next day or two. The day was bright and unseasonably warm. He chatted with Greta and Terrence while he rode along. There were many people on the road this morning. It made Zarcon nervous. If someone were following them, it would be difficult to tell. He kept a wary eye on those going in the same direction. He tried to watch those coming up from behind as well. It was difficult to do that without drawing attention to the fact. He had them stop frequently so he could keep an eye on anyone who kept the same pace. He didn't notice anyone and began to feel more at ease. He whispered to the soldiers to keep a look out as he passed them once. He hoped they would do so.

Voltar followed Zarcon. He would alert them if the wolves came within two miles. He was grateful for Voltar's sense of smell. He was hyperalert as they traveled. He had stayed with the horses when they were in a village or town. He followed them through the trees as they traveled on the roads. It would be difficult to identify him as belonging to Zarcon for that reason. Yet when they camped for the night, Voltar was next to Zarcon for the whole night. He would not leave his side unless Zarcon sent him out to scout the area. Zarcon had grown to depend on Voltar for many things in the years they were together, but like Zarcon, Voltar was aging and slowing down. There was a lot of white in Voltar's muzzle, but he was strong and had almost as much endurance as ever.

They had just rounded a curve in the road when Voltar suddenly stopped and started growling. It was a deep rumble in his chest. His hackles were raised, and his teeth were bared. The group looked ahead and saw what looked like a very large cat. It was crouched to spring at Voltar.

Zarcon decided it was time to intervene. He said a few words of a spell and waved his arms at the cat.

Just as it was about to spring, it looked at Voltar like he was the biggest monster it had ever seen and sprang away, howling into the forest. "Just a little trick I learned. I couldn't very well have Voltar hurt over some silly cat, could I?"

The others were stunned by what they had just seen. They didn't know whether to laugh or throw up.

Greta gave him a hug. "If that cat had attacked Voltar, it would have been a disaster for us all. I'm so glad you acted so quickly to end the danger before it really became such. Thanks from all of us, Zarcon."

"Well, if a wizard can't help at a time like this, what good is he?"

Everyone smiled. No one would ever think Zarcon was of no value, but they were certainly grateful for his powers.

"What was that exactly? I've never seen a cat so large." Greta was very concerned about the surprise attack, especially where there were so many other people.

Zarcon replied, "It looked like one of the big cats that are known to inhabit the Backlash Mountains. Donavan, would you agree?"

"I have seen cats that large, but there was something very unusual about that one that I have never seen before. The color was all wrong. It should have been tan with black-tipped ears and tail. That one was more golden without the black tips. Also, the snout was too long. It almost looked like a very large fox, but we don't have anything like that in the mountains where I lived. I wonder where it came from. Do you have any ideas, Jasmine?"

Jasmine was thoughtful, trying to remember something from a long time ago. "You know, I think I heard of a cat like that once in the Landpur hills. Do you think someone might have brought it with them? Could it have been trained to attack? I didn't think you could train a cat, but stranger things have been known to happen in Landpur."

Zarcon said, "I think you may be on to something, Jasmine. Remember the man named Black Hawk who was asking about us at the inn? Didn't one of you suggest that he had a large cat that traveled with him? I would not have thought it was something so large. Have any of you heard of that?"

Micah said, "All the rumors I've heard are very bad. Apparently he is a spy or assassin, depending on what skills you are looking for. He works for the highest bidder. He has no loyalty—only to himself. If he is in the area, we are in big trouble. If anyone can find us, he can. The trouble with him is that we don't know who he'll sell the information to. It could be that Prince Curzon is just fishing for information—or the witches have hired him. Maybe he's working on his own. We can't know any of that without catching him, and I would not want to do that. He is far too dangerous."

Donavan said, "What if we set a trap for him, assuming it is him? We need to know for sure and deal with him before we try to take on the witches, don't you think? If he gets to the witches before we do, it would ruin the surprise party we have planned."

Zarcon looked concerned and said, "You have an excellent point, Donavan. What are you thinking?"

"I would like to have a few of us walk ahead of the rest. We'll find a place to hide and wait for him, and then we'll ambush him as he passes. I have enough magic now to help if needed. What do you think, Zarcon?"

"Sounds like a good plan to me. Take a one of the soldiers with you. Will you need anything else?"

"I'll take Micah with me. He's good with a bow and can hide in the trees. I'll be behind the trees and try to take him by surprise. Anyone have questions?"

No one spoke.

Jasmine walked up to him and said, "Donavan, you will be very careful, won't you? I couldn't bear it if—"

Donavan said, "I'll be careful." He was warmed by the concern in her eyes. He gave her a quick kiss and headed off up the road.

Jasmine was surprised at the kiss, however quick it had been. Her knees went a bit weak.

Black Hawk saw the group stop as they were making the next turn. He was hoping that meant that his cat was busy with them. Then he heard the dog growling. He was just about to run forward and watch his cat take out that dog when he heard his cat howling and running away. This was unexpected. His cat had never backed down from a fight. He moved further into the brush at the side of the road and waited to see what would happen next. He was fearful that the cat might have given him away. There were people who knew that he had the cat.

He kept watching the group as they rounded the next bend in the road. When they were out of sight, he moved ahead carefully. The forest was rather thick at this point near the road and would be for the next mile or two. He must keep them in sight. As he caught up to them—at least close enough to see what they were doing without being seen—he noticed that some of the men had gone ahead. He just made out their backs going around the next bend. This made him nervous. What were they planning?

He walked ahead and stayed to the side of the road as usual. He would have been difficult to see—even if they knew he was there. He watched the group move on. The dog was running ahead and barking at them to hurry. They were all having a great time, laughing and talking like they had no cares. He was not happy. He would be thrilled if Curzon would allow him to kill at least some of them. He specialized in slow, painful deaths. If they had done anything to his cat, they would pay for it—whether he got paid to do it or not.

Donavan found a copse of trees that was about a mile up the road from where they had met up with the cat. It was two bends in the road, so there would be no visual of them from where they had been either.

Micah climbed up into an oak tree about ten yards into the trees. He had a good line of sight all the way to the road so he could watch Donavan and look out for Black Hawk if he was following them. They had decided they didn't really want to kill him. They wanted to find out what he was after and who he was working for. It seemed fairly obvious that he wished them no good since he had sent his cat after them.

Donavan hide behind a large maple tree that had to be at least fifty years old. It was just off the road about ten feet, and he was partially concealed by the underbrush that was next to the road and close to the tree. In about ten minutes, the others walked past them. They didn't see them and kept going as they had planned. Now, the wait for Black Hawk began.

Several people walked or rode past them, but it only took a moment for a man in black to step quietly through the trees along the side of the road. It had to be Black Hawk. When the man was alongside Donavan, he stepped out from the tree and said, "Sir, may I presume that your name is Black Hawk?"

Black Hawk spun toward him and drew his knife. Micah saw him, drew the arrow, and fired at Black Hawk's arm. He hit him in the back of his right arm, and the knife went flying. Donavan grabbed the man's throat and pushed him into the trunk of the tree he was standing by. Black Hawk hit his head hard on the bark. "You have two choices here.

You can either talk to me now—or you can die this instant. What do you prefer?"

Black Hawk struggled for a moment, but Donavan was very strong and kept his grip on the man's throat. Finally, Black Hawk realized that the more he struggled, the tighter Donavan's grip would get. He was blacking out when he finally gave up the fight and raised his hands in surrender. "Get his weapons, Micah."

"With pleasure, Donavan."

Micah had climbed down from the tree as soon as he hit Black Hawk. He patted the man down and came up with several interesting weapons. Some he had never seen before. He said, "My, my, Mr. Hawk, you certainly are prepared! I wouldn't want to meet you in a dark alley."

Black Hawk sneered at him and locked eyes with Donavan, "So, you're Donavan. I've heard rumors about you. I've also got many clients looking for you. Could we strike a deal?"

"That depends. Tell me who you're working for first and what you want."

"I can't do that. It's against my principles to divulge that information. Besides, it would no doubt get me killed."

"Then we can't deal, can we?"

"Aren't you even going to listen to my proposal? I could make us both rich. You have information I need, and I have information I'm sure would benefit you and your friends."

Donavan said, "What do you know of my friends? You'd better talk fast—or Micah will put many holes in your pathetic body."

"I know that you travel with Zarcon and Jasmine. I know that the witches aren't the only ones who would pay dearly to know that you are in the area. Now can we deal?"

Donavan was very skeptical of Black Hawk's words. He was pretty sure only the witches would be interested in his group, but it would be much safer to find out what Black Hawk knew than to discount it out of hand. "I am not interested in any sort of deal with you, but I am interested in what you know. Will you give me your word of honor that if I release you, you will not harm me or anyone else here?"

Black Hawk smiled to himself. It was exactly what he was hoping for. Once he was released, all he had to do was kill this idiot and be on his way. He wasn't worried about the other man. He obviously had no power over him, and he was too fast for his bow and arrows. He said, "I give you my word."

Donavan loosened his hold just enough for Black Hawk to jerk away. He drew the slim knife he kept up his sleeve and was about to stab Donavan when Jasmine threw a knife into his back. She had followed Donavan, not trusting that he would be safe—with or without Micah.

Black Hawk had a look of complete surprise on his face as he hit the ground. He did not move.

"Sorry, Donavan. I was worried and followed you. I hope you aren't upset that he's dead."

"Upset? You just saved my life—and you wonder if I'm upset? You're amazing! He was trying to tell me that there were more people than the witches who are interested in our whereabouts. I seriously doubt that, but we'll have to play it very carefully from here on out. I suspect he might have been referring to Prince Curzon in Landpur. If that is the case, we really do need to be wary. He is very powerful and would not hesitate to sell us out to the witches. The good thing is that Black Hawk is gone and can't report to anyone now. I do wonder about his cat though."

"Me, too. I'm not sure of the cat's loyalty to him. I have never heard of a loyal cat, but they were together off and on for many years from the stories. Hopefully, the cat will never come back."

Micah was still trying to recover from the shock of Black Hawk trying to kill Donavan and Jasmine saving them all. "Jasmine, I am beginning to understand where all the stories about you come from.

You really are amazing. I was about to shoot the guy with an arrow, but I knew it would be too late to save Donavan even then. You saw that coming, didn't you? I was much too trusting. I hope never to make a mistake like that again."

Donavan, Jasmine, and Micah walked out of the trees and headed for the rest of the group. It would take them some time to catch up, but the walk would help dissipate some of the adrenaline from the situation. They left Black Hawk where he had fallen. It was far enough off the trail that no one would see him for days, maybe years, especially with his black clothing. In death, he would continue to blend in with the shadows.

The three of them caught up with the others after about an hour of walking. They mounted their horses and rode on with the rest of the group.

Zarcon asked, "So how did it go with our friend Black Hawk? I assume you saw him?"

"We saw him all right." Donavan told the others what had happened.

Zarcon said, "It was fortunate that Jasmine worried about you. I was unsure whether it was wise for her to go. Now I'm more than grateful that she did." He turned to Jasmine. "Excellent work, as usual, Jasmine."

"Thank you, Zarcon."

"It's a good thing we are so close to Synkana. I would be much more concerned if we had far to go. I'm wondering about the wolves. We really haven't seen anything of them yet. Do you think they have gone on to Synkana to be with the witches? If so, should we be concerned about that?"

Donavan answered, "I really don't know. I have been listening to any conversations I could get close to. There has been no mention of the wolves at all, which is unnerving in a way. There would be some rumor by now if they had moved on past those villages. Could they have gone to the forest around Synkana without anyone noticing the passage of a pack of wolves?"

Jasmine said, "They tend to travel at night. It is possible, especially if they didn't kill any animals as they passed through."

Micah said, "I lived in an area with wolves for many years. They would move through the forest at night, and no one would see them for days. They always came back to their territory. These wolves are probably completely different. They are under the spell of the witches and probably go wherever the witches go. At least that is what I suspect."

Zarcon said, "You're probably right, Micah. They could no doubt make it all the way to Synkana without taking down any animals if they knew they were going to be fed when they got there. I hate to think what that might mean. We are now about three miles from Synkana, and Voltar hasn't sniffed out the wolves yet. Let us hope he won't until we are closer."

After another mile or so, Voltar started to growl. His hackles were raised in anger. It was the warning they had feared for the entire journey. The wolves were close now—probably somewhere close to the two-mile limit Voltar could detect. If they were closer, Voltar would have started barking. They rode on, watching Voltar very carefully. It seemed to confirm that the wolves were closer to Synkana.

The group separated into their smaller groups as they neared Synkana. They were still concerned about the witches recognizing them as one large group. They watched for anyone who seemed unusually interested in their movements, but no one was. The people traveling into Synkana with them were more interested in their own problems at the time. Voltar was getting more and more anxious as they neared the city, but he did not give any sign that the wolves were closing on them.

Finally, they saw the city gates in the distance. The large city had three-foot-thick walls around it. The gates were ironwood with brass hinges and braces for the ironwood bar that would hold the gate shut at night or in times of attack. In addition, there was a moat and a drawbridge. The moat was at least twenty feet deep with spikes at the bottom to discourage anyone foolish enough to try to cross it. The drawbridge was down during the day and was about thirty feet wide. This allowed the many travelers and merchants to get into and out of the city without crowding the bridge.

Zarcon and his group blended in with the rest of the travelers and merchants. They walked through the gates and into the city without a problem. They split up as they entered and found rooms in separate inns as they had agreed to do. They would meet at the Flaming Orange on the east side of the city near the wall. The tavern was not so large that they would have no privacy, but it was large enough to admit larger groups without notice.

It was just past midday when they were finally able to meet at the tavern. They went in and found a large table at the back of the main room. The soldiers took a separate table so they could watch for anyone too interested in them. They needed to go over their plans, have a meal, and get ready to face the witches.

Getting Ready for Battle

Now that Zora and the others were settled in their inn, they were about to send for Magg to come to them. Then they realized she could never get to them in time. The more they thought about the coming battle, the clearer reality finally seemed to be setting in. Zora realized she hadn't thought this through as thoroughly as she should have. Magg would not be with her for the coming battle.

Zora was getting concerned. They had not heard anything that would indicate that Zarcon's group was in the area. They had spies throughout the Synkana region. There were no reports of any large groups headed their way. She realized her mistake. They would probably have broken up into smaller groups as they traveled so they would not attract undue attention. She had been an idiot not to think of that. To top it off, Zarcon would not be traveling in his red robe of office. How could she have been so foolish? She would have to decide what to do. They could arrive in Synkana at any moment. She had no idea how far they may have been behind them. "Sisters, I think we have a problem. I had not figured that Zarcon's little group of thieves would come in smaller groups. They could already be here. What should we do? The wolves are out hunting and won't be back until tomorrow morning.

I'm hoping that will be soon enough, but what if it isn't? I have spies all over the country—but not many here in the city. How can we find out where they are?"

Heleren said, "I think we will know soon enough if they are here. I don't think they will wait long to let us know. Like us, I think they want to get this over with."

Anesthia said, "I certainly hope so. This is really getting on my nerves."

The witches were anxious to end it and get the orb back. They didn't seem to realize what was going on. They could all be dead by nightfall. They seemed to have no fear.

Myshella looked around the room and said, "I wonder where they will meet. They must meet as a group someplace in the city. Do we have spies we could send out to all the taverns and inns in the area large enough to hide a large group? There couldn't be more than a dozen of them."

"Great idea. How much time do you think we have to get them together and send them out before it's too late?" Zora asked.

"Send out what we can get here in the next hour and have them go from inn to inn and tavern to tavern until they find something. That shouldn't be so hard."

"Okay. Each of us has spies in the city. Let's get out there and talk to as many as we can find right now. When you have spoken to at least three, come back here. We'll report what we know."

Myshella, Heleren, Anesthia, and Zora left the room. They split up and went to the places where they had stationed their spies. Each of them was surprised to see the witches out and looking for them. None had anything to report since they were looking for a large group with a wizard in red among them. Now that the witches had refined the search, they headed out one at a time until the witches had found at least three of their own spies. They should cover most of the city within the hour.

The witches had told the spies to meet back at their inn as soon as they found anything, but regardless, they were to be back within the hour. The witches returned to the inn and waited.

Half an hour later, one of the spies returned with a message. "I found the group you are looking for. They actually found me first. They had been watching for us. They told me to tell you to meet them at the city's central square at dawn tomorrow. They want to talk."

Zora screamed, "Talk? What do they mean? I want the orb back, and I want it back now! What are they thinking? It's our orb after all!" Sparks flew from her fingertips and started a fire on the opposite wall. She struggled desperately to regain control of her rage, but she could only mumble some particularly foul curses. Anesthia ran to the fire and threw water on it from the washbasin. She had never seen Zora so angry.

The spy became very afraid and started to back out of the room. He didn't get far.

Zora shrieked, "Where do you think you're going? I'm not finished with you yet. You must take a message back to them." She gradually calmed her voice enough to say, "Tell them that we will meet with them … but not to talk. We just want the orb back … and maybe we will let them live." She had a particularly evil smirk.

The spy bowed his head and said, "I shall do as you say." He left very quickly.

The witches were enraged at the nerve of Zarcon and his band of thieves. Now that they knew Zarcon and his band were in town, they had to prepare a plan to deal with them.

Zora was still in a towering rage. "We will not allow even one of them to live. We will eliminate them all from the face of the earth. Now, what do you think we should do when we see them in the square? I say we just blow them away, but that won't get us the orb. So we must plan carefully to get the orb and then blow them out of existence, but how?"

Heleren said, "I vote we just walk to the meeting place, listen to what they have to say, bargain for the orb, and promise them whatever they want. Then, once we have it, we eliminate them. Simple, but effective." Her smile would freeze the heart of a snake.

Zora looked at Heleren as though she had just grown another head. "And, dear Heleren, you really think they'll just hand it over with no tricks? I know it won't be that easy. They've got something much more than that up their sleeves. I know Zarcon better than that. He's up to something, and I don't like the smell of it at all. We really don't have a choice. We'll meet with them, see what happens, and react accordingly. You all remember your most horrible spells, do you not?"

The other witches said, "Yes, of course."

"Then meet me just before dawn. We need to consider some options. I will send a runner to let the men know to meet us as well. We all need to be together on this important occasion."

After they calmed down a bit, they went to their rooms for the night. They had their own concerns about the coming battle and spent a sleepless night. Just before dawn, they rose and gathered together.

Zora said, "Well, today is the day we regain the orb, my sisters. Are you ready to face your future as queens together? Are you ready to rule the world? I am ready to do battle. Are you?"

Anesthia, Heleren, and Myshella were eager to begin the battle as well. They all knew what they needed to do when they got to the square. Their men arrived and were prepared.

Cardeegan was anxious to face Donavan again. It would be a good day to fight. The other men were ready to get it over with. They were not really motivated to help the witches, but they knew they would not live to see another day if they did not. That was something they were all aware of.

Zora and the other witches left the inn and called their men to join them, and went out into the city. None of them took into account that without the orb their powers were diminishing.

16

Fair Warning

Zarcon and the others had spent a few days making final preparations and plans for the coming battle with the witches. They knew that Zora and the other witches had spies in the city. They were fairly certain that they would be around soon, looking for them. They decided that the best defense would be to get the witches out into the open. The sooner, the better. Zarcon had made certain that everyone knew his or her part in the defense and ultimate destruction of the orb. They felt ready for the witches when one of Zora's spies came into their inn and started asking obvious questions about them. Zarcon had called the man over and started a conversation with him. He finally got the man to admit he was asking on behalf of Zora. Zarcon told him to give Zora a message. He was to tell her that he would meet her in the central square at dawn to have a conversation about the orb. He knew in his heart that it would only serve to enrage Zora and the other witches, but that was exactly what he wanted. He knew that Zora was almost completely insane from lust for the orb. He was relatively certain it would make her more likely to make mistakes.

With some satisfaction, he sent Zora's spy on his merry way to deliver his message to Zora. He wished he could be a fly on the wall when it was delivered. He thought there would be fireworks if she lost control. He did hope not, however, since it might mean damage to the city of Synkana. He and his group would watch for such things nevertheless.

Zarcon returned to his group after the spy left and told them what he had done. Jasmine and Greta were sure that what Zarcon had done would cause Zora endless rage and frustration. Like him, they hoped it would anger Zora and the other witches enough that they would make mistakes. Greta had been practicing her ability to affect the moods and feelings of others as they traveled there. As she practiced, her power was getting stronger. She could now affect larger groups of people. She hoped that she would be able to motivate the people of Synkana to help them when they were needed.

Donavan had also found that he had great powers as he had practiced. He could block spells and send much of the power back to the sender, which was unheard of in circles of wizards. There had not been a wizard who could do such a thing since Xyrene. No one told Donavan of this, but Zarcon was somewhat fearful that he could have such power in such a short period of time. He hoped he lived long enough to help Donavan learn to control it and use it for good. He was confident about Donavan's good heart but not his maturity in using magic. He was also confident that Donavan's magic would be the deciding factor in this last battle for the orb. Between them, they had much more power than the witches. He had not been so confident at the beginning of this adventure. He was amazed at how much things had changed in such a short time.

Zarcon gathered his men and talked with them about their positions for the battle. They would line the roofs of the inns near the central square for the meeting. If there were any signs of treachery, the men were to fire on the witches. They were also told to watch for Zora's soldiers and make sure they were incapacitated if need be. Zarcon was confident that Voltar would warn them if the wolves came. Plans were made for what would be done if they did.

Zarcon sent everyone to bed early so that they would be rested for the battle at dawn. Greta helped him to bed and sent comforting feelings and thoughts his way so that he might be able to at least rest. She also used her powers to help the others relax. It would be a long night, but it would pass all too quickly when dawn came.

Donavan and Jasmine spent the night in the same room to comfort each other and hope for a future together. They curled up like spoons and held each other all night. Jasmine had never felt so comforted and so safe.

Donavan had never felt so close to another person. He had loved his first wife, but it had not felt as good as this. They spoke quietly of the things they must do in the morning, but they did not discuss anything about the future. They did not want to jinx it. They held those things close in their hearts.

Morning came early and found them up and ready for action. Zarcon's group met in the inn's common room and had a light breakfast to prepare for what was to come. They ate quietly and tried to contain the anxiety they all felt about what would happen.

When they were finished with their meal and were ready to leave the inn, Zarcon gave them some encouragement. "This morning will decide the fate of so many by so few. Stay strong and we will prevail against the evil that is the witches."

In their hearts, they were ready to face whatever fate brought them.

The witches made their way to the central square and looked for Zarcon. They were so enraged by what Zarcon had said and done that they could hardly contain themselves. Zora knew in her heart that she would win this day and get their precious orb back. It was meant to be that she and her coven would rule the world. Nothing must stand in the way of their destiny. They didn't wait long.

Zarcon and Greta appeared on the opposite side of the square. He was holding up a black velvet bag with a round object inside. "We have the orb, as you know. What are you willing to give up for it?"

"We are not willing to give up anything for it. It is ours!" Zora was enraged at the effrontery of the man.

"Then you shall not have it, Zora. One must sacrifice for what one wants most in this life. We have had this orb long enough to know that you shall not have it."

Zora was outraged. She said, "If you think you can keep me from my precious orb, you are sadly mistaken. I will have what is mine!"

She began a spell to incinerate Zarcon where he stood. She was pretty sure it would not affect the orb. The other witches joined her.

Unknown to the witches, Jasmine and Donavan were across the square with the real orb in a plain burlap bag that included other articles to disguise its shape. The witches didn't notice them.

Zora sensed something close at hand with real power in it, but she was too consumed with rage to realize what it meant.

Donavan began chanting quietly in response to the witches. He created a counterspell that would direct their power to the orb as planned. Jasmine had set it down closer to the witches, which was dangerous but necessary. The witches released their spell toward Zarcon and the bag, but it suddenly veered toward the real orb close to the witches. They were shocked that this could happen. They had never seen anything like it.

Donavan increased the power of the spell.

Zarcon started his own spell. It joined them all and changed the working just enough to enter the orb and send it to another dimension. The real orb vanished in a bolt of lightning that went up into the sky and flashed once before it disappeared.

It took a moment for the witches to realize what had happened. They were in a state of shock. They all began screaming. Zora screamed at Zarcon and turned to Donavan. "What have you done? What have you done? My beautiful orb can't be gone!"

Zarcon said softly, "Oh, Zora, but it is. Your plans are over. You will never possess the orb again."

Zora raised her hands to cast another spell at Zarcon. Donavan sent out his spell that blocked hers before it could do any damage and sent it back to her. She was just able to duck before she was hit. When she realized Donavan was doing it to her, she yelled, "Not you again! I thought I was rid of you and that horrible freak Jasmine. I can't stand it!"

Before anyone could stop her, she drew a knife and threw it at Jasmine. One of the soldiers on the rooftop let an arrow fly. It hit Zora in the chest and threw her aim off just enough that the knife only grazed Jasmine's arm. Zora was dead in the middle of the square. Her own blood started pooling beneath her. The people in the square started to cheer.

The other three witches looked at each other and tried to conjure a curse for Zarcon and the others, but their powers were greatly diminished after the orb was gone. They hadn't realized how much the orb had bolstered their strength until then.

The soldiers who were supposed to protect the witches saw Zarcon's soldiers surrounding them, realized what was happening, and ran to their horses. Even Cardeegan could see the futility of staying now that Zora was dead. The men ran off in terror, not wanting to find out what the other witches would do to them. It was their chance to get out of the situation they had endured for so long. They were gone before anyone could stop them.

When the witches realized they couldn't make enough magic to harm those who had wronged them, they decided to run. They couldn't imagine anyone killing Zora. They didn't know what else to do. They knew they couldn't win without hope of getting the orb back.

Greta was alarmed to see them fleeing. She sent out courage to the people around the square to go find them and bring them to justice. About twenty of the men ran after the witches, yelling that they would not let them go. It was time to take action against them. Voltar started barking and growling. He could sense the wolves coming. Zarcon's men on the rooftops nocked their arrows and prepared to fight. The wolves came running into the square and found Zora's body on the cobblestones. The big gray male forgot about Voltar and started to howl. It was the most mournful sound anyone had heard. Then he suddenly turned and attacked Voltar. The other wolves started circling him. The men let their arrows fly into the wolf pack, taking out two more wolves. The other wolves saw what was happening and ran from the square. They clearly had enough. The big gray wolf finally realized that he had no mistress and no pack and left with his tail between his legs. Voltar had also wounded him in the fight. Voltar barked and growled to send the wolf away. He ran to Zarcon to guard him in case he was needed.

Donavan held Jasmine close while Zarcon came running over. "Let me see what happened."

"She is only grazed, but I fear there may be poison on the blade of the knife. Jasmine has fainted. Her pulse is weak, and she's panting."

Zarcon opened one of her eyes and checked her pulse. "You are right. Let's get her into the inn over there. I will do all I can to counteract the poison."

They carried her to the inn and the innkeeper—who had been watching everything—showed them to the nearest empty room. He told them they could have it as long as they needed it.

Zarcon went to work and sent tendrils of power through her body. He found the poison and identified it. He had brought his bag of potions with him. That was what the witches thought was the orb. He pulled out the antidote and poured it between Jasmine's lips. She was barely able to swallow it. She was fading rapidly. It was a very potent, fast-acting poison.

Donavan sat on the side of the bed. He felt helpless. This was not something he had any power over. He said, "Jasmine, this is Donavan. I'm here. Please stay with me. You know how I need you. I can't live alone again. You have meant so much to me. Please stay."

Greta sat in a chair and sent out feelings of peace and comfort to Donavan and Jasmine. Greta knew that Jasmine would need to relax for the antidote work. If she fought it, she would waste valuable energy and might not survive the cure.

Donavan held Jasmine's hand and kept talking to her. He did not leave her side all night. They brought dinner in so that he could eat, but he refused. "It will just make me sick. I'm too upset to eat." The next morning, Jasmine seemed to be a little better. Her breathing was quieter and more even. She wasn't panting anymore. Greta's spell seemed to have calmed her. Greta also spooned a bit of soup between Jasmine's lips occasionally so she would not dehydrate.

Donavan was so relieved to see her improve that he almost collapsed. But he would not leave her side.

The next two days were much the same. Jasmine gradually improved. She was very weak from the poison and needed time to heal. Donavan spent his time by her side and kept talking to her to let her know he was there and loved her. However, he ate so little and rested only in small snatches.

Finally, on the second day, Zarcon told him to go rest. He would be sick himself if he did not do so. He assured Donavan that Jasmine was much better and was not going to die any time soon.

Donavan was so exhausted he couldn't argue with that. So he went to the next room to get some sleep. He was able to sleep for several hours in complete exhaustion. The next morning found him at

Jasmine's side holding her hand. Later that day he fell fast asleep in his chair.

A few hours before nightfall, Zarcon woke him quietly. "Donavan, Jasmine is moaning in her sleep. It looks like she might be coming around."

Donavan shook his head and was instantly awake.

Jasmine was just coming around. "Where am I? Where's Donavan? I'm so thirsty."

Donavan held her hand and kissed it. "I'm here, Jasmine. I'm here. I'm so happy to see you awake. It's been a rough time for all of us."

"What happened?"

"Zora threw a knife at you. It just grazed your arm, but it was tipped with poison. Zarcon had the antidote, but the poison was very fast. We were so worried. Greta was able to help you relax so the antidote could work better. We've just been waiting for you to wake up. Don't ever do this to me again. I've been scared out of my mind. Jasmine, I must have you with me forever. Please marry me. I love you more than I can say."

Jasmine smiled. "Well, let me think a minute … hmmm … sounds good to me. Of course I'll marry you! Just don't ask me to live in the mountains. I've had enough of that for a very long while."

Donavan laughed. "You know—I'm inclined to agree." He bent over Jasmine and gave her a long, lingering kiss. "That's a promise of more to come. I can hardly wait to share my life with you, Jasmine. It has been such an adventure being with you."

Jasmine said, "I love you, Donavan, and I want to be with you too. Do you think I could maybe have something to drink and something to eat? I'm really, really hungry."

Zarcon said, "Well now, you really are feeling better! You've been through an awful lot in the past few days. Greta and I will bring you something to eat right away. There's some warm soup and fresh bread in the kitchen. We'll be right back. The rest of you will just have to leave these two alone for a while. Let them eat and talk alone together. Come on, all of you."

Terrence had been standing just inside the door, worrying about Jasmine. He was so glad to see her smile again. It had been hard to see her hurt and not be able to help. It was his job to protect, and he felt that he had failed. He would not let that happen again. He reluctantly left the room, but he didn't go far.

Micah had been tending the horses and had just come in to check on Jasmine's condition when he heard Donavan proposing to her. He knew then that all would be well. He walked back out of the room with a big smile.

Greta was so happy to see Jasmine up and talking that she shed silent tears of joy. Jasmine had become a dear friend as they traveled, and she couldn't bear to think of her being hurt so badly. She left with Zarcon and went to help with the meal that Jasmine and Donavan both needed. They were both in need of strength after this ordeal.

As a group, they were all so relieved to be rid of the blue orb. It had been such a burden for so long. It truly was a weight off their shoulders. Everyone was happy to be alive. They did not, however, forget those they had lost on the journey. Their joy was tempered by a touch of sorrow for those left behind.

Epilogue

Heleren and Anesthia were caught as they tried to get to their horses and escape. With the orb gone, their powers were much diminished. They screamed when the men caught them and tried to use what powers they had left to control the men, but it was no use. Greta had given the men courage, and Donavan had been able to blunt their powers further just before Jasmine was hit. The witches were dragged to the city prison to await trial and probable hanging.

Myshella ran the other way and found a horse tied near a tavern. She got out of town and made it out into the open country near Synkana. It was then that the Black Wind found her. She was said to have tried to make it to the next village, but some travelers reported seeing a woman who looked much like Myshella with boils all over her body and screaming for someone to kill her because of the pain. No one would, of course, because they knew who she was. She finally died alone and in great pain. Someone said they saw a Black Wind blow across her body and disappear. They hoped it had exacted its revenge and was gone.

Magg was waiting in the castle for any word from her sister, Zora. No word came, of course. She finally went out into the village to see if anyone had heard anything. It had been such a long time. She had started wearing light- colored clothing and changed her hair so that no one would recognize her. She listened at the local inn for any news. She had been doing so for weeks.

Finally, one night she heard a traveler speak of a battle between "those nasty witches and the wizard Zarcon." He said that the head witch had been killed and the others caught before they could escape. Everyone in the country was celebrating.

As Magg listened she was stunned. How could her sister have failed? She was so powerful. Yet Magg knew that her strength had weakened once the orb was gone. She thought she would be sad when her sister died. But it was not so. If anything she was relieved.

Magg decided that she would find Zarcon and see if she could be an apprentice to him if he would have her. Her heart was good in spite of having Zora for a sister. She never did like Zora's ways or her cruelty to others.

She had grieved for the old dog that Zora killed. She had even grieved when she found the small animals that Zora killed so coldly. Maybe she could make up for some of the bad that Zora had done in the world. She could only hope. She felt guilty that she was so relieved that Zora was dead. Her life was her own now, and she would make something better of it.

The blue orb was never seen again … not in this world.

www.ingramcontent.com/pod-product-compliance
Lightning Source LLC
Chambersburg PA
CBHW060917190726
48286CB00002B/543